I HAVE WHAT I GAVE
The Fiction of Janet Frame

I have

what I gave

THE FICTION OF
JANET FRAME

Judith Dell Panny

George Braziller   New York

First published in the United States of America
in 1993 by George Braziller, Inc.

First Published in New Zealand
in 1992 by Daphne Brasell Associates Press

For information, please address the publisher:
George Braziller, Inc.
60 Madison Avenue
New York, New York 10010

Library of Congress Cataloging-in-Publication Data
Panny, Judith Dell.
  I have what I gave: the fiction of Janet Frame/ Judith Dell Panny.
p. cm.
  Revision of the author's thesis (Massey University).
  Includes bibliographical references.
  ISBN 0-8076-1308-8 (hard) — ISBN 0-8076-1309-6 (pbk.)

  1. Frame, Janet—Criticism and interpretation. 2. New Zealand in literature.
I. Title.
PR9639.3.F7Z83 1993   93-16386
823—dc20   CIP

Printed in the United States
First U.S. Edition 1993

To Rolf

ACKNOWLEDGEMENTS

In an earlier form, the present work was a thesis
supervised by Dr William Broughton of Massey University.
I would like to thank him for his careful attention and advice.
Thanks are due to Andrew Mason for his invaluable guidance
in transforming the thesis into a book.

I HAVE WHAT I GAVE
The Fiction of Janet Frame

Contents

AUTHOR'S NOTE

I use the full range of punctuation marks to distinguish quoted material.

Direct quotations are indicated by double quotation marks. Single quotation marks are used to isolate or highlight a word or phrase.

Where my sentence ends with an incomplete quotation, the concluding punctuation is placed outside the quotation marks. For example, the words chosen as the title of this book are "I have what I gave". The complete quotation from p 212 of *Daughter Buffalo* is as follows: "What matters is that I have what I gave; nothing is completely taken; we meet in the common meeting place in the calm of stone, the frozen murmurs of life, *squamata, sauria, serpentes;* in the sanctuary." Here, on the other hand, the end of my sentence coincides with the end of the quotation. Frame's concluding punctuation is thus included within the quotation marks.

In Frame's texts, some words are italicised, indicating the special, often equivocal, significance of a particular word. Where I have drawn attention to certain words in Frame's quotations, I have underlined them and acknowledged that.

Square brackets [. . .] indicate a gap of several lines or sentences in a quotation. Ellipses are mine unless otherwise indicated.

I

Introduction

Looking back over his accomplishments, the elderly writer in *Daughter Buffalo* concludes, "I have what I gave"[1]. His paradoxical remark reverses the usual acquisitiveness of a materialistic age. Although Janet Frame has often been at pains to distinguish between thoughts expressed by her characters and her own distinct and different views, she admits that, on occasion, a character may voice an opinion or enunciate a belief with which she agrees. "I have what I gave" suggests a philosophy which, I believe, Janet Frame herself could embrace. Her gift is her contribution to the corpus of world literature. It is also her own supreme accomplishment. To date, she has given 11 novels, 80 or more short stories, a volume of poetry, three volumes of autobiography and one book for children. She has received international acclaim and prestigious awards. Recently, the public awareness of her life and work has increased with the worldwide success of the film *An Angel at My Table*, derived from her autobiography.

Frame's gift has not always been enthusiastically received. She once explained that she sees things "In an imaginary light—which is a bright light, without shade—a kind of inward sun"[2]. This vivid image led to the critical judgement that "a world lit by an inward sun is difficult for others to see clearly."[3] Frame's idiosyncratic imagination has been blamed for difficulties encountered in her texts. Misled by the widespread, though erroneous, belief that she had suffered from mental illness, some readers and critics have assumed that answers to the puzzling questions in the texts could never be found; contradictions and ambiguities have not been seen as part of a deliberate patterning and purpose.

Yet, in spite of their acknowledged difficulty, Frame's novels hold a fascination that has been variously attributed to the poetic quality of her prose, to the immediacy of her narration, or to the sense of mystery that pervades her writing. But there are few extended studies of her work. Until now, two monographs and one book are the only publications devoted to Frame alone and written by a single critic. Patrick Evans is the author of the book and one of the monographs. In 1973 he made an observation which has held true for nearly 20 years; he said that, although Frame was "probably New Zealand's most successful contemporary novelist, she has reached this position, curiously enough, without the impetus of unified critical understanding . . . . This dereliction of critical duty seems to have stemmed from the difficulty of sensing immediately where the centre of her work lies."[4]

Articles and essays on Frame abound. It is a tribute to her stature that her work has continued to generate readings from many perspectives, whether feminist or Freudian, mythical or Jungian, Marxist or modernist or even postmodernist. While not denying the validity of the range of possible readings, this book offers a new perspective from which to view each of the novels and the extended story "Snowman, Snowman".

My intention, originally, was to study Frame the myth-maker, and to pay particular attention to the obscure aspects of her work. I began with *Living in the Maniototo*, a novel I admired for its humorous and perceptive view of human interaction. Its lively episodes in various settings juxtapose contrasting ideas. Many words and images are reiterated. There are, for example, repeated references to an underworld. Knowing little about the subject, I turned to Dante's *Divine Comedy*. The result was the surprising discovery of parallels between *Living in the Maniototo* and *Hell*, the first volume of Dante's trilogy. There is an amusing and bizarre likeness between an imaginary suburb of Auckland and a region Dante calls Upper Hell. Furthermore, Frame's depiction of the American city of Baltimore features astonishing parallels with Dante's Lower Hell.

I was determined to pursue the most intractable questions raised by the text: why should a deceased daughter be character-ised as a wolf-child, why should so many characters die or dis-appear, why are certain words italicised, and why should the business of exacting payment and being in debt recur in different contexts? The answers to all these questions emerged gradually to form a pattern. I found that, in this and in other works by Frame, there is a deliberate patterning which is not mythical or metaphysical; it is allegorical.

Since allegory and the allegorical are no longer familiar terms, a brief explanation is called for. Allegory involves a system of double meaning that is sustained throughout a work. The Greek word *allegoria* means to speak otherwise than one seems to speak. Angus Fletcher's initial definition, in his authoritative book on the subject, is: "allegory says one thing and means another."[5] While this has been criticised as an over-simplification, it never-theless indicates clearly the paradoxical nature of the concept. Allegory functions through puns and riddles and through phras-ing which carries both an obvious and an alternative meaning. In each of Frame's novels, there are clues linking plot, situation, character or setting to an earlier book or myth, to a well-known sequence of events or to an established idea. The parallel may form quite a simple structure. One example from mythology is the descent of Orpheus into the underworld and his eventual return. In *The Edge of the Alphabet*, the voyage of Toby Withers to London and back is patterned on the Orphic descent and return. London, with its fogs and odours and misery, can readily be seen as an underworld. Thus, the Orphic descent and return is an extended metaphor that structures part of the book. Within this structure, however, Frame inverts anticipated details. Toby is no hero, and the object of his search is the antithesis of Eurydice.

"We have allegory", writes Northrop Frye in his encompassing definition, "when the events of a narrative obviously and continuously refer to another simultaneous structure of events or ideas, whether historical events, moral or philosophical ideas, or natural phenomena."[6] To see the "simultaneous structure" requires comparison and contrast between the work being read and the earlier story, myth or idea. To make matters more complex (and distinctly more amusing) a writer like Janet Frame will often parody the earlier text through exaggeration or inversion. She alludes to biblical stories, archetypal patterns, Greek mythology and religious allegories of the past but selectively inverts or subverts these familiar models.

Parody in literature is comparable to caricature in art. It can tell a terrible truth with a smile. Its mockery or criticism is usually quite obvious. Allegory, on the other hand, involves concealment. In Frame's fiction, parody is often hidden. Until the allegorical aspects are disclosed, the humour of the parody remains locked away.

Many of Frame's characters have an obvious role while embodying a hidden allegorical idea. It is possible to view Snowman of "Snowman, Snowman" as man or as Christ. An even more complex character is Edward Glace from *Scented Gardens for the Blind*. His obvious role is that of an anxious father who is a genealogist by profession. His allegorical role is Death, who, in order to achieve his sinister intentions, pretends to be a saviour. This novel is one of three which draws on different aspects of relationships within the satanic family (Satan, Sin and Death).

Into the texture of language conveying everyday life or exploring feeling and imagination, Frame weaves her version of an ancient and venerable mode. Allegory is a timeless, universal concept. It has long been out of favour, though. Last century it was condemned by Coleridge because *reason* (as opposed to *imagination*) organised its material. This century, it has been condemned because many readers associate allegory with texts like *Pilgrim's Progress* where commentary and interpretation are incorporated into the narrative, indicating a character's worth or otherwise, commending or censuring actions. Bunyan's allegory affirms a body of Christian belief, as does *The Divine Comedy*, which illustrates graphically the religious concepts of sin and expiation. Moral instruction of this kind is disliked today. In the work of many 20th-century novelists, allegorical elements are significant but inconspicuous, having been cleverly concealed. Carolynn Van Dyke's study of narrative and dramatic allegory, published in 1985, considers that "the work of such writers as Hawthorne, Kafka, Mann, Beckett and Pynchon is haunted by allegory." Van Dyke observes that "the writing of the past century preserves the allegorical tradition in so radically changed a form that it should be called not allegorical but postallegorical."[7]

In modern allegory, it is likely that the work's moral purpose will be achieved through contrasting examples and highly equivocal situations. In this age which questions all absolutes, allegory expresses and engenders doubt. The reader is impelled to think and judge. My discussion of Frame's novels unfolds allegorical dimensions, leaving space for each reader to connect images and ideas and to draw individual conclusions. Where readings are given, they are suggestions only, offered in the knowledge that another reader might well interpret the allegory differently. The potential diversity of response is a measure of the richness of the allegorical component in Frame's work.

Allegory emphasises the power of language to deceive or mislead by drawing attention to its own word-play, clues and equivocal phrasing. In two novels, there are characters who deliberately misspell words to expose underlying truths: "masheens" (machines) are frequently destructive; "citysins" (citizens) may sin collectively, condoning inhuman conduct to safeguard themselves; the need to send "maw men" (more men) to war suggests soldiers who are hungry for killing. Milly Galbraith from *Intensive Care* says, "I wanted to use my special spelling to make the words show up for what they really are the cruel deceivers."[8] In each of her novels, Frame conveys a profound mistrust of language. At the same time, she delights in its infinite and seemingly magical capacity to create.

An awareness of language as magical developed during Frame's childhood: "In my family words were revered as instruments of magic." She claims to have been three years old when she composed her first story to relate to her sisters and brother; as an adult she has described the story as her best: "As I still write stories I'm entitled to study this and judge it the best I've written."

> Once upon a time there was a bird. One day a hawk came out of the sky and ate the bird. The next day a big bogie came out from behind the hill and ate up the hawk for eating up the bird.[9]

One can only wonder whether, in singling out this story for special approval, she was speaking truthfully or perpetrating a fiction which would engage a succession of academics in the analysis of a three-line tale by a pre-school child. It should be noted, though, that it was a remembered story and a remembered childhood situation; the memory of the adult Frame is surely to be taken seriously. Already present in the story is a kernel or an inkling of Frame's adult view of life and death. For this reason alone it warrants study. But it will also serve to demonstrate the process of close reading that I shall apply to each of Frame's novels.

The first step is to examine the most literal significance of the text, and then to compare and contrast key words and images. The next phase is to consider the figurative implications, especially within the context of Frame's *oeuvre*, but also in the context of literary tradition. At each stage, the text will raise questions to be addressed. Contradictory signals, which are often ignored, will receive special attention.

A bird is able to create song. If it is small enough to be the prey of a hawk, it is a fragile creature. The hawk is a predator, an instinctive killer. The bogie, an apparition from the netherworld, has unknown powers, being governed by forces outside our comprehension. In comparing and contrasting the three elements, it seems that each is more powerful than the last. Paradoxically, as long as the fragile bird still lives and sings, the bogie stays behind the hill.

In Frame's work, the image of the bird is often equated with the writer, its song being the story or novel.[10] Inspiration and song-making have often been regarded as divine attributes, as has the beauty of a creature that rides currents of air. By tradition, the singer has the power to tame the world as Orpheus tamed the beasts. But the singer needs to be valued and protected or he will be overcome, as indeed Orpheus was finally overcome and torn to pieces by the women of Thrace. The hawk can allude to human predators who would silence the singer. If bird and hawk suggest the artistic and the aggressive members of a community, all must perish when the bogie takes its revenge. We tend, with little thought, to applaud revenge. The story persuades us to question such an assumption. In the tale, revenge simply results in total destruction.

There is a contradiction implicit in the action of the bogie. It metes out justice; the hawk is punished. But this does not transform the bogie into a power for good. Without bird or hawk there will be silence. However, every archetypal story offers a sequence to be repeated any number of times. If we return to the beginning, we can assume that in the time-of-the-bird, which is infinite, the dark power is held in check. While the bird sings or while the poet speaks, the magic of song or the magic of words has the power to restrain the hawk or the force lurking behind the hill, or both. James Bertram comes to the same conclusion, though he identifies the bird with Frame herself. Referring to hawk and bogie, he says that Frame "has learnt how to keep them at bay with the magic spell of words."[11]

Jeanne Delbaere notes that Frame's "fable certainly lends itself to more than one interpretation."[12] But misinterpretation is also possible. When exploring the range of figurative meanings, failure to keep in mind the literal significance can produce an inconsistent reading. Robert Robertson, for instance, suggests that "Janet Frame finds her 'hawk' in the average New Zealander."[13] This cannot be denied, though in Frame's work people *everywhere* are predatory and jealous. New York, London and Baltimore have communities which are just as destructive of artists as those in Waimaru, Dunedin or Wellington. But the bogie is regarded by Robertson as "the spirit of fantasy and dream which can destroy the hawk"[14]. This is difficult to justify; the "spirit of fantasy and dream" is not necessarily a destructive force, whereas the bogie is.

Delbaere has called the story a "fable". A fable often has a moral lesson to convey and suggests that, with good conduct, things might have turned out differently. However, in the "Bird Hawk Bogie" story, the cruelty of an ineluctable sequence places it outside the realm of fable: something divine is destroyed wantonly; retribution, which could assume fearsome proportions, follows. Allegory gives expression to universal truths and eternal patterns, but the tale is not an allegory either.

Myth, like allegory, is concerned with eternal patterns, with the mysteries of the universe, and in some cases with the embodiment of a unique cosmic view. In its primitive and simple expression, Frame's tale is an original myth. An allegory would take a different form, but it could embody the same truth. Indeed, this very sequence of cause and effect is explored allegorically in two of her novels.

Given its cryptic nature, the allegorical part of Frame's work requires systematic investigation. Study of her 11 novels and "Snowman, Snowman" will reveal that all include allegorical features. In the first three novels, *Owls Do Cry*, *Faces in the Water* and *The Edge of the Alphabet*, sequences derived from mythology or from the Bible provide an allegorical framework. In all three, however, the focus is on characterisation, depicting the anxiety, pain and inner conflicts of the central characters, rather than on foregrounding the text in the manner of allegory. Allegorical patterning receives greater attention and emphasis in the later novels.

The extended story "Snowman, Snowman" inverts traditional ideas and values. Most of the novels from *Scented Gardens for the Blind* to *The Carpathians* employ this strategy. While continuing to explore character, human interaction and the human heart, they are allegorical in their extended allusion to particular aspects of prior texts. *A State of Siege* is different in that it embodies an ancient conflict between heart and mind, life and death. It is allegorical in the broadest sense, being linked to a structure of ideas.

Once discovered, the allegorical component of Frame's work cannot be ignored. It provides access to much of her irony, to her most subtle and amusing parody, and to the provocative questions implicit in her work.

1   Janet Frame, *Daughter Buffalo*. Page number refers to the Century Hutchinson edition, Auckland, 1986. "I have what I gave" is spoken by Turnlung, p 212.

2   Janet Frame, "Artists' Retreats", *NZ Listener*, 27 July 1970, p 13.

3   Patrick Evans, *Janet Frame* (Boston, 1977), p 204.

4   Patrick Evans, "Alienation and the Imagery of Death", *Meanjin* XXXII 3 (1973), p 294.

5   Angus Fletcher, *Allegory: The Theory of a Symbolic Mode* (New York, 1964), p 2.

6   Northrop Frye, cited by Samuel Levin in "Allegorical Language", *Allegory, Myth and Symbol*, ed Morton W Bloomfield. *Harvard English Studies* 9, p 23.

7   Carolynn Van Dyke, *The Fiction of Truth: Structures of Meaning in Narrative and Dramatic Allegory*, pp 290 and 291.

8   Janet Frame, *Intensive Care*. Page numbers refer to the Century Hutchinson edition, Auckland, 1987. Misspelt words: pp 206, 225, 208. "I wanted . . . deceivers.", p 193.

9 Janet Frame, "Beginnings", first published *Landfall* XIX (1965), pp 40 and
   42.

10 For example, the writer-narrator in *Living in the Maniototo* is Mavis,
    which means 'song-thrush'.

11 James Bertram, Review of "*The Reservoir and other stories*. Janet Frame",
    Landfall XX 3 (1966), p 292.

12 Jeanne Delbaere, "Introduction", Bird, Hawk, Bogie, p 7.

13 Robert T Robertson, "Bird, Hawk, Bogie: Janet Frame, 1952–62", *ibid*,
    p 19.

14 *Ibid*, p 22.

2

O w l s   D o   C r y

Owls Do Cry, Janet Frame's first novel, questions the values guiding our lives. Winston Rhodes, in his 1972 survey of Frame's novels, described *Owls Do Cry* as "a recurring parable based on search for treasure. [. . .] . . . the search for treasure implies a reappraisal of the value of life and the meaning of death"[1]. In his 1957 review of the book, Rhodes noted that, in this quest, "Frame brings us close not to the average New Zealander but to common humanity in its suffering and search."[2] These universal implications are suited to allegory. But the book has none of the deliberate duplicity of allegory, for it does not cloak its intentions in ambiguity or word-play.

The fall of Adam and Eve and the fall of Lucifer from heaven contribute to the structuring of five of Frame's novels. In *Owls Do Cry* the characters suffer the metaphorical fall from a heaven to a hell, simply by growing beyond childhood. They are not guilty of sinful conduct, though they are betrayed by the deceptions of the adult world. For Daphne, the central character, the progression from heaven to hell requires a narrative time of more than 20 years. The novel's structure derives from the Bible, though, in embodying the myth of a lost paradise, it reflects an archetypal pattern found in many mythologies. The novel also alludes to sequences of cause and effect that occur in *Grimms' Fairy Tales* or in Greek myths, though the anticipated effects are usually subverted. Characters are not freed by prince or hero, nor

are they saved by prayer or magic incantation; they may, however, be changed into something less than human.

The opening chapter of *Owls Do Cry* is a poetic first-person
'song'. The singer is Daphne, a character whose poetic monologues or 'songs' appear at intervals throughout. However, the
book is mainly a third-person narrative, with the perspective
shifting, often swiftly, from one character to another. Daphne
takes her place among them as the one whose perspective we
share most often. The novel is divided into two parts: "Talk of
Treasure" depicts the childhood of three sisters and a brother,
and the transition of one sister from childhood into the adult
world; "Twenty Years After" deals with the adulthood of the
other two sisters and the brother. It concludes with a two-page
"Epilogue".

Childhood is seen as a time of freedom, though intimations of
the constraints of adulthood—clocks, calendars and bills—create
apprehension. The world of the Withers children, Francie,
Daphne, Toby and Chicks, is enriched by "treasure" in various
forms: items found at the rubbish dump, "first and happiest,
fairy tales" (p 11), the "*bigness and sweetness*" (p 118) of the
mother, and the imaginations of the children which give them a
mythical understanding of the world. In a time of shared story-
telling and shared discovery, the children take care of one
another: removing stones from the shoes of Chicks, the smallest,
giving Toby room to lie down when he has an epileptic fit,
sharing stolen fruit, and making plans together to combat the
tyranny of their father, Bob. The children enjoy the freedom of
being 'outside' where "the shrubs and children (including the
Withers family) remained happily planted on the hills surrounding the town." (p 16) Even on a school day, Toby is able to say,
"I don't wanner go to school . . . I wanner go to the rubbish
dump an' find another book." (p 11) Neither he nor Daphne is
punished for truancy. The instruction of Bob Withers to his
wife, Amy, "Make sure you keep those kids away from that rubbish dump" (p 22), is unheeded.

Books are the most significant treasure provided by the rubbish dump, for there the children find *Grimms' Fairy Tales* and a volume by Ernest Dowson. Impressions gleaned from literature discovered at the dump and encountered at school interact with the children's observations of their own world, helping to shape their interpretation of it. Places and people in Waimaru become richly endowed with fairy-tale attributes of menace and magic. The sea is "the roll-down sea" where "the rush of pebbles [is] sucked back and back into the sea's mouth each time it draws breath." (p 18) Ice-cream is bought from "the mountainous woman who moves like faith from town to town, leaving behind her a trail of sweet and ice-cream shops, almost as if they dropped from her pocket, like crumbs or seeds" (p 18). Both quotations allude to "Hansel and Gretel". Crumbs dropped by Hansel to mark the way home are eaten by birds, but the pebbles he drops shine in the moonlight. The image of Waimaru's sea is more alarming, as even pebbles are consumed. The children explain occurrences in terms of spells, challenges, promises, rewards and punishments. In their own myth-making, they use the same logic as they have encountered in the fairy tales: "when the mill siren sounded she was to say a special charm, from the fairy-tale book, so that Francie would not be captured for ever" (p 31).

The mill and the rushing sea are dangers well beyond the place of safety chosen by the Withers children. They return repeatedly to the rubbish dump which was

> ... like a shell with gold tickle of toi-toi around its edges and grass and weeds growing in green fur over the mounds of rubbish; and from where the children sat, snuggled in the hollow of refuse ... they could see the sky passing in blue or grey ripples, and hear in the wind, the heavy fir tree that leaned over the hollow, rocking, and talking to itself saying firr-firr-firr, its own name ... (p 11)

In safety and warmth, amid the green and gold of youth and the gold and blue of heaven, the children enjoy a dump which has become, in their perception, a paradise. Here they can sing their 'songs of innocence'. There is a supreme irony in the location of a paradise in a rubbish dump. But it is the imagination of the children that creates a heaven from a "hollow of refuse".

Imagination allows the Withers children to answer many 'why', 'where' and 'how' questions easily. "But how [on Judgement Day] shall there be room for the dead? They shall be packed tight and thin like malt biscuits or like the pink ones with icing in between that the Withers could never afford" (p 21). Other questions can be postponed until a time of greater understanding and wisdom: Toby, afflicted by epilepsy, wonders if his teacher Andy Reid understands "why some people are given a private and lonely night, with a room of its own but no window that the stars . . . may look through?" (p 14) To the children, questions are not frightening: "And we sat, didn't we, Toby, Chicks and Francie, as the world sits in the morning, unafraid, touching how and why and where, the wonder currency that I take with me, slipped in the lining of my heart" (p 134).

But the family is rich only in "wonder currency". Their poverty compels Francie to leave school at the age of 12, a girl of talent who sings at the school garden party and takes the part of Saint Joan in the school play. In true fairy-tale fashion, Francie is transformed by "silver helmet and breastplate" (p 20) into a heroine. The day of the play is her last day at school, after which she is taken

> . . . beyond Frère Jacques . . . and Shakespeare, there I couch when owls do cry,
>> when owls do cry when owls do cry . . . (p 20)

The night sounds of owls in the macrocarpa and cabbage trees become mingled with the thought that "it is raining for ever and there will be no more sun, only quee-will and dark." (p 22) Having left the "cowslip's bell" (p 22) of childhood, Francie is placed among the predatory owls of the adult world.

It is the transition into the adult world, rather than poverty as such, which drains the imaginative richness, the enthusiasm and spontaneity that characterised Francie. With every step into her grown-up condition, Francie's expectations are proven false: "the free book had cheated and was not free and you had to pay twenty guineas for learning opera." (p 44) Her belief that Tim Harlow's father was "a surgeon in his spare time" (p 40) disintegrates with her realisation that he works for the local council and attends to rubbish disposal. Boys, new slacks, lipstick, the local "hop" draw Francie into new, unoriginal roles. She changes, adopting artificial 'adult' language. The other children complain: "—Before you left school . . . everything was different." (p 40) She no longer finds the rubbish dump interesting: "I'm sure I'm not going to sit here all day in a dirty old rubbish dump." (pp 39–40) Francie becomes more and more silent and Daphne wishes for "gold and green clouds of birds to help her fight the armies of tangled wool, oh it was all tangled, being alive was tangled, and there was Francie going by herself every day to face it and fight it." (pp 36–37)

Francie's development as a young woman of the world is cut short. She dies by rolling down a steep slope into the flames of the rubbish dump. Francie's death signifies the waste of her considerable imaginative capacity, though the 'burning' of her individuality began when she became a worker in the adult world. In contrast to her enactment of "Saint Joan", her death is a descent, not an elevation. It lacks all mystery and ennoblement:

> And then no one can describe exactly what happened, but it happened, and Francie tripped over a rusty piece of plough and fell headfirst down the slope, rolling, quickly, into the flames.
>
> (p 40)

The magic that is part of the imaginative world of the Withers children loses its power:

> And Daphne and Toby and Chicks ran forward, calling out,— Francie, Francie, Francie, as if her name, three times said, would bring her alive, like magic. (p 41)

Unlike the Grimms' characters who die but reappear at night or are restored by the kiss of a prince, Francie does not return.

The fire into which Francie has fallen signifies the hell into which each member of the family will fall on reaching adulthood. Like leaves in a rubbish fire, each of them 'withers' in a different and distinct way. Francie's progress reiterates an archetypal pattern whereby treasure is found and paradise is found, but both are subsequently lost. While Francie's death by fire can be seen as a release from the adult world, there is no expression of hope that the paradise can ever be regained.

In the section entitled "Twenty Years Later", we find that Toby, though an adult, has not found his place in the adult world. Because there are no answers to the questions raised by his condition and situation, the questions become terrifying:

> *Now Toby, what will you be, what will you be,*
> *in freezing works west-coast mine or foundry?*
> *Now Toby where will you live, where will you live*
> *—in hovel or bungalow God forgive.*
> *Now Toby how will you die how will you die*
> *—dug and dumped in the pit of why.* (p 54)

This rhyme is reminiscent of those chanted in *Grimms' Fairy Tales*. The simplicity is in keeping with Toby's unsophisticated understanding, for his capacity to learn has been impaired by recurrent fits. As an adult, Toby lives "*in a half-world . . . where neither the wind blowing the way forward nor the way back . . . could feed or make you whole.*" (pp 53–54) Toby has been singed by a fire which has condemned him to a half-life or half-death, to be "there and not there, journeying half-way which is all torment for *The singe on the sleeve is worse than the fire*" (p 83). In his nostalgia and loneliness he dreams of an ideal state in which he is "not ever . . . on the outside of the circle that whirled round and round faster than any light and letting no part break for a man to squeeze in and be warm" (pp 61–62). His hell is his exclusion. He aspires to acceptance in the adult world but has a place only in the home of his mother, where his childhood relationship to her is preserved. Chicks (called Teresa as an adult) complains that, if he should stay with her, "He lazes around and expects to have everything done for him, and he won't eat this and he won't eat that, like a spoilt child, the way he acts at home." (p 108) When his mother dies, he does not belong anywhere. The Epilogue finds Tobias E Withers "convicted for being a vagabond and lacking visible means of support." (p 172)

Toby's childhood pursuit of treasure at the rubbish dump is subverted in his adult years into an obsessive gathering of items that can be sold, turned into "Hard cash." (p 54) Like the traditional miser, he counts his money repeatedly and is reluctant to part with any of it. He abhors the thought that he may have to care for his parents in their old age, as he expects to have "his hands full to control the treasure of money that would help him to fit in and know where and why and how." (p 86) He is regarded by Daphne as a "*Poor trafficking child, with no treasure.*" (p 83) Though not illicit, "trafficking" contributes to Toby's *withering*; it has made him its victim or addict. He is one of those pursuing blindly "the wrong magic and the wrong fairy tale." (p 32)

Chicks (or Teresa) also 'withers' in an adulthood that becomes a hell. In the Epilogue her fate is reported: "A society woman found shot in the head, and her husband arrested for murder." (p 171) Chicks becomes the mother of three children and gathers "all the modern devices my mother never dreamed of" (p 117). She longs for "luxury and clothes and travel" (p 114) and aspires to be "popular and sought after." (p 109) It is clear that nothing she has already brings happiness to Chicks.

Frame is employing irony in her manipulation of the events in this section of the novel. Through her diary, Chicks presents her own idealised self-image. She presumably intends to communicate this version of herself to her husband, whom she fully expects to read the diary, for she leaves it where it will be 'found' (and indeed it is found, but by Toby): "dear Timothy, he is so honest that I could leave it lying anywhere in the house and he would never open it." (p 96) The one thing we know for certain about Tim Harlow is that he tells lies; many years earlier he told Francie that his council-worker father was a surgeon. The ideal-wife-and-mother mask worn by Chicks slips from time to time: "We are not having any more children. Later, we shall send Peter and Mark and Sharon to boarding school." (p 114) Tim wants Sharon's rocking-chair to be brought up from the garage, but Chicks says, "I find I have to refuse, for the carpets and linoleum will be ruined." (p 114) Thus she discredits her subsequent remark, "Dear Sharon. I would do anything in the world for the child!" (p 114) For Chicks, the adult world is a hell of petty deceptions, jealousies, dissatisfaction, and a marital disharmony which is confirmed in the Epilogue.

Ironically, Chicks plans to return to Waimaru with her family to live in a new house on the filled-in site of the old rubbish dump. This event consigns Chicks to the dump, along with all her 'goods'. It suggests the replacement of childhood values with those learnt in the adult world. Paradoxically, the plan also reveals a desire, perhaps subconscious, to return to the special childhood place in the hope of finding a paradise that has been lost.

Toby, once he learns of his sister's attitudes through reading the diary, pronounces her "dead" (p 125). A letter which Chicks has written to Daphne is returned with "the words Help help help at the end" (p 101). It is clear that Daphne considers Chicks to be in need of rescue "from a terrible doom" (p 101); she is both blind and trapped "*under a big dark box, not being able to see*" (p 95). Blindness, imprisonment, a state of 'death' characterise those who pursue the false treasure of money, goods or social status esteemed by the adult world.

There is a refrain which suggests the effect of adult life on the inner world of Amy Withers: "The hollow house will never be filled" (p 92). Amy herself is the "hollow house", emptied by being the refuge or treasure for birds and children:

—Kiddies, kiddies a little waxeye has come to us in the cold weather, and meaning, Kiddies, a waxeye had come to her *to hide from the snow and find honey in her . . .* (p 118)

A remnant of imagination allows Amy only brief travel in the "warm half-minute escape from the forever problem of facing up." (p 84) Her creative energies have flowed out in the service of others, until she has become an ageing woman with a "thin time and child-stolen lap." (p 84)

Amy holds fast to religious faith, believing, or trying to believe, that "the people walking in darkness" must have "seen a great light?" (p 93) But the vision of light has not been revealed to her. She has shared and endured her husband's imprisonment as well as her own, in the form of his "child-like dependence" (p 118), and his continual frustration and despair at being besieged by bills. The calendar is his prison demanding impossible payment by particular dates. And the clock demands early or late shift in the service of the railway. Time is an imprisoned and imprisoning force in the adult world: "and the clock making a stifling ticking that hops round and round droning, like a swarm, in the sack, and is never let free." (p 26) "Time and death" (p 9) claim Amy who "should have died long ago she was so tired with sweeping out her house and the world" (p 118).

Daphne, in contrast to all the other characters, suffers physical imprisonment, but not mental or imaginative constraint. Because she has refused to embrace the aspirations of the adult community, she is committed to a mental hospital where she is given shock treatment "in practice for the world." (p 45) Daphne and other patients are compared to rubbish that is deposited to be burned. Each electric shock treatment takes the form of a re-enactment of Francie's death by burning at the rubbish dump: "the pink people come to unlock the door, and . . . the frozen bodies . . . are heaped on little trolleys . . . and wheeled to the rubbish dump, to be scattered amongst the toi-toi or burned." (p 128) While awaiting treatment, Daphne describes her perception of the passage of time since her childhood: "the sunniest of days, coloured like a single toi-toi with a sunflower in its heart of seedcake . . . had driven on and on through a million years to a world of blindness" (pp 45–46). Having been asked to climb on to a bed, she climbs a "shadow of mountain and finds on its summit a golden hollow, her own size, for lying in." (p 47) The hollow recalls "a shell with gold tickle of toi-toi . . . where the children sat, snuggled in the hollow of refuse" (p 11). Before every treatment, Daphne re-creates the paradise and then endures its loss. Shock treatment is a descent through burning and ash to a state in which her "seeing", like Francie's, "will be blinded" (p 45). After each treatment she is returned to a hospital room which she calls "*the dead room.*" (p 9)

We learn in the brief Epilogue that Daphne has undergone a lobotomy. She anticipates the operation in the preceding chapter, envisaging the darning of "the believed crevice of my world." (p 170) The "crevice", the flaw to be repaired, contains Daphne's imagination and individuality. After the lobotomy's 'success' in the eyes of the adult community, Daphne becomes one of the workers at the woollen mill, "a whirling spiritless machine that makes the same speech day after day till its life ends." (p 73) Daphne has been transformed, not into a laurel tree like the nymph Daphne in the Greek legend, but into an automaton. Her new imprisonment is to be contrasted with physical incarceration in a mental institution which nevertheless allowed freedom to dream and imagine.

Frame's inclination towards allegory is apparent in her first novel. There is a reiterated pattern springing from a prior idea, which has both mythical and biblical associations. The fall from a paradise to a hell forms an allegorical pattern which is repeated by Francie, Toby and Chicks. At great cost, Daphne holds fast to her paradise, singing for 20 years after the death of Francie, until she is compelled by "God or the devil" (pp 45, 46, 47) to 'wither' in the hell she has resisted for so long.

A true allegory would include two features in addition to an allegorical framework. The first is a distance between reader and characters; the second is equivocal language. On both counts, *Owls Do Cry* is not allegorical. The characterisation of Daphne, in particular, appeals to our emotions. She is so convincing as a character that we are easily seduced into thinking that the novel must be about the author herself. We are altogether too involved with the fortunes of Daphne and her family to see them as allegorical figures. As Joan Stevens has put it:

> Daphne ... expresses explicitly in a poetic monologue, what
> *Owls Do Cry* means symbolically; she is also a character within
> the story; she is also very obviously the voice of the author. This
> is too great a burden to place upon any device of character or
> plot, and the novel suffers accordingly.[3]

Stevens has noted Daphne's symbolic significance. While other readers may not find her multiple role problematical, there is an expectation, established with the first song, that she will be a bearer of ideas. But, for the most part, she develops in the manner of the central character in a psychological novel. It is not until the Epilogue that we are encouraged to view the characters as examples of "humanity in its suffering and search."[4] A newspaper report which discloses the fate of each is followed by an italicised statement like this: *"And the name was Daphne Withers though the paper said another name."* (p 172)

Allegory depends on deliberate manipulation of language. Far from playing verbal tricks in *Owls Do Cry*, Frame tries to speak as plainly as possible. She conveys complex ideas through metaphorical language and through recurrent and contrasting images. The greatest complexity occurs in the condensed language of Daphne's songs. Though arranged to look like prose, the songs have the rhythm and sound-patterning of poetry.

The page-long song which opens the novel and which concludes "sings Daphne from the dead room" (p 9) encapsulates its most significant ideas. Daphne expresses a view of time which

changes from the youthful "The day is early", with its sense of
the vast expanse of the day, and "the days above burst
unheeded", suggesting a lack of awareness of time's passing, to
"buy a caterpillar that is wound up and crawls with rippling back
across our day and night." From a knowing or disenchanted perspective, the days seem concertinaed together like the ripples of
the caterpillar's back, while days and nights are reduced to
miniature proportion in contrast to the size of a caterpillar which
traverses them easily.

The passage's opening depicts a new paradisal world with
birdsong, warmth, colour, intense movement of insects, lush
growth, and grass blades that are "crippled" or mown, having
lost their power to sever or harm. The failure of the carrot seed to
grow is explained mythically: "the wind breathed a blow-away
spell". These impressions are replaced by knowledge of the truth
of death; the carrot seed "sank too deep or dried up".

With the knowledge of death comes the knowing view of
Santa Claus as "dyspeptic", embodying over-indulgence and
emphasis on the material. Debasement of Christmas is suggested, an idea developed later in the mental hospital when Santa
presents Daphne with a gift of perfumed soap. But Daphne seeks
an entirely different gift: "she cannot fully tell its name or shape
or size but she wants it, needs it, and waits for Santa, the red and
white God . . . to understand her need." (p 138) Santa is shown
to be no God, and Christmas offers no reverent celebration of a
birth or promise of hope or salvation.

Santa personifies a misdirection of Western values. It is
implied that we imprison ourselves as we "wrap our life in cello-
phane with a handkerchief and card." (p 9) Daphne's "dead
room", literally a cell-like room with a high barred window, is
like any person's imprisoning parcel or cocoon; from this sealed
position, the colour, sound and movement of the natural world
are unheeded or undervalued. The "dead room" is not simply
Daphne's prison; it is the world viewed as a void, empty of spiritual significance.

Owls Do Cry as a whole addresses a question posed on its opening page: *"what use the green river, the gold place, if time and death . . . not rest from taking underground . . . rose . . . bean flower and . . . song in pepper-pot breast of thrush?"* (p 9) As Winston Rhodes comments in his 1972 study, the novel explores "the meaning of death" [5], revealing the profound effect of the loss of a sister on Daphne. The closeness of death to life is demonstrated in the cosmos of the rubbish dump by Francie's plunge from the blue, green and gold into flames and death. In the space between lie the discarded goods, signifying a community's values and endeavour and final achievement. The dump is "the living and lived-in wound" (p 11): literally the earth's wound, figuratively the wound of decay and time that gradually destroys every living person. The wounding, the beginning of death, occurs at puberty with its image of blood: "—You will drop blood when you walk, Francie said." (p 11) For those who embrace adult values, a lifetime is spent digging the pit, labouring, using, dumping, dying. In a dream, Daphne tells Toby, "We have dug the pit and he who diggeth the pit shall fall into it" (p 83).

As well as exploring "the meaning of death", the novel is, in Rhodes's words, "a reappraisal of the value of life" [6]. *Owls Do Cry* questions the effects of "man's ignorance of the human compass and where the hand of the star points him to follow." (p 139) At the time of transition from childhood to adulthood, human beings seem to lose their sense of direction and embrace goals that are intrinsically destructive. The result is encompassed in the image of a burning pit filled with goods consumed and discarded, in contrast to an image of sky, gold toi-toi and "clouds like white slippers or silk fish" (p 117).

To find the "use" of the "green river, the gold place" requires a journey into an inner world. Daphne sings: *"we walk like Theseus or an ashman in the labyrinth, with our memories unwound on threads of silk or fire"* (p 52). She chooses to absent herself from the 'real' world, where things decay continuously, in order to reside in a more enduring realm. The golden petal that Daphne plucks from the high place "further than the sky" (p 41) on the afternoon of Francie's death serves to light her way to her own treasure, the memories and dreams and songs within the labyrinth of her own mind. No other "great light" (p 93) will be discovered. Treasure resides within the mind and the imagination of the seeker.

Owls Do Cry was first published by Pegasus in Christchurch, 1957. Page numbers in this chapter refer to the edition published by Sun Books, Melbourne, 1967.

1   Winston Rhodes, *Landfall* XXVI 2 (1972), p 142.
2   Rhodes, *Landfall* XI 4 (1957), pp 328–329.
3   Joan Stevens, *The New Zealand Novel 1860–1960*, p 100.
4   Rhodes, *Landfall* XI, p 329.
5   Rhodes, *Landfall* XXVI, p 142.
6   Rhodes, *ibid.*

3

Faces in the Water

Faces in the Water is a first-person narrative in three parts describing the ordeal of Istina Mavet, who suffers incarceration in New Zealand psychiatric hospitals for nine years. The book has frequently been regarded as autobiographical, as Mark Williams observes.

> The formula warning in *Faces in the Water* that the book is a work of fiction and that 'none of the characters, including Estina [*sic*] Mavet, portrays a living person' has not deterred all those readers of the 'tragic disordered power' school who recklessly conflate narrator and author. They imagine themselves listening directly to the voice of Janet Frame . . .[1]

Many details recorded in *An Angel at My Table* confirm the belief of such readers. Physically, Istina and Janet Frame have much in common, sharing frizzy hair, acquiring infections and sores while in hospital, and becoming very thin during treatment. Both suffer at the hands of staff who resent their levels of education and their knowingness. Like Istina, who often panics, Frame admits to a "feeling of panic simply at being locked up"[2].

> What I have described in Istina Mavet is my sense of hopelessness as the months passed, my fear of having to endure that constant state of physical capture where I was indeed at the mercy of those who made judgements and decisions . . .[3]

Nevertheless, Janet Frame has rejected the notion that Istina is herself "under a different name"[4]. Frame's own experiences provide source material for the novel: "The fiction of the book lies in the portrayal of the central character, based on my life but given largely fictional thoughts and feelings, to create a picture of the sickness I saw around me."[5]

Emphasis on the autobiographical has tended to pre-empt more searching criticism of the novel. Furthermore, *Faces in the Water* takes us into the hidden world of mental hospitals. Visits by the public to the London asylum of Bedlam last century testify to a morbid interest in the manifestation of insanity. Mark Williams observes the "awful fascination that attends mental illness in New Zealand"[6]. The novel is a compelling account of an individual's struggle to survive in psychiatric hospitals.

That there is more to *Faces in the Water* than most critics have seen is implied in Janet Frame's attempt to point one of them towards the ideas it contains. In a rare revelation, she wrote in a letter to Patrick Evans that the name Istina Mavet "links the Serbo-Croatian word for 'truth' with the Hebrew word for 'death'"[7]. Indeed, *Istina* is Serbo-Croatian for 'truth' or reality, while *Māwet* is Hebrew for 'death'. Frame is suggesting the need for an analytical reading focused on language. The title promises an allegory, though the work's most obvious patterns of imagery do not immediately seem linked to "faces in the water". Nevertheless, there are parallels between patients and the dead, hospitals and hell, staff and devils.

Allusions to hell form an indictment of conditions in two fictitious mental hospitals, emphasising the punishing nature of Istina's treatment during her first stay at Cliffhaven, near Dunedin, and at Treecroft, in Auckland. Cliffhaven is comparable to Seacliff and Treecroft to the Auckland Mental Hospital where, Frame writes in *An Angel at My Table*[8], conditions were worse than those described in *Faces in the Water*. In the first two parts of the book, the hospitals, not unlike hell, are places of incarceration, mental anguish and physical punishment. Electric shock treatment (EST), surely comparable to any of hell's torments, is administered as a punishment: "Every morning I woke in dread, waiting for the day nurse to . . . announce . . . whether or not I was for shock treatment, the new and fashionable means of quieting people and of making them realize that orders are to be obeyed" (p 15). Istina repeatedly suffers the loss of her identity as she is plunged by EST into "the darkness of not knowing and of being nothing." (p 24) Those in control are portrayed as having the power, the callousness and even the physical attributes of devils. Matron Glass moves with "pegging footsteps . . . on her tiny blackshod feet" (p 17), an image suggesting a devil's goatsfeet.

The sense of human identity lost is intensified in Part Two. Treecroft is a hell even worse than Cliffhaven. "<u>Wild</u>" lilies, "<u>blown</u> roses", a "<u>weeping</u> willow" and "<u>slow-burning</u> ivy" (p 66, emphases mine) present a disquieting veneer. Certain Cliffhaven conditions are mysteriously echoed at Treecroft. Istina notices that "both the doctor and Sister Creed were limping" (p 68), recalling that species of devil which bears a club foot or cloven left hoof. Matron Borough of Treecroft is seen as a replica of Matron Glass of Cliffhaven, for both are large corseted women. The bones of their corsets, visible through their uniforms, suggest the ribs of a skeleton, or death personified. The doctor in charge of the EST machine has a "quick evil glance" and a neighbouring ward has a "haunting smell" (p 71).

In Part Three, however, which forms the second half of the book, allusions to hell are abandoned. Istina returns to Cliffhaven to find that, in the refractory ward, there are flowers, paintings, large windows and good food. Although some of her worst experiences occur in this section, they are not compared to punishment inflicted on sinners in hell. The doctors are referred to as "Gods" (p 234), but when Dr Portman rescues Istina he calls to mind folk tales in which a prince arrives in the nick of time. Dr Portman, in keeping with his name, opens the door to freedom. He does not conform to the usual conception of princeliness, but is "the tubby loud-voiced intelligent intuitive prince in the forbidden castle." (p 242)

Although allusions to hell do not provide an allegorical structure, a second, less obvious pattern of imagery develops in the course of the novel. The progress of Istina from Cliffhaven to Treecroft and again to Cliffhaven is paralleled by three phases of a *catabasis* or descent, in which Istina descends into her own being. Although he does not describe *Faces in the Water* as allegorical, Mark Williams notes the "pattern of descent, discovery, and return", and compares it to that which "turns up in Homer's *Odyssey* when Ulysses goes down into the underworld. It is the informing structure of Dante's *Divine Comedy* and of Conrad's *Heart of Darkness*."[9] Istina makes the descent to seek her own imprisoned soul.

It is one of the doctors who asks, "My God what means the hospitality of the soul?" (p 101) We are to consider what kind or quality of care and comfort the soul requires, and what its proper nourishment might be. In a play on words familiar in Frame's later work, the meanings of 'hospitality' and 'hospital' become closely and ironically linked. Istina's soul, instead of receiving her care and hospitality, is hospitalised or incarcerated. In considering the opposite extreme, we can see that the human being might provide a place of refuge (a hospice, hostel, hotel, house) where the soul can be secure. Istina recalls the old men of Cliffhaven "sitting outside their dreary ward, and no one at home, not in themselves or anywhere." (p 114) She compares this impression with the condition of the many "'Poor naked wretches'" lamented by King Lear: "'*How shall your houseless heads and unfed sides, / Your looped and windowed raggedness defend you*'" (p 114). It is the 'souls' of the old men at Cliffhaven that are not at home; according to a reading suggested in the Arden edition of *King Lear*, it is the 'souls' of Shakespeare's "'Poor naked wretches'" that are unprotected[10].

The house of the soul is represented at times by "a small locked room" (p 204) and at other times by a ward, or an entire

mental hospital. The buildings, with their remote rooms, surprising doors and corridors, provide an image of a person's physical intricacy, corridors being comparable perhaps to "miles and
miles of intestines" (p III). The staff and inmates, many hidden
away, can be regarded as the multiple facets of one complex
identity. Memories, conflicting impulses, sensitivity, imagination lie beyond the reach of conscious thought but determine
each personality. We can visualise parts of the human psyche
that have been repressed or sealed off, "immured and left to rot
in an abandoned dwelling" (p 137). Ward Seven is compared to
the depths of the mind: "What if Ward Seven were but a
subaqueous condition of the mind which gave the fearful shapes
drowned there a rhythmic distortion of peace . . . ?" (p 69)

During Istina's first stay at Cliffhaven, the interior sections of
the hospital remain unknown to her. Aware only of her inability
to find her way, Istina learns little more than to go "dutifully for
treatment on nearly every morning when it was required of me"
(p 54). Individuality is suppressed. Under such conditions, the
soul is fettered. Istina observes other inmates "being driven . . .
their bodies half crouching, as if they faced a driving blizzard, as
if they pushed on to a kind of One Ton Camp of the soul, with
no hope of getting there." (p 44) The Scott-of-the-Antarctic
image suggests the effort required to become united with one's
soul, and the likelihood of failure in accomplishing that goal.

Istina is fascinated and appalled by the inmates of the neighbouring refractory ward and ponders the possible "meaning of
the gifts or rejects which they threw over the park and yard
fence—pieces of cloth, crusts, faeces, shoes—in a barrage of love
and hate for what lay beyond?" (p 46) The mystery surrounding
her own inner being is externalised through this image. It is also
personified through fellow patients like Mrs Pilling who displays
an "eternally calm" surface which "one watches . . . for evidence
of the rumoured creature inhabiting perhaps 'deeper than ever
plummet sounded'.[12] One needs a machine like a bathysphere to
find Mrs Pilling. A bathysphere of fear? Of love?" (p 36)

The move to Treecroft signals a development. It could be said that Istina enters the submersible observation chamber, the "bathysphere of fear", as part of her inner journey. She asks, "was I inhabiting, as it were, as a guest for the weekend, my own mind and becoming more and more perturbed by its manifestation of evil?" (p 75) She becomes aware that much is hidden beyond the bright camouflage of Ward Seven, which corresponds to the aspect of the mind capable of deception. At a deeper, invisible level, "fearful shapes" lie "drowned" [27] (p 69). Gradually, Istina makes a further descent, first to Ward "Four-Five-and-One" (p 83), its odd name suggesting the movement of a lift. There, people move like "automatons . . . fearful lest whatever or who-ever controlled them should tire of giving them distraction, and let them run down like broken toys and have to find in their own selves a way of overcoming the desolation in which they lived." (p 87) It is implied that learned patterns of continual busyness without thought lie immediately below a façade of apparent choice. Istina's 'descent' continues until she finds herself in Lawn Lodge, a ward where there are "raging screaming fighting people, a hundred of them, many in soft strait jackets, others in long canvas jackets that fastened between the thighs" (p 89).

Having reached the deepest level, Istina observes patterns of behaviour that parallel her own confusion. The crowd of inmates in Lawn Lodge are "like a microfilm of atoms in prison dress revolving and voyaging if that were possible, in search of their lost nucleus." (p 90) Istina tries to find her way, not among unrecognisable people, but among "unrecognisable feelings" (p 92). The fighting people represent a jumble of feelings that Istina has experienced but has hitherto failed to confront. Having descended to those depths, she "wanted the peeled layers of human dignity to be restored, as in one of those trick films where the motion moves backwards" (p 92). The descent into Lawn Lodge makes inner conflicts and emotions visible.

From her Lawn Lodge experience, Istina develops the under-standing that many humans suffer insanity as "the product, in the beginning, of crude longing dug out from their heart." (p 103) What has been destroyed may be described as "crude", elemental or basic human needs which 'civilisation' has often linked with 'evil', unless expressed within strict conventions such as holy wedlock. Istina's "crude longing" is not "dug out" with the "ice pick of a lobotomy" (p 161). Instead it is repressed, surfacing from time to time as a desire for human warmth and closeness, and a longing for children of her own. She yearns for the attention of someone who might write her a love letter and, on hearing of her sister's third pregnancy, asks why she, by contrast, should be so "empty" (p 130). She sees other patients, too, suffering from "a kind of starvation" (p 251) for husband, wife, child, family and love.

With Istina's return to Cliffhaven in Part Three, the journey into the profound areas of her own being continues. She is relegated to the refractory ward and to the inner reaches of the hospital complex. Eventually, she emerges from the depths to be placed in the more open wards and is finally pronounced well enough to leave.

Structurally, the novel follows the broad archetypal pattern of a descent and a return to the upper world. However, the intermittent images encouraging the impression that the hospital is a body housing a diseased mind and a sick soul are not reiterated in Part Three, though the analogy between hospital and person is not negated. Istina here is less often an observer and more often concerned directly with her own thoughts and emotions. She involves herself in a childlike and sensuous response to another person, Sister Bridge, who is in charge of the refractory ward.

Love is the emotion from which care-givers protect themselves. In Sister Bridge, love is concealed beneath scorn and sarcasm. She has become an overweight woman who shouts and mocks, though as a young nurse she "cried most of the night" (p 139) after her first day of duty among patients in locked boots and strait-jackets. Istina's perception transforms her negative approach into something positive: "words which came from her

as sarcasm and mockery . . . seemed in the air to undergo a trans-formation . . . so that they arrived without seeming to hurt."
(p 139)

The sister's self-conscious awareness of Istina's attention prompts an embarrassed rejection. " 'You're studying me are you, Miss Know-all?' " (p 140) Istina's intensity of feeling is clear: "I hated her, I hated her, but I wanted to pummel her mounds of flesh . . . Was she my mother? I wanted to hit her and to climb crying on to her lap and plead to be forgiven." (pp 172–173) Just as Sister Bridge's love has been subverted into sarcasm, Istina's love is subverted into anger and violence. Having spoken to Istina as a human being outside the hospital, Sister Bridge reverts to her customary manner once back in the ward. Istina's response is to push her down a flight of steps: "our contract of enmity was signed and sealed, surprisingly enough, with my love which I had shown by rushing at her and thumping her soft belly" (p 176).

Like Sister Bridge, Istina attempts to hide from her own human response. Her love cannot find release or expression. It seeps through the walls of her imprisoned self and is transformed into something negative:

> But I have never seen so much love in the storehouse; confined and sealed and lowered in price, it seeps and fumes through the wall as a mephitic presence; one wipes the trace of it like a mist from the mirror. (p 201)

It seems that, thus confined, love itself rots and exhales the fumes of a compost. The "storehouse" Istina refers to is her own inner being. It is that "storehouse" which will be "politely ransacked" (p 216) should she be subjected to a lobotomy; it is the "central storehouse—that self . . . to be assaulted, perhaps demolished" (p 219), which for almost 30 years has stored her awareness of time, her memory and her soul.

A lobotomy would supposedly enable Istina to join the ranks

of those in the outside world who have been shaped by society. As she contemplates "The World, Outside, Freedom", she visualises people as "giant patchworks of colour with limbs missing and parts of their minds snipped off to fit the outline of the free pattern." (p 38) That is the 'death' which Daphne from *Owls Do Cry* must endure after her lobotomy; it is the fate of many of Istina's fellow inmates. The memory of all those she encounters at Cliffhaven and Treecroft will inhabit forever the recesses of Istina's soul as "faces in the water", the drowned remnants of individuals. They are people considered by the nursing staff to be "to all intents and purposes ... dead." (p 105) The "bathysphere" and the references to drowning reinforce the pattern of Istina's descent, a search for her own 'truth' and for "that self" (p 219) with its own integrity to be valued and saved from death. The image of drowning recurs as Istina listens to the piano-playing of fellow patient Brenda, once a talented musician. After two lobotomy treatments, she is usually confined to the "dirty dayroom" (p 151).

> Listening to her, one experienced a deep uneasiness as of having avoided an urgent responsibility, like someone who, walking at night along the banks of a stream, catches a glimpse in the water of a white face or a moving limb and turns quickly away, refusing to help or to search for help. We all see faces in the water. (p 150)

Compassion itself may be too immured to offer any response to the needs of others. But many individuals are beyond all help; they are 'drowned' like Mrs Pilling " 'deeper than ever plummet sounded' " (p 36). Through listening to Brenda, Istina becomes aware of a loss comparable to the witnessing of "the kind of earth tremor that in two instants uncovers and reburies the lost kingdom." (p 151)

As part of her search for her own "lost kingdom", Istina must endure long weeks of solitary confinement, in which her only resources are memories and remembered poems and songs. Her greatest hunger is for reading and writing material. Earlier in the novel, she would not admit to the need for literature which is so strongly a part of her nature. Her copy of Shakespeare has "pictures falling out and pages unleaving as if an unknown person were devoting time to studying it." (p 114) Later, through access to the library, she discovers her own "land of meaning" (p 241). But it is through her writing that she is able to accept her "crude longing" (p 103) and to dispel dreams that were once "festering" (p 10). At the book's conclusion, she is able to enter at will her formerly "lost kingdom"; it is the source of her creativity and identity. It is the realm which, throughout the novel, is under threat from a lobotomy.

Faces in the Water does include an allegorical dimension in the recurrent analogy between hospital (with its outer and inner wards) and person (with outward appearance and inner complexity). In addition, the *catabasis* structures the entire novel. But the reader's empathy with Istina's traumatic experiences runs counter to an allegory's demand for "an analytical frame of mind" [12]. Nevertheless, allegorical devices are cunningly used to enrich the literary account of a disturbed human character.

The novel does not include deliberate dissimulation on the part of the author. If it poses difficulties, that is because *Faces in the Water* is concerned with the freeing of what Jung has called "the dark uncanny recesses of the human mind" [13]. This is the source writers draw on when they produce work in the "visionary mode". Jung is referring here to a mode "that derives its existence from the hinterland of man's mind, as if it had emerged from the abyss of prehuman ages, or from a superhuman world of contrasting light and darkness." [14] This is the territory which Frame enters.

In 1964, Allen Curnow singled out just two New Zealand novels which could justify the existence of an indigenous literature. *Faces in the Water* was one. Frame, he believed, had discovered "'the insider'", the "'all human'",[15] or the naked, defenceless human being. In this novel, Frame is concerned with the inner person and with that which determines and defines humanness. Curnow considered that "for New Zealand literature the way out is the way in;" this is the way to truths that are "'embrac'd and open to most men.'"[16] These are the truths that Frame is seeking in her concern with "dark, uncanny recesses of the human mind" (Jung) and with "the hospitality of the soul." (p 101)

Faces in the Water was first published by Pegasus Press in Christchurch and Braziller in New York, 1961. Page numbers in this chapter refer to The Women's Press edition, London, 1980.

1   Mark Williams, *Leaving the Highway: Six Contemporary New Zealand Novelists*, p 58. Williams earlier cites (p. 44) the *Encyclopaedia of New Zealand* entry on Frame's work which refers to her "'tragic disordered power'".

2   Janet Frame, *An Angel at My Table*, p 99.

3   Janet Frame, *ibid*, p 109.

4   These are Donald Hannah's words, from his essay "*Faces in the Water*: Case History or Work of Fiction", *Bird, Hawk, Bogie*, p 45. Frame does not respond to Hannah specifically, but to the many commentaries which have assumed that this novel is autobiographical.

5   Janet Frame, *An Angel at My Table*, p 73.

6   Williams, *op cit*, p 36.

7   Patrick Evans, "The Muse as Rough Beast: the autobiography of Janet Frame", *Untold* 6 (Spring 1986), p 1.

8   Janet Frame, *An Angel at My Table*, p 102.

9   Williams, *op cit*, p 37.

10   Shakespeare, *King Lear*, ed Kenneth Muir (Arden, London, 1961), p 115. In this edition, the editor cites in a footnote D G James, *The Life of Reason* (1949), p 147: "If also [the reader] will consider the phrases 'unfed sides' and 'loop'd and window'd raggedness,' he will see what a fusion of ideas is here; the body as the house of the soul and the house as protection for the body are ideas fused in the way I have spoken of."

11   The reference is to *The Tempest*, Act III, Scene 3. Alonzo, believing his son to have been drowned, says, "I'll seek him deeper than e'er plummet sounded,/And with him there lie mudded."

12 Angus Fletcher, *Allegory: The Theory of a Symbolic Mode,* p 107.

13 C G Jung, *The Spirit in Man, Art, and Literature,* p 91.

14 *Ibid,* p 90.

15 Allen Curnow, "New Zealand Literature: The Case for a Working Definition" (1964), in *Look Back Harder,* pp 207–208.

16 *Ibid,* p 208

The Edge of the Alphabet

The Edge of the Alphabet is a journey of "self-discovery" (p 223) venturing into "the dark seas of identity" (p 68). Janet Frame is again concerned with "the dark uncanny recesses of the human mind" [1], exploring a different aspect of a vast territory.

This is the first novel in which Frame employs a narrator. In sections which usually include the words "I, Thora Pattern" (p 13), she offers poetry and reminiscences. Her name suggests a god-like (or goddess-like) creator and pattern-maker. Thora creates for her characters an imagined world in which they act and interact. She announces her achievement on the first page of the book: "I made a journey of discovery through the lives of three people—Toby, Zoe, Pat." (p 13) She has "bequeathed" (p 208) to these characters parts of herself.

Toby is the epileptic Toby Withers from *Owls Do Cry*. Initially, the "journey" seems to be a voyage from New Zealand to England in which the three characters meet aboard the *Matua*. Allusions to Orpheus, however, prompt us to see the journey as allegorical. As in *Faces in the Water*, Frame is concerned with a *catabasis*, but the image of the descent is quite different here. The long sea journey to London parallels the descent of Orpheus into the underworld. At the same time, this dangerous journey, in which the "water lapping the sides of the ship was dark with blood" (p 40), is symbolically the beginning of a dangerous inner journey, a descent into Toby's mind.

Allusions to the Orphic myth raise particular expectations, but these are soon subverted. It is Frame's sense of irony which casts Toby Withers as Orpheus. He is given this role at a shipboard party together with the task of finding his partner. Far from charming trees, animals or people with his song, as Orpheus did, "Toby all his life had teased animals and birds and people" (p 20). Instead of making music, he embarrasses others with his unpredictable shouting and uncontrolled guffaws. He does not win the love of Eurydice but instead is rejected by Evelina. He does not journey to another world to find Eurydice or Evelina; he goes in search of his mother, Amy, "who spent most of her time caring for him and sheltering him." (p 122) The novel opens with Toby's grief at her death. As the *Matua* is about to sail he imagines her voice: "You will visit me one day in your voyage—In October?—lemon light, giraffe shadows, children let out of school" (pp 45–46).

The sea journey is an extended crossing of the Acheron. The ferryman Charon is Pat Keenan, who is "doomed to have no relationship with the living animal." (p 56) He dreams that he ventures "underground by the dripping rivers and caverns" (p 61). He sees himself as a "white-haired" (p 61) man bearing a huge safety match which is said to resemble a faggot or walking-stick but also resembles the oar used by the "white-haired" Charon to propel his bark. Ironically, "Pat needs desperately to recruit people." (p 131) Dante's Charon is said to round up lingerers, beckoning with his hand and thumping any reluctant passengers with his oar.[2]

Pat avoids the task of self-discovery. Though smug and self-satisfied, he is one who "never 'came into his own'" (p 55). As ferryman, he does not ever enter the depths of the underworld. Coming 'into one's own' he sees as "a difficult process anyway, rather like entering the parlour of oneself while the spider is waiting." (p 55) He remains a man inhibited by prejudice and prudery. "I've seen the book on your shelf, Zoe . . . To tell the truth I've had a quick look at it. It's not the kind of book you should ever read. [. . .] And steer clear of sex. Have nothing to do with it." (pp 189–190)[3]

Once the sea journey is over, Pat resumes his regular employment, ferrying passengers around London by bus before choosing a 'safe' occupation in stationery (the homophone 'stationary' is also implied). Pat seeks a contrast to the dangerous mobility of his earlier job, hoping, it seems, to halt the passage of change. He does not discover his identity.

In legend and folk tale, the hero finds his heroine and the heroine her hero, if only for a brief time. In Frame's world, there is no Eurydice for Orpheus. Toby first meets Zoe at a shipboard party where she has been given the label "Minnie Mouse" (p 69). The role coincides with her sense of life's cartoon quality. Unlike Toby, she is an ironist. With an awareness of herself as the invention of an author, she says to Toby:

> "It doesn't make you afraid, does it, that you are fiction, that you are not really aboard the *Matua* sailing to England, that you exist only in someone's mind, some poor writer who cannot do better than bring forth the conversation of musicians, poets, mice?"
>
> (p 70)

Thomas Crawford, reviewing the newly published novel in 1963, complained sharply at this question. "We just aren't able to believe in [Toby, Zoe and Pat] after Zoe's Berkeleyan remark to Toby at the ship's fancy-dress party."[4] He also dislikes "Thora's irritating questions and apostrophes" which "destroy our faith in the reality" of the characters. A credible characterisation is indeed at variance with Zoe's consciousness of the writing process and with Thora's detached commentary. Later critics would see exposure of the writing process as a postmodern feature that Frame will use more extensively in *Living in the Maniototo*.

At the shipboard party Zoe predicts, "Some day—did you say your name is Toby Withers?—you will be torn to pieces." (p 70)

The 'underworld' visited by Toby is London in winter. "People walking had wreaths of smoke or fog rising about them . . . like people sleepwalking in hell." (p 144) Whereas Orpheus is torn to pieces after his return to the upper world, Toby is under attack while still in the underworld. Indeed, he has been under attack all his life. The clearest image of his fragmented mind occurs through an impression of mirrors which surround him "sidling and circling" (p 215). Bizarre reflections replace his own identity which is "nowhere to be found" (p 217). Body, legs, face, hair are unrecognisable.

Toby is not alone in suffering fragmentation and dispersal. He becomes fascinated and appalled by goods displayed in the "Lost Property Great Railway Sale"—offering "the bits and pieces of travellers . . . a store of human leavings" (p 144). In London, Toby feels driven into the open, "unhoused, like a rabbit alone under a sky of circling hawks, with hungry identities preying upon him." (p 217) Much of what he assumed to be his own identity is a mere reflection of patterns gleaned from others "—the boy down the road . . . aunts . . . family . . . father . . .— and his mother." (p 217) All of these inhabit the 'underworld' that is, figuratively, his mind. In order to make repairs to his own distinct being and to assert authority over himself, Toby, "on his mother's advice" (p 218), returns to New Zealand. For Toby, as for any living being changing over time, the process of discovery and repair will continue until death.

Toby does not speak directly of the task of self-discovery. He knows intuitively that if he is to realise his ambition to write a book, for which he has already chosen the title—"The Lost Tribe" (p 18) — he would need ready access to his mental faculties, his memories, ideas, language. When his father complains, "Beats me with all your talking about this Lost Tribe why you haven't written about it and got it over with" (p 31), Toby's response is to think to himself, "My father doesn't understand the subject at all, there are precautions to be taken, menaces to be foreseen and overcome, slits in the roof to be mended" (p 32).

The "Lost Tribe" is an intriguing idea, but it is difficult to discover where, or whether, it belongs within the novel's allegorical structure. Toby seems unable to explain the concept: "No one but himself knew or understood the real meaning of it . . . and no one must ever share it." (p 29) But he offers a number of clues. "They live, he says, behind a mountain approached through a secret pass." (p 164) Earlier, he imagines himself to be "an entire forest, with the Lost Tribe inhabiting him as if his head were a secret gully somewhere up-country" (p 14).

Toby's idea is probably derived from at least two sources. There is much evidence that Maori tribes once lived on the shores of the southern lakes in New Zealand's South Island[5]. Toby seems to link local (South Island) history with religious belief in the survival of the Ten Lost Tribes of Israel which would, in time, be reunited with their brethren. Toby's idea has been nurtured by his mother "advising him, warning him, appearing to him at night and talking of the Lost Tribe and the Latter Days, quoting *Nation shall not lift up sword against Nation, neither shall they learn war anymore*" (p 161) (the reference is to *Isaiah* 2:4).

When asked why he has not written his book on the Lost Tribe, Toby replies that he is "an ambassador" (p 33). He also imagines himself to be a king: "The lad that's born to be king . . . Why, that's me!" (p 43) Later, Toby is asked if he is a lawyer. "—To do with law, Toby said earnestly." (p 70) But when he is asked, "—What do you have to do with the law?" he replies, "—Law? . . .—Nothing to do with law. I'm selfemployed—" (p 71). These conflicting statements may derive from Toby's secret wish that he should be the Christ of the second coming. The "law" he has "to do with" may be that law which is the divine commandment of God. His mother's tendency to quote from the Bible has provided material for Toby's myth-making. Having in his imagination placed the Lost Tribe among the southern mountains of New Zealand, Toby might be playing the imaginary role of Christ the ambassador who carries "out of Zion . . . the law."

(*Isaiah*, 2:3) But this is an assumption for which the text offers no clear confirmation. Such a mission is neither demonstrated nor explicitly parodied by Toby's actions.

While Toby's father mocked him, his mother gave encouragement: "Many of our greatest men were no good at school or games" (p 19). Wishful identification with Christ would have arisen from his mother's reverence: "Toby resented his mother's dream that the Second Coming would occur in her home, in the kitchen of the house at Waimaru. In Amy's mind Christ appeared conventionally as a swagger wandering up to the door and asking for food and shelter"[6] (p 167). In his dream, Toby returns to Waimaru, but he is not received with joy and reverence. Amy tells him, "—We're all dead Toby." (p 126) The dream-visit concludes with his father's appearance: "Still got your fine fancy ideas?" (p 127) In the course of his London sojourn, Toby does indeed lose his "fine fancy ideas". And he does find his mother; he hears her voice again and again giving advice and comfort. She seems to "sneak in and stiffen and sharpen his shapes of memory" (p 169). The *catabasis* takes Toby into his own mind with its thoughts of Christ and the "Lost Tribe". There, too, his mother continues to 'live'. As a result of the descent, Toby listens to, and takes note of, his mother's words, perhaps for the first time. He accepts her concept of the second coming and promises to give "the swagger" food and a cup of tea, "—perhaps a piece of salmon or trout or a whitebait patty." (p 218) Thus, he has given up the daydream of himself as Christ. His arrogance diminishes; on returning to New Zealand, he makes himself useful to an ailing aunt. Nevertheless, she says, "mysteriously,—There's more to Toby than you think." (p 220)

The characterisation of Zoe is less complex. She is linked only briefly and tenuously with the Orphic myth. In Toby's mind, a series of girls or women are interchangeable: Minnie Holloway—Evelina—Eurydice—Zoe—Minnie Mouse. The book's allusion to Eurydice is not developed.

One event lies at the heart of Zoe's characterisation. When she is prostrate with sea-sickness in the semi-darkness of the ship's hospital, someone places a kiss on her lips. She sees only a crew member "in a striped jersey" (p 85). The stripes signify the ribs of a skeleton. The "Kiss of Death" transforms Zoe. She asks, "Can what happened in the ship's hospital have transferred another world to me?" (p 106) The imagery does not suggest that "another world" is an underworld. Zoe looks back at life as if she is speaking from the very margin between life and death—from the "edge of the alphabet". The fact that her name means 'life' offers an ironic comment on the precariousness of life. The kiss reminds her of her desire for love which has never been fulfilled. Just as Istina in *Faces in the Water* laments her emptiness and contrasts her condition with that of her third-time-pregnant sister, so Zoe reveals her longing for a child by knitting a tiny white baby's dress. She waits in vain for a hero or prince. As an usherette in a London cinema, a place of dreams and illusions, she laments that she works in a "Palace where Princes are unknown." (p 181)

After the kiss, Zoe is conscious always of the "burgle and runnel of decay" (p 78). Drains and vacuum cleaners contribute to the sucking out and 'extraction' of life, and therefore of identity. Zoe is tormented by the uncertainty of her own identity and that of everyone else, "for no one really *knew*, for people were all the time being extended, distorted, merged, melted" (p 195). She is one of a multitude. When she wears a brown imitation-suede jacket, it is "as a last refuge of identity; at one with the tribe, in lion-skins, dancing around the circle of darkness." (p 198)

Zoe's intense awareness of death's imminence impels her to define or discover her own identity before being lost forever: "Shall I engage in private research of identity?" (p 81) Since the only sure way to affirm her existence is to make something, Zoe creates a forest from silver paper in which there are "silver faces of dead people, the layers of snow on their faces, their clothes bunched, hiding the loneliness of their body." (p 202) She peers into a realm comparable to the "mirror city" into which a person may send an "envoy"⁷ to make enquiries and discoveries. She sees her own being reflected among the icy solitary people caught in her silver forest. It is an image of sterility. This dead world is a simplified version of the world Thora Pattern creates.

The silver forest is shaped at the "Serpentine" (p 198), the name of the curved lake in Hyde Park. Frame transforms the entire Serpentine into a public swimming pool and park entered through a revolving gate with "staccato teeth" (p 199). On a figurative level, there are links between this venue and hell, whose entry is often depicted as a monster with gaping jaws. The serpent is a synonym for Satan, known as the "old serpent" (*Revelations* 20:2). The scene inside is described as a "summer battlefield and all the bodies, wounded in one place or another, strewn there . . . Some screamed. With joy. Or leaned in languor upon their death." (p 199) Zoe's visit to the Serpentine, comparable to Toby's underworld journey, enacts her descent into the hidden places of her own mind. It is as if Zoe faces her own forbidden dreams as she journeys with unknown men and finds herself in the company of a prostitute and homosexuals.

— . . . I don't even know you . . .
— I know you Zoe Bryce, he said, again accusingly, and Zoe blushed. He guesses, she thought. He guesses everything. (p 198)

The spiked gates at the entrance to the Serpentine suggest the danger implicit in inner exploration.

Having defined and accepted the particular nature and limitations of her world, Zoe decides that the right time for her death has arrived. She commits suicide, plunging "from the small cliff-area where she lived at the edge of the alphabet and achieved that most dramatic and convenient change in habits which we call Death." (p 205) "The edge of the alphabet" is a place where "all streamers are torn or trail into strangeness" (p 42): it is the infinitesimal yet infinite space separating speech from silence, light from darkness, and life from death. This ambiguous con-

cept is reiterated through a series of images suggesting transition
between levels or territories: stairways, gates, waiting-rooms,
doorways and the sea are all dangerous dividing spaces which, at
the same time, link one realm with another.

The novel was to have been a "journey of discovery" (p 13). At
the book's conclusion, Thora speaks of "self-discovery" (p 223).
Though we have encountered the fruits of a writer's imagination
and creative ability, we know little about Thora the woman. As
she says, she has "bequeathed" to her characters only parts of
herself, and those are the very parts she rejects: "I bequeathed to
them the parts of myself which I cannot invite as guests to this
lonely house" (p 208).

While revealing little of Thora, the journey allows Toby and
Zoe to explore their own identities, though Pat makes no such
exploration. The Orphic descent reveals Toby's secret dreams,
fears and limitations. Once in the underworld of his own mind,
Toby finds that he has lost a veritable tribe of faculties. (As a
result of epilepsy, he has suffered brain damage, he is almost
blind in one eye, his hearing is impaired and his walk is a "clam-
ber" (p 164); to marshal the language he needs for speech or writing is extremely difficult for him.) The text indicates that he is
"lost, inside and out." (p 141) But imagination can transcend all
deficiencies. It is possible that, in Toby's dream, humankind is
the Lost Tribe to be led by Toby Withers the chosen son, the one
with a special destiny who is "born to be king". Understandably,
the descent into Zoe's mind discovers an entirely different set of
hopes and values. Her sense of the futility of continuing her life
springs from a lack of future purpose or vision.

The work's wider significance is declared in the concluding
pages by Thora Pattern. Thora's death is announced in an introductory Note which states that her manuscript has been found
and submitted to a publisher. We are never told of the circumstances of her death. As the book comes to an end, Thora

despairs at being "haunted by death and the dead!" (p 223) The "dead" could be regarded as another "lost tribe", but the text does not identify them as such. Thora laments that humanity is divided into so many people "when one birth, one mind, one death would be enough to end the tributary tears" (p 223). The statement has a biblical echo, calling to mind the salvation promised by Christ's birth and death.

Thora notes the way people in city or forest "fight to kill one another" (p 224) and asks, "Where is the Keeper of the Merry-Go-Round?" (The "Merry-Go-Round" is presumably the world, and its Keeper, God or Christ.) The answer is that "He is away" (p 209). There is an implicit longing for the promised age in which "*Nation shall not lift up sword against Nation*".

Like *Owls Do Cry* and *Faces in the Water*, *The Edge of the Alphabet* foregrounds the exploration of character. The allegorical framework of a descent provides an unobtrusive structural element. Allusions to Orpheus (or the opposite of Orpheus) illuminate only one facet of Toby. He is a credible character who changes and develops as the novel progresses.

Thora, as the creator of the three characters and the fiction within a fiction, survives the silence beyond the "edge of the alphabet". By writing the novel, she makes a statement that recurs throughout Frame's *oeuvre:* a work of art can transcend death. The dead follow Thora persistently—as if she might be the one to allow their resurrection or immortality through her writing. They hope to be led home. "Home? The edge of the alphabet" (p 224). The only home Thora can offer is the novel itself—*The Edge of the Alphabet*. As she tries to look beyond the edge, she fears that, at the end of her life, she will confront only herself, her own reflection. "And what if the person who meets us for ever is ourselves?" (p 223)

The question is not answered. The small, well-made allegory published less than a year later entitled "Snowman, Snowman" will ask a question which falls into the same area of ontological enquiry.

The Edge of the Alphabet was first published by Pegasus, Christchurch, Braziller in New York and W H Allen in London, 1962. Page numbers refer to the Pegasus Press edition.

1   C G Jung, *The Spirit in Man, Art, and Literature*, p 91.

2   It is always interesting to consider Frame's reasons for choosing a particular name. The Irish pronunciation of 'Keenan' (K non) is quite similar to the sound of 'Charon' (K ron). Charon is "white-haired" in the Sayers edition of *The Divine Comedy, I: Hell* III 83. His rounding-up of passengers is described in III 110-111.

3   Pat Keenan is reminiscent of the friendly, 44-year-old Patrick Reilly, a bus driver, described in *The Envoy from Mirror City*. "He was a natural helper. He was also dependable, self-satisfied, bigoted, lonely, religious with an endearing Irish accent." (p 16).

4   Thomas Crawford, " *The Edge of the Alphabet.* Janet Frame", *Landfall* XVII 2 (1963), p 193.

5   Artefacts and burial grounds indicate that three hundred years ago, several Maori communities lived on the shores of the southern lakes in New Zealand. The reason for their departure or demise is a matter for conjecture. Belief in their presence in the region continued into the 19th century. In the 1830s, sheep farmers moving into the vicinity of Lake Wakatipu "were warned that there was a tribe of natives who had their location in the forest between Lake Wakatipu and the sea. Nothing, however, was seen of these." (Robert Gilkison, *Early Days in Central Otago*, Christchurch, 1961, p 6.)

6   The idea derives from *Revelations* 3:20. "Behold, I stand at the door, and knock: if any man hear my voice, and open the door, I will come in to him, and will sup with him, and he with me." The image of the swagger recalls R A K Mason's poem "On the Swag", which describes "the cold wet deadbeat" and concludes "'for this is Christ'". (*A Book of New Zealand Verse 1923-50*, ed Allen Curnow Christchurch, 1951, p 114.)

7   The image is taken from the title of Volume Three of Frame's autobiography, *The Envoy from Mirror City*.

8   There is a lighthouse "Keeper" in *Scented Gardens for the Blind* who, according to my interpretation, is a Christ figure: "Year after year so many lives were saved by the use of the lighthouse and the powerful beacon restlessly turning and flashing in the dark, controlled and guarded by the Keeper . . ." (p 45)

5

S n o w m a n ,   S n o w m a n

Whom we might meet as we pass into the "for ever" of death is
one of the questions posed in *The Edge of the Alphabet*; the story
"Snowman, Snowman" considers the nature of the destination,
the "place" where one is to live "for ever and ever." (p 102) After
the complexities of *The Edge of the Alphabet*, it is instructive to
consider a much smaller work, a skilfully composed allegory
focused on fundamental human concerns. Other stories by
Frame can be read as parables or fables, but the near-novella
length of this one sets it apart. In "Snowman, Snowman" there is
no emphasis on character to mask or detract from the allegorical
intention: the protagonists are a snowman and a snowflake.

Published in 1963, "Snowman, Snowman" was the title story
in the volume *Snowman, Snowman: Fables and Fantasies*. Frame's
longest story, it was one of those she chose to be reprinted in the
1983 collection *You are now entering the human heart*. It is a tale
of a talking snowman who looks on the world with wondering
eyes and a questioning mind. His mentor, the Perpetual Snowflake stationed on a nearby windowsill, helps him to interpret
what he sees. The action is confined to part of a street that is
within Snowman's range of vision, although the Perpetual Snowflake provides histories and anecdotes about neighbourhood
families. The story's tension derives from the irony of Snowman's
belief that he is immortal, and the reader's knowledge that he will
soon melt.

If the story is read as an allegory, Snowman corresponds to man, who is thus depicted as shapeless, cold and inflexible. Ironically, humans like to see themselves as versatile, warm and distinctive. Furthermore, man's tenure on earth is scarcely more secure than that of Snowman. There is an invisible "germ cell" waiting to claim human victims: "a germ cell like a great sleeping beast lies curled upon the . . . doorstep, tethered to past centuries" (p 33). The sleeping beast, which at any moment may awaken to infect or consume, mocks human complacency. In the context of "past centuries", a man's life becomes as brief as a snowman's.

Though a critic of human self-deception, Snowman unwittingly deceives himself: "I talk of the sun but I do not believe in it." (p 92) In spite of his apparent disbelief, he tries to protect himself against its heat. The Perpetual Snowflake is impatient with him: "'You are a fool of course. As self-centred as any human being. You imagine newspapers are printed to shelter you from the sun.'" (p 85) But Snowman believes himself to be superior to man. Though told by a passing sparrow that he is in prison, Snowman, with specious reasoning, arrives at a conclusion he finds comfortable. He considers immobility advantageous. Instead of the danger of being whirled through the air as drifting snow, Snowman is "preserved, made safe against death" (p 31). He thinks that humans, by contrast, are mortal and vanish swiftly: "I would not believe vanishing was possible if I did not observe it happening each day—around corners, into the sky, behind doors, gates, hedges" (p 52). There is wit and charm in Snowman's candour. But the fixity of his perception and his limited mind and vision are recognisable as human failings.

We are amused that Snowman should consider himself "preserved" until, with a certain shock, we come to see that his attitudes mirror our own. Snowman's complacency is shared by those who consider themselves to be privileged, 'made safe', if not in this world, then in the next. Snowman asks, "I should like to know of the place where I am to live for ever and ever. Tell me." (p 102) But the request is not answered. Snowman does not associate his own future dwelling-place with that of Rosemary, who died shortly after making him. The Perpetual Snowflake asserts that "the rain will treat her as earth . . . and new streams form and flow from her body to the clay and back again with circular inclusion flesh clay flesh" (p 91). She survives in the memories of those who have known her: "the dead . . . drop like parachutists to the darkness of memory and survive there because they are buckled and strapped to the white imperishable strength of having known and been known" (p 89). Many people, like Snowman, prefer to imagine an ideal dwelling-place.

This, however, is only one aspect of Frame's allegory. Snowman also says: "I have been made Man . . . Is it not a privilege to be made Man?" (p 35) The words echo the Nicene Creed:

> Who for us men, and for our salvation came down from heaven,
> And was incarnate by the Holy Ghost of the Virgin Mary
> And was made man,[1]

The suggestion is that Snowman is also a Christ-like figure. Christ is "as white as snow" (*Revelations* 1:14); Snowman is 'innocent'—"I am the white page." (p 32) In *Revelations*, Christ "cometh with clouds." (1:7) Snowman descended to earth with other flakes that could be seen "paratrooping in clouds of silk" (p 31). *Revelations* suggests that Christ's "eyes were as a flame of fire." (1:14) Snowman has "coal-black pine-forest eyes." (p 32) Fire is his enemy: "I have been so afraid of fire. I did not know that I contained it within the sight of my eyes and that when I gazed upon the sun the dreaded fire would originate from myself . . . all my life I have carried fire." (p 102) Dying is, indeed, an integral part of living. Snowman's words, spoken as he is melting, render ironical the earlier lines: "I have no passion. Is this why I shall live forever?" (p 32) "Passion" takes on the Christian implication of suffering and death as part of a divine purpose. As he melts, Snowman discovers his own kind of suffering which bears upon him like a weight, bowing his shoulders. He is also threatened by a sharp rod-like weapon, suggesting the spear that pierced Christ's side. It is an icicle whose melting mingles with the black blood from his body. His snow bleeds from its "wounds of light" (p 93). There is reference to "weeping" (p 91), "thorns" (p 95), a halo of light: "this bright light surrounding me." (p 99) Although unaware of his identification with Christ, Snowman re-enacts a crucifixion, his adversaries being the forces of nature, the warm wind and the sun.

The significance of the link between Snowman and Christ is reinforced by the role of the Perpetual Snowflake. Snowman asks, "Who is the Perpetual Snowflake? I never knew him before, though our family is Snowflake." (p 35) The Perpetual Snowflake is not mocked. His wisdom seems infinite. A "visitor from beyond the earth" (p 61), he is aware of people's inner thoughts and subtle motivations. "People do not cry because it is the end. They cry because the end does not correspond with their imagination of it." (p 48) At one point, Snowman announces that he no longer trusts the Perpetual Snowflake: "Since he spoke of the gap in the sky and the sun I have not trusted him." (p 91) The remark casts no doubt on the integrity of the Perpetual Snowflake, but makes Snowman look foolish. The contrast between the two is sharpened by the ridiculing of Snowman through irony.

The voice of the Perpetual Snowflake is like a voice from heaven. "'Snowman, Snowman,' my creator said." (p 30) These words appear on the story's first page. One assumes that they are spoken by Rosemary Dincer who, Snowman tells us, "made me to stand in her front garden" (p 31). But the voice at the story's conclusion reiterating "Snowman, Snowman!" (p 103) is that of the Perpetual Snowflake, implying that Snowman was called to life by the Perpetual Snowflake, his 'real' creator. The double appellation appears in the Bible when the Lord addresses a specially chosen person; "Moses, Moses" (*Exodus* 3:4) and "Samuel, Samuel" (*1 Samuel* 3:10)[2] are two examples. An allegorical parallel is suggested, therefore, between the Perpetual

Snowflake and the Creator.

The image of a Perpetual Snowflake is fraught with paradox and therefore open to different interpretations. Pure (in the most literal sense) he may be transformed into a vapour. His physical presence manifests perfect order and crystalline beauty, which depends on the capacity to reflect light. Like any remarkable work of nature, a snowflake occasions wonder and respect. In addition, the Perpetual Snowflake, as old as the world itself, is an example of nature's ancient and enduring memory.

The Perpetual Snowflake is indeed immortal, since he re-forms with the same beauty and perfection every winter. By mingling with the elements after he melts, Snowman too may be said to live "for ever and ever" in the form of ice, water, or cloud particles. In an ironic reversal, the photograph of Snowman that did not "turn out" shows "Solid brick, wood and stone" (p 78) as "unsubstantial", while everything covered with snow becomes "strong and bold . . . capable of withstanding ordeal by season and sun." (p 79) Winter snow will return season after season, but buildings will be worn away.

Like the Perpetual Snowflake, Snowman is an equivocal image. He might be viewed as a travesty of Christ. Or he could be said to mock a simplistic concept of Christ. There is a caustic edge to the statement, "You ought to be proud, Snowman, to have so changed the face of the earth, to have reduced it to such a terrible simplicity that people are blinded if they gaze upon it." (p 69) The words are an obvious and innocent statement of fact, for snow can cause blindness and it does indeed transform the surface of the earth. But they almost certainly mock the way Christian beliefs, worldwide in their influence, have been reduced or modified to fit human requirements. Christ is 'made to measure' in the same way that children make snowmen to whatever size and shape they choose. "Some are seven feet tall and others are only three feet tall . . . And all have been made by children or by those whom others regard as children." (p 44) A middle-aged woman named Tiny, four feet high and with the understanding of a child, makes a snowman exactly her size. When he refuses to respond as she had hoped, Tiny destroys him. Likewise, people have conceptualised Christ to fit their own expectations and have rejected him if he failed to fulfil those expectations.

Human activities provoke disparaging judgements from the Perpetual Snowflake. He mocks warmongering by likening a navy to children at play: "they press buttons which open snow-white umbrellas above the sea ... the candy floss of death licked by small boys from the hate and fear blossoming on the tall wooden sticks." (p 88) He is alluding to H-bombs and rocket-fire.

"Snowman, Snowman" examines the concept of immortality. It also re-enacts the story of Christ's death in such a way as to demand reappraisal of its significance, while allowing a range of readings. One would be that the spiritual and immortal exist, not in theological constructs and conceptions, but in the miraculous forms of nature and the energies of the changing seasons. The divine resides in the mysterious memory stored in seeds, spores and ova, and in human memory with its endless capacity for re-creation. This philosophy is reiterated in *The Carpathians*, Frame's most recent novel. Here, she describes memory as "a naked link, a point, diamond-size, seed-size, coded in a code of the world, of the human race; a passionately retained deliberate focus on all creatures and their worlds to ensure their survival."[3] To the Perpetual Snowflake, it seems that "seed is shed also at the moment of death" (p 83). The dead are part of the earth's inheritance; it draws "new forces of life from the mingled grass and sand and dead human flesh." (pp 57–58)

"Man is indeed simplicity" (p 30), for it seems that he resists or misinterprets the more profound truths. Nonetheless, Janet Frame has shaped a story of considerable complexity. Instead of endorsing a body of knowledge in the manner of traditional allegories, "Snowman, Snowman" questions old certainties. The tale subverts our expectations, making the allegory ironical. Though he considers himself knowledgeable and competent, modern man is shown, in his "simplicity", to depend on material goods: "Coal, brass, cloth, wood" (p 30). By contrast, a snowflake needs only the elements. The Perpetual Snowflake is powerful and enduring; humans, by contrast, have a brief life. The paradoxes are startling.

Snowman Snowman: Fables and Fantasies was first published by Braziller, New York, 1962, 1963. Page numbers in this chapter refer to the volume *You are now entering the human heart,* Victoria University Press, Wellington, 1983.

1   *The Book of Common Prayer.* This creed is part of the service of holy communion.

2   For example: 1 *Samuel* 3:10: "And the LORD came, and stood, and called as at other times, Samuel, Samuel. Then Samuel answered, Speak; for thy servant heareth."

3   Janet Frame, *The Carpathians* (Auckland, 1988), pp 171–172.

6

Scented Gardens for the Blind

Scented Gardens for the Blind has been described by Winston Rhodes as "impressive but 'difficult'"[1]. Patrick Evans, in considering the novelist's achievement up to 1985, found it to be "in many ways the most important of her books."[2] Jeanne Delbaere has also acknowledged its significance:

> It joins the choir of all the great voices of the modern sensibility which prophesy the ruin of Western civilization and equate the death of language with the death of man. If Dante's or Bunyan's quests ended at the top of the stairs in a vision of God or the Celestial City, Janet Frame's ends at the bottom.[3]

In her perceptive reading, Delbaere compares Frame's work with that of the two great allegorists Dante and Bunyan. The themes she identifies are the stuff of allegory. Rhodes finds in this novel a concern for "the long struggle of human beings to emerge from darkness into light, how they have used and wasted their gift of language, nurtured and abandoned great aspirations"[4]. These, too, are themes that are suited to allegory.

Scented Gardens for the Blind gives the initial impression of being a study of three members of a family. It invites us to consider why Vera Glace should feign blindness, why her husband Edward has chosen to absent himself from his New Zealand family to live in London, and why their daughter Erlene has lost her ability to speak. The answers cannot be discovered without exploring the allegorical identities these characters possess.

Vera Glace is the first-person narrator. Her anxieties form the subject of the first chapter. The second chapter is devoted to Erlene and the third to Edward. Both are third-person narratives. We do not know that Vera is the narrator until the book's final chapter. She is entirely unobtrusive as she enters the consciousness of her characters, offering extensive passages revealing the thoughts of Edward and Erlene. The structural sequence—Vera, Erlene, Edward—is repeated until the end of Chapter 15. The 16th and final chapter looks at the characters differently. They are discovered to be the invention of Vera, a 60-year-old inmate of a mental institution who has not spoken for 30 years. The characters, with their contradictions and many-sidedness, live only in her deranged mind. The insane, like Daphne Withers in *Owls Do Cry* (and the many Fools of literature), always speak truthfully; at the same time, they cannot be held responsible for views that may be outrageous. Paradoxically, the tale Vera narrates justifies her speechlessness. Language has become so alienated and abused that silence is preferable. Vera projects herself into a highly complex role, though at first we are aware only of a woman tormented by guilt.

She reflects on silence, blood, death, blindness and fear. The suspicion that she may be responsible for Erlene's muteness sets up tension in the narrative. However, the only misdemeanour to which she admits is the drowning of a sackful of kittens. She takes Erlene to the hospital for treatment by Dr Clapper and informs Edward of his daughter's condition. Meanwhile, we discover how Edward occupies himself in London. He responds to Vera's news by booking a flight to New Zealand in the hope that he may encourage his daughter's recovery. When Edward finally arrives in her room, the silent Erlene turns her back on him.

On the surface, there is little action, but the novel's ambiguities conceal a surprising complexity of motivation. The work alludes to the characters and the metaphoric universe of Milton's *Paradise Lost*. The parallels between the two works are not precise; Frame has transformed ideas and images from the epic poem to fit her own purpose.

It is confusing to find that repeated allusions link Edward to five different characters in *Paradise Lost*: Adam, God, Christ, Death, Satan. Nevertheless, a consistent characterisation is gradually disclosed. From one point of view, Edward embodies the aspirations and shortcomings of man. Like so many of Frame's male characters, he has an inflated sense of his own importance. Erlene wonders if he is "Adam sitting at his desk in the Garden of Eden, totting up the generations, gloating over them, trying to preserve their future by making lists of them" (p 224). To Edward, a genealogist by profession, preserving the human race involves keeping detailed records. To represent humanity, he chooses an " 'ordinary family' " (p 61) named Strang. The word has somewhat sinister associations with strangle, strange, danger; in German, *der Strang* is the hangman's rope.

Edward enjoys wargames with plastic soldiers. At first we do not know that the battle he describes is imaginary. He relishes "the battlefield . . . strewn with the bodies of the enemy, the dead, and the wounded who were left to die" (p 35). The discovery that Edward is playing a game allays for a time the suspicion that there is something demonic about him. Erlene's understanding is that "My father has promised to save us, that is why he went away and left us, so that he could return and save us. [. . .] My father is very powerful." (p 189) This remark seems to associate Edward with Christ, the Saviour, until it is recalled that Satan, too, promised to "seek/Deliverance for us all" (*Paradise Lost* II 464–465)[5].

Edward mocks the concept of Father, Son and Holy Spirit within a single entity by having eyes in which "people . . . saw themselves reflected three times" (p 60). This suggests that man may have created God in his own image, mocking the biblical assertion that God created man in his image. Edward's account of a voice which usually tells him no more than he already knows parodies the Holy Spirit. Vera complains, "The affair of the voice in his left ear is troubling, and a cause for jealousy on my part" (p 156). The allusions linking Edward to God and Christ can be read as the attempt by one of the satanic family to emulate or mock the members of the Holy Family.[6] Edward, rivalling God, makes genealogy his profession, for God is considered responsible for the biblical genealogies such as those in *Genesis* 5. God produced a rainbow as a sign of his covenant[7]; so Edward dreams of a devastated earth with its "well-kept rainbow perfect in the sky." (p 69)

Edward's obsession with the "Bomb" (p 68) indicates that his hopes and intentions are indeed malevolent. Description of the earth after devastation by the "Bomb" is related alluringly, like a cherished dream.

> He talked of the Bomb, of soft white ash like talcum powder clogging the pores of the earth—like a deodorant, though not like lilies or jasmine, only the smell of nothing removing without trace the smell of humanity, all its pools of blood, sweat, tears, semen, milk; a mere dusting of talcum powder; and trees with white hair; and a blue flame in the valleys; and night falling as usual with the stars coming out in their correct places and shining, and frost visiting . . . (pp 68–69)

Edward's perspective is indicated when he compares "bodies after death" with "tiny packets of hairpins between my finger and thumb . . ." (p 121).

It might be surmised that Edward's counterpart in *Paradise Lost* is Satan; however, in *Scented Gardens for the Blind* that role is played by Vera's father, Grandfather Bertram. He is a dreadful-looking fellow whom Erlene feared: "He was ugly, like a goblin, with no top teeth and blackened bottom ones, and even when he walked his knees seemed to bend giving him the appearance of dancing and sometimes of suddenly having to submit

to a pain inside him, as if he had been eating green gooseberries."
(pp 55–56) This description is in keeping with medieval drawings
of Lucifer or Satan which show him to be stunted, blackened and
contorted. It is also in keeping with Milton's account of Lucifer's
punishment: "lasting pain/Torments him" (*Paradise Lost* I 55–56).

In Milton's epic poem, Sin and Death, daughter and son of
Satan, are sent to earth. Satan gives them the following
instructions:

> . . . on the Earth
> Dominion exercise and in the Air
> Chiefly on Man, sole Lord of all declar'd,
> Him first make sure your thrall, and lastly kill.
> My substitutes I send ye, and Create
> Plenipotent on Earth, of matchless might
> Issuing from mee: on your joint vigour now
> My hold of this new Kingdom all depends,
> Through Sin to Death expos'd by my exploit. (X 399–408)

There are strong links between Frame's Edward and Milton's
Death. Exercise of "Dominion . . . in the Air" is alluded to when
Vera mockingly refers to Edward's "paper-and-paste wings"
(p 150) and to "headroom, enough for the demons to fly back
and forth" (p 68). Edward also has plump cheeks "in a way that
does not quite match his body, as if he carried a hamster com-
partment packed with pieces of torn—words? Certainly not food.
Paper, people?" (p 212) The image belongs to Death; it was once
commonplace for bodies in funeral parlours to have cheeks filled
out to restore their appearance.[8] Furthermore, the reference to
"people" suggests the image of Death devouring humankind.
Milton's Death says, as he contemplates his food supply on
earth, "here, though plenteous, all too little seems/To stuff this
Maw" (*Paradise Lost* X 600–601).

Discovery of Edward's allegorical identity is made difficult by
the deception that is part of his demonic nature. Since he pretends to have lofty motives, alert reading is required to perceive

his malevolence. His choice of imagery often betrays his attitude: "I do wonder if I should not have chosen a form of art—vivid, swift (like death)" (p 120). Vera's equivocal remarks contribute to the difficulty of deciphering Edward's role. When she says that he "keeps people, like hens or pigs, in an enclosure of Time, hoping to protect them from extinction; he feeds and fattens their histories" (p 156), she is alluding to the care with which he keeps his records and to his food supply. Furthermore, she chooses an image which indicates his disdain for the human family.

In the modern world, the Devil is no longer regarded as a threat. Death is his successor. In *Scented Gardens for the Blind* awareness of the Devil and Death as the antithesis of God and Christ helps to account for Edward's frustration with his human role: "Edward could not understand why he who had so much power . . . should be forced to endure the petty mutilations of time and light, should have no defence against the perpetual assault, . . . and the trip wires to death which gradually surrounded him . . ." (p 108). Having been sent to carry out a mission on earth, even he is susceptible to death. And as Satan's son, he resents the light.

Equivocation characterises Edward's remarks. When he speaks of himself as being "truly at war now" and envisages "death encroaching on all sides piercing defences, destroying communications" (p 114), he refers at one and the same time to his own life on earth, to his involvement in the fantasy of war games, and to his allegorical role of Death, who orchestrates and manipulates the encroachment of death "on all sides".

As Death, the Devil's son, Edward is a demon and a Prince of Darkness. Like any demon, he can change his shape. Edward manifests himself in two other forms. He can be identified with Uncle Blackbeetle, who lived on Erlene's windowsill. "She was related to the blackbeetle who sat outside on the windowsill." (p 32) Edward's first words after his long absence are, "Erlene,

speak to me Erlene. Don't you remember Uncle Blackbeetle?"
(p 237) Dr Clapper is another of Edward's guises, since Erlene
mistakes him for Uncle Blackbeetle: "fear began to grow in her
mind that Uncle Blackbeetle was Dr Clapper in disguise, trying
to get at her and spy on her" (p 191). The two are interchangeable. Uncle Blackbeetle asks: "Would you like me to put on a
white coat and come here to visit you? And would you like to
talk to me, using words?" (p 81) At a literal level, these confusions
have a different validity. Erlene is entirely credible as a deranged
young person.

Within the allegorical dimension, Edward adopts several
guises to exert pressure on Erlene to speak. Erlene is expected to
become the Antichrist, the beast. Edward asks, "Who from his
throne will save the world?" (p 203) and five pages later is
answered: "I will choose to sit with a beast upon the throne"
(p 208). Erlene wonders whether "ancestral voices prophesying
war" would come from "lumbering beasts" who, like herself,
"cannot speak with words"⁹ (p 224). Like Yeats, Frame is anticipating the antithesis of the promised second coming. Edward
hopes for a "significant message" (p 150) from Erlene which she
will "pronounce like an oracle" (p 151). He dreams of a return to
New Zealand which will successfully prompt "his daughter to
regain her power of speech and utter prophecies." (pp 199–200)

Erlene's mother Vera is Sin personified—hence her obsessive
guilt. Although in *Paradise Lost* Sin is the mother and the mate
of Death, as well as the daughter and mate of Satan, Frame does
not imply that the relationship between Edward and Vera is
incestuous or that there has been an incestuous relationship
between Vera and her father. Frame uses only those aspects of
Milton's epic that fulfil the requirements of her fiction. Vera's
salient characteristic is malevolence. Of Erlene, she says, "if I
knew that her first words were to be judgement upon me I would
kill her, I would go now to the little room where she sits alone in
the dark, and kill her, and she would not be able to cry for help."

(p 9) Vera seems to have spilt blood in the past: "I hear blood. [. . .] I could not escape from the tumult; drums, parades, congregations of scarlet [. . .] the terrible babbling of blood." (p 21) Milton's Sin is a fallen angel; she was once an "Inhabitant of Heav'n, and heav'nly born" (*Paradise Lost* II 860). Vera muses nostalgically: "I believed, in my powerless state, that I had once been in control of the world . . . I had helped to fix the sun and the sky in their right place." (p 18) In her new abode, Vera finds herself deprived of perfumes she once enjoyed. "I could not smell the first smell so dear to me—the flowering currant plunging its violent uncouth waves of presence in the fresh spring air" (p 27). Fragrance, like light, is an attribute of heaven: "while God spake, ambrosial fragrance fill'd/All Heaven" (*Paradise Lost* III 135–136).

In *Paradise Lost*, Christ undertakes to redeem humankind, without which "all mankind/Must have been lost, adjudg'd to Death and Hell." (*Paradise Lost* III 222–223) This situation is parodied in *Scented Gardens for the Blind.* Vera tells of a Christ figure who is portrayed as a lighthouse keeper, "one of the happiest men alive. So they said." (p 45) He would wait for night to descend, then he would "save men from death" (p 45). However, on the pretext that the "Keeper" has gone mad, "marooned for too long with Light" (p 47), two men take him into custody and bring him ashore. Vera does not see whether he then "changed to a bird flying round and round under the sun, or whether they . . . locked him safely in another tower" (p 47). In the continuing absence of Christ as keeper, humankind is condemned to the darkness of hell and to the ministrations of Sin and Death.

Vera's human counterpart is Eve, who, like Sin, is responsible for bringing death to humankind. Eve acknowledges, "I . . . first brought Death on all" (*Paradise Lost* XI 168). Milton's images of Satan's flight to earth, followed by his taking the form of a serpent and creeping secretly to tempt Eve, are evoked when Erlene asks why she can no longer speak. She imagines: "There must be so many reasons flying in swarms around the sky and creeping secretly with their belly to the earth" (p 82). The fall is the reason for her muteness. Erlene represents the multitude of children who must die following Eve's fall. Her silence is the silence of death.

When Erlene asks Uncle Blackbeetle, "why has it all happened, that I am not allowed to speak anymore?" (p 82), she does not receive an immediate answer. But eventually, Uncle Blackbeetle presents an image of death in the form of

> " . . . soldiers thin as the wind, in twos and threes in the dark."
> "Is it death then?"
> "Yes," said Uncle Blackbeetle. (p 84)

Erlene often behaves like one who has died. She lies flat "with her arms folded across her breast, as if she were dead." (p 88) Her mother asks, "Does Erlene speak to me and am I so afraid of death that I cannot hear?" (p 161) Erlene no longer knows her age—a person's years are not added to after death. She complains that

> once you have lost your place, your special hanger in the dark coat cupboard that fills the world of time, then there is nowhere for you to go to keep clean and free from dust and the moth grubs which chew your face in the dark and spit out the wishbones behind your eyes. (p 79)

These are images of the grave. Nevertheless, Erlene continues to think and move.

The place in which she does so is beyond the grave. It is hell, where "the air is full of spikes" (p 164) and she feels the "ghost of the pressure" (p 99) of the doctor's hand on her shoulder. She believes his head to be "empty, the wind whistl[ing] in the spare rooms between the walls and the torn wallpaper and under the threadbare carpet" (p 168).

It is possible to see the hell experienced by the Glace family as an inner or figurative hell. From a different perspective, hell and earth are one and the same place, as they are in *The Adaptable*

Man and *Living in the Maniototo*. In *Paradise Lost*, Hell and Earth are two places which are connected when Sin proposes to Death that a bridge should span the abyss that lies between:

> . . . let us try . . .
> to found a path
> Over this Main from Hell to that new World
> Where Satan now prevails . . . (*Paradise Lost* X 254 and 256–258)

Whereas Milton's "Main" is the abyss, Frame's vast " 'main' " is hell-on-earth, a mainland from which people try desperately to escape across a perilous bridge to some ideal, imagined place.

> I have seen the desperate people of the "<u>main</u>" crowded at the edge of the slight swinging bridge, trying to balance their escape to the island . . . while the <u>loaded·sun of noon</u> picked out with <u>merciless light-shot</u> the few swaying fearfully near the end of their journey. (p 28, emphases mine)

The underlined words allude to *Paradise Lost.* Frame's quotation marks around "main" indicate a direct, though unacknowledged, quotation. The "loaded sun of noon" refers to the unshadowed light which becomes dangerous because, at noon, Satan's sight is unimpeded. There is "an ancient fear of the noonday devil"[10]. Satan's sight may well be the source of Frame's "merciless light-shot" which fells those trying to escape across the "slight swinging bridge".

The intention and hope of the satanic family and other fallen angels is the "utter destruction of the works of God".[11] The "Bomb" is the ideal weapon for such a mission. Erlene, a prophet of doom not unlike Cassandra, is a herald of things to come after the Bomb. Erlene's prophecy is her silence. Edward wonders why Erlene has been "chosen to represent the terrible silence which threatened mankind?" (p 113) He considers that Erlene may have "strayed into the future . . . where few human beings have survived" (p 118). It is just a matter of time before everyone is silenced. Soldiers without swords, medals, uniforms, will have their teeth "cleaned with people ash." (p 84) One suspects that the beans placed in coffins by Uncle Blackbeetle are not simply beans, but 'human beans' (human beings) or 'has-beens', a macabre yet childlike play on words suggesting that humans are insignificant. The invisible soldiers, the people ash, the beans in coffins and the silent Erlene all serve to foreshadow the death of the entire human family.

Jeanne Delbaere has observed that, instead of the possibility of redemption, this novel conveys the message that "God has deserted for good the post-Hiroshima sky"[12]. Reliance on a deity is mocked in the parable of Albert Dungbeetle. He allows his family to starve to death while he waits "to seize the Treasure of All Time when it falls from God" (p 176). His awaited treasure is a ball of sheep-dung, a travesty of the 'Word of God'. The dung finally crushes and buries Albert. Preoccupation with imagined treasure, "dreams of the glory of his gift", bring only "darkness and death" (p 187). The disillusionment demonstrated here is echoed by Erlene:

> . . . there had just been a time when the human race grew up suddenly and panicked at the sight of the empty sky which they had once filled, for comfort, with fat old men wearing beards and smiling blue-eyed smiles and dropping promises that disintegrated when they reached the atmosphere . . .[13] (p 235)

There is a parallel between the ball of dung which destroyed Albert Dungbeetle after his years of waiting and dreaming, and the Bomb. Language has misled Albert into ignoring the needs of his family; language has allowed Edward to justify to himself the need for the Bomb, just as words like 'peace' and 'defence' have lulled people into accepting nuclear weaponry.

Edward envisages "the time of the flash in the sky, the deep burn of words which destroy all power to create, the time of a first-degree language so articulate that the vision of it results in physical blindness, and those who have spoken one word of it are struck dumb" (p 118). He is depicting a scene of annihilation in the interest of a vivid, new, but final statement. His choice of language presents the "flash in the sky" in positive terms. Edward demonstrates the danger of language, its capacity to justify extreme positions.

It is by means of language that deceit is most often practised. The name Vera means 'truth'; ironically, she is intent on hiding the truth, with language her accomplice. Jeanne Delbaere observes that Glace is French for 'mirror': "Vera Glace is . . . the 'true mirror' of mankind"[14]. It is sobering to place this judgement alongside the proposition that Vera is Sin personified. It follows that all humans stand accused of sin against humanity.

After the Bomb, there will be silence or a return to the language of the beast. Erlene imagines a new language arising from the wasteland, not a new articulate language, but the "voice of the beast", making sounds she conceives of as "true", "rising at last from ice and marshland, ancient rock and stone, the ultimate denial of cities and people and rich stores of language skimmed century after century from the settled civilisation of human beings." (p 227) When, at the book's conclusion, Vera speaks after 30 years of silence and after the detonation of a bomb in the northern hemisphere, it is with sounds that cannot lie or deceive: "Ug-g-Ug. Ohhh Ohh g. Ugg." (p 252) Milton believed that "Languages . . . are without doubt divinely given."[15] *Scented Gardens for the Blind* takes us into a time when a chaotic jumble of sounds replaces language. At the conclusion of *Paradise Lost*, Adam and Eve, now possessing a moral conscience, are assured that there is "A paradise within thee, happier far." (XII 587) Frame's novel concludes with a pessimistic negation or reversal of this redemptive vision. She offers an inversion of selected aspects of Milton's allegory.

The novel's title is cryptic. Scented gardens for the blind are provided in several New Zealand towns and cities by charitable organisations like Rotary or the Lions' Club. Frame's title mocks the concern displayed through such projects, for many individuals are less beneficent than they imagine themselves to be. In this novel, degrees of blindness are related to degrees of self-deception. Figuratively, Vera lives in darkness, her voluntary blindness an attempt to hide the truth. In Milton's Hell, a place of "darkness visible" (*Paradise Lost* I 63), each person, like Milton's blind man, is condemned to "ever-during dark ... from the cheerful ways of men/Cut off" (III 45–47) Vera's father complains: "we're cut off. I always knew we'd be cut off." (p 77) Edward's poor eyesight troubles him continually.

Just as those in the "darkness visible" of Milton's hell attempt to feign the conditions of heaven, so do those in the hell of the Glace family remember and try to re-create a scented environment to emulate the "ambrosial fragrance" that fills heaven when God speaks. Edward longs for lilac and Vera longs for the perfume of the flowering currant. Vera places richly-scented poppies, flowers of sleep and death with their "deadly" (p 30) centres, in Erlene's room. Uncle Blackbeetle masks the smell of death: "in the room where the finished caskets lay he would sprinkle a perfume collected from the heads of the grasses" (p 86).

The novel expresses a nostalgia for the scented gardens of a paradise or Eden where death is not an ever-present threat. Gradually, we come to understand that the nostalgia is our own. We who have sanctioned the Bomb in the name of peace are the ones who are blind. The name Edward means 'rich guardian'; death, our ward or guardian, will reap a rich harvest. Having viewed Edward as comparable to Milton's Death, it is important to see him also in human proportions.

Scented Gardens for the Blind is one of the two novels which convey, through their allegorical dimension, the "Bird Hawk Bogie" myth. The bird is the silent Erlene. She has been attacked by the "hawks"; they have "speckled Erlene's mind with Death" (p 103): "between *havens* and *hell* there are *hawks*; that way the world goes." (p 182) The bogie, in the form of the Bomb, has emerged from behind the hill, wiping out "Britain" (p 251). The dust with which Erlene is "speckled" is like the "talcum powder" that falls after the Bomb; "the world was still numb with fear, tasting people ash in their mouths" (p 251).

Delbaere has spoken of "the absence of plot and the apparent confusion in the monologues of the three 'characters'"[16]. The confusion at the most obvious narrative level led Owen Leeming, reviewing the book for *Landfall*, to complain of "indulgent lapses into sheer meaninglessness"[17]. Many passages are not meaningful unless they are seen in an allegorical context. The judgement of Winston Rhodes, that there is "imperfect control of the technique of plot-character structure"[18], is valid only to the extent that access to an intricate plot-character structure is difficult. The novel's allegorical dimension has startling coherence. However, one needs imaginative agility to switch back and forth from a realistic, psychological investigation of characters as figments of Vera's disturbed imagination to an appreciation of their complex allegorical roles. Both perspectives are necessary if we are to perceive our human blindness and to link the threat of holocaust with human ruthlessness and self-deception.

Scented Gardens for the Blind was first published by Pegasus in Christchurch, Braziller in New York and W H Allen in London, 1963. Page numbers in this chapter refer to The Women's Press edition, London, 1982. Spelling has been anglicised.

1   Winston Rhodes, "Preludes and Parables. A Reading of Janet Frame's Novels", *Landfall* XXVI 2 (1972), p 138.

2   Patrick Evans, "Janet Frame and the Art of Life", *Meanjin* 3 (1985), p 378.

3   Jeanne Delbaere, "Beyond the Word: *Scented Gardens for the Blind*", in *Bird, Hawk, Bogie*, p 77.

4   Rhodes, *op cit*, p 139.

5   John Milton, *Complete Poems and Major Prose*, ed Merritt Y Hughes. References give book then line numbers.

6   Milton, *ibid*, p 177. Merritt Hughes suggests that in *Paradise Lost* "Satan, Sin and Death are now seen to be a parody of the Trinity of Heaven". He is referring to the response of 20th-century critics.

7   *Genesis* 9:9.

8   An interview with funeral director Colin Griggs (of Thos Griggs and Son,

Palmerston North) has confirmed that placing of cottonwool or tissue paper in the cheeks of the dead was commonplace until the 1960s. Modern embalming techniques have replaced this practice.

9   Erlene's musings recall the "rough beast" from the poem by W B Yeats, "The Second Coming", in *Collected Poems of W B Yeats*, p 210, and "Ancestral voices prophesying war!" from "Kubla Khan" by S T Coleridge, *Poems and Prose*, p 89.

10 Milton, *op cit*, p 273. In the following from *Paradise Lost* (III 614-620), the "eye" is Satan's:

> far and wide his eye commands,
> For sight no obstacle found here, nor shade,
> But all Sun-shine, as when his Beams at Noon
> Culminate from th'*Equator*, as they now
> Shot upward still direct, whence no way round
> Shadow from body opaque can fall, and the Air,
> Nowhere so clear, sharp'n'd his visual ray

Merritt Hughes notes that Satan's vision is supposedly sharpened when no shadows fall.

11 *Ibid*, p 183, from Hughes's commentary.

12 Delbaere, *op cit*, p 77.

13 Consider, for example, Murillo's painting, *The Holy Family*. God, attended by cherubim, reclines upon clouds above the representation of Christ, Mary and Joseph. This painting has been popularised as one of the coloured plates in *The Book of Common Prayer*.

14 Delbaere, *op cit*, p 75.

15 Milton, *op cit*, p 455. Hughes, footnoting lines 52–59, cites *Logic I* XXXIV (CEXI, 220).

16 Delbaere, *op cit*, p 68.

17 Owen Leeming, review of *Scented Gardens for the Blind*, *Landfall* XVII 4 (1963), p 389.

18 Rhodes, *op cit*, p 145.

7

The Adaptable Man

In her autobiography, Frame records critical responses to *Scented Gardens for the Blind,* ranging from "This book is unreadable in the worst sense" to "likely a work of genius".[1] Her publisher Mark Goulden claimed that, though her novels "had excellent reviews, they did not sell"; he hoped she would "write a 'bestseller'"[2] one day. *The Adaptable Man*, Frame's next novel, could well be her response to those remarks, for it mocks the 'bestseller'. Early in the work there is a murder. The reader anticipates a web of intrigue to be revealed gradually. In its unfolding, however, the novel refuses to comply with the expectations of those familiar with 'bestselling' murder mysteries. 'How' and 'why' remain unanswered until the novel's allegorical dimension is discovered.

Frame again uses *Paradise Lost* as a foil and prior text, drawing further on the memorable pattern of relationships within the satanic family. New versions of Satan, Sin and Death appear. Frame continues to depict the modern world as hell.

The Adaptable Man begins with allusions, not to *Paradise Lost*, but to the opening scene of *Macbeth*, where the witches around a cauldron intend to brew mischief. The narrator speaks of the "cauldron world of the witch novelist" (p[8])[3]. We are warned that this novel will be unpalatable. In a mood that simmers with defiance, the "witch novelist" is "mixing a cauldron of uneatables for others to observe, admire, shrink from" (p[8]).

In the Prologue, each of the characters speaks in the first person. But the body of the work is a third-person narration in which the perspective shifts from one character to another. Unity Foreman is an unobtrusive narrator who does not interact with any other character. Her name reminds us that, behind the intricacies of the work, there is an invisible writer who guides, shapes and unifies. The setting is Little Burgelstatham in East Suffolk.

While writing of "roses, honeysuckle, blackberries" (p 46), Unity Foreman finds her imagination turning to "spurt of blood, the adder, grinning rat, deadly nightshade" (p 47). Though she pretends to write from a country cottage, her abode is London where a jet "screams" overhead, the June traffic is "harsh" and the room is "stuffy, full of carpet dust and invading soot. [. . .] —Hell, she said.—Hell" (p 47). London, as depicted in this novel, is hell; with its smog and chained windows, it is "a wild city full of bankrobbers, murderers"[4] (p 219), or "dissolute models, playboy dukes, pimps, touts, sly foreigners" (p 223). There are "slums; more slums" (p 24). But the countryside is also a hell: "the first thatched cottages, some derelict, fingers of dark poked through their torn eyes, the thatch rotting, riddled with bird and rat-holes, the gardens overgrown." (p 24)

In the land around Little Burgelstatham, scarecrows are typical inhabitants—"an outlandishly dressed ineffectual race." (p 17) They crackle "as if they devoured their own poor dry skeletons." (p 17) Such imagery is reminiscent of the way in which death and hell are characterised in *Grimms' Fairy Tales*:

"dry-boned Death came striding toward him".[5]

Hans looked terrible, worse than a scarecrow. "Where have you come from?"
"From Hell."[6]

Frame's crimson-faced scarecrows which "crackled like thriving flames" (p 17) recall the "Devil with a fiery head"[7] who is disguised as "Frau Trude" in the Grimms' tale of that name. The underworld characters in these tales are in the habit of visiting the earth, while earth-dwellers visit hell from time to time. Into the land of scarecrows comes Botti Julio, a foreign worker from Andorra employed to pick fruit. He is murdered on his way from railway station to farm, but the novel pays little attention to the discovery and exposure of the culprit.

The name Little Burgelstatham contributes to the ghoulish atmosphere. A "burgel" is "a burial place of the heathen" (p 15). All the inhabitants are figuratively buried. One of the central characters, Greta Maude, laments that her husband Russell, a dentist, "bought a practice in Murston, a cottage in Little Burgelstatham, and began to bury her, himself and Alwyn [their son] in the depths of East Suffolk." (p 81) She complains to her brother-in-law that "We're dead here" (p 34). The notion that the populace is "heathen" seems to be confirmed by a harvest festival service in a church opened once a year and attended by a congregation of three people and one dog.

The Maudes—Russell, his brother Aisley, Greta and Alwyn—could be considered to be members of the 'Death' family, for Maude evokes the German *der Mord* meaning 'murder' and the French *la mort* meaning 'death'[8]. Among New Zealand children of Janet Frame's generation, the school dental clinic was popularly known as 'the murder house'. Indeed, Russell's drill sounds like a road drill, re-creating the impression of the "dentist as villain, the childhood tortures, cloves, cocaine" (p 139). There is a childlike humour in the visual link between the word 'corps' and 'corpse'—during the war, Russell Maude was stationed with the "Dental Corps" (p 80).

Aisley is the "late vicar of St. Cuthbert's." (p 10) As well as meaning 'former' vicar, "late" suggests that he no longer lives. Aisley finds his Christian faith to be burdensome and imprisoning. When he speaks of "my Christian faith set strongly behind me" (p 10), he is betraying his own equivocal attitude, for the statement could imply either support from, or rejection of, his faith.

Aisley has an ethereal appearance:

(Aisley was so thin; his feet moved like planks or flat paddles along the summer-dusty lanes. The dust rose in a thin cloud about him; he looked like a portrait of an aloof creature, new to earth, skimming along the lately-abandoned surface of hell).
(p 89)

We catch a glimpse of Aisley, enveloped by something like a halo. He is thin because he has been ill with tuberculosis. Greta invites him to stay for this ostensible reason. She considers that he had "seized her invitation too readily, or had been seized by it like a man who circumspectly pacing the floor of truth treads suddenly upon a loose board that gives way" (p 86).

His journey to Little Burgelstatham seems to have involved a descent. The impression is reinforced by the image of his going "to earth":

> . . . after his ordination, Aisley, like his fellow clergymen, 'came down to earth'; but Aisley went further, he went *to* earth, like a fox; he burrowed into the past. (pp 94–95)

The words 'came down to earth', placed in quotation marks by Frame, evoke the familiar carol "Once in Royal David's City", which includes the words "He came down to earth from Heaven". Several veiled allusions like this support the notion that Aisley is one of Frame's representations of Christ. Another such allusion is Russell's remark: "I haven't the complex My Son My Son which, if the truth were known, is perhaps the reason behind Aisley's pursuit of religion." (p 205) If Aisley is a Christ figure, it may be to suggest that Christ himself would become ill, dispirited and doubting if he were to find himself in the 20th century.

Aisley attempts to escape a simplistic perception of God. Like Erlene in *Scented Gardens for the Blind*, he rejects the image of God as an old bearded man with "peaceful countenance" or "righteous anger" (p 210). He also rejects the notion that God's eye is upon him; he becomes "embarrassed by personal photography" (p 10).

In the quiet of the countryside, Aisley gradually arrives at "himself" (p 77) and wonders then "if . . . there is room for God to return to the picture." (p 77) He comes to see God as

> the adult image of a powerful invisibility; the final Power and Pressure: less a superhuman creature than a marvel of engineering precision which, ultimately, will provide us with the power to develop wings though the heavens cry, Fall powerless on rock and stone. (p 210)

Aisley progresses from illness and doubt to new health and new resolve to follow the example of St Cuthbert in living a simple, contemplative life where he can be at one with the earth and sea. He had never felt at home in this century; it is an age of darkness and spiritual poverty. As a time-travelling Christ figure, Aisley's emulation of St Cuthbert is fitting. St Cuthbert died in 687, but his body remained miraculously incorrupt for hundreds of years[9]. In choosing to resist 20th-century progress and to follow the path of St Cuthbert, Aisley is suggesting that, to hold fast to Christ-like principles in this era, a person would need to become a recluse. His or her way would be the opposite to that taken by Jesus Christ, who preached to the multitudes. In a lonely place, Aisley "would be Man returned to stone, to communion with stone and sea and the first forms of life." (p 239) He quotes from the Anglo-Saxon poem "The Wanderer", sharing its nostalgia for a past golden era:

> 'Whither has gone the giver of treasure? Whither has gone the place of feasting? Where are the joys of hall? Alas, the bright cup! How that time has passed away, has grown dark under the shadow of night as if it had never been!' (p 263)[10]

The allegorical identity of Russell, Aisley's elder brother, is betrayed by his aspirations:

> Perhaps Russell . . . was more concerned with the present and the future than he supposed, was rehearsing the time when the

hero emerges not as poet, philosopher, statesman, but as *dentist* with the task of identifying, classifying, the sand– and ash-buried teeth, the tiny white pyramids erected as almost the last tomb enclosing the human race? (pp 150–151)

Russell's perspective encompasses time until the world's end. He imagines that teeth will outlive all other traces of humankind. He admits that he cares "only for monuments—teeth as tomb-stones, as sculpture—I see a vast deserted world of burnt earth, with these tombstones rising from it to speak" (p 205). Like Edward Glace in *Scented Gardens for the Blind*, Russell is looking ahead to a time which will see the destruction of God's work.

Unlike Edward, however, Russell does not play the part of Death. He takes a passive role, "setting up camp in the human mouth" (p 149) rather than launching an attack. In medieval art and drama, the mouth of hell was often depicted as a huge gaping mouth lined with teeth[11]. As a dull old-fashioned dentist with a terrifying drill, Russell, like Grandfather Bertram in *Scented Gardens for the Blind*, is the Devil, whose power and influence were greater in a past era.

The name Russell means 'fox'. One link between Devil and fox occurs in a medieval Bestiary where Vulpis the Fox is described as

> ... a fraudulent and ingenious animal. When he is hungry and nothing turns up for him to devour, he rolls himself in red mud so that he looks as if he were stained with blood ... The birds ... think he is dead ... Well, thus he grabs them and gobbles them up. The Devil has the nature of this same.[12]

On one occasion, Russell comes to have lunch with Greta "blood-spattered." (p 166) Details of this kind are always significant in Frame's work. The implication that Russell, like his brother Aisley, has gone *"to* earth, like a fox" (p 95) is subtle and deliberate.

Greta complains bitterly: "If only he hadn't buried himself in

the country! He would have been at the top, the top!" (p 60)
This possible allusion to Russell's 'fallen' condition is reiterated
as Greta speaks of "Russell's metamorphosis" (p 90) once he settled in Little Burgelstatham. Though he may once have been on
the side of the angels, "He was now on the side of the Great
Dull" (p 201). He lives among "bores" who "contribute by their
own actions to the denial of their soul." (p 202) The era in which
the Devil fought to win souls seems to be long past.

The 20th century is described as "an age in which genocide is
the basis of survival" (p 147). Unlike his father and uncle, Alwyn
Maude is a modern young man. He has taken

> . . . the first step towards being the truly adaptable man, a Child
> of His Time, by murdering someone whom he did not know,
> whom he had never seen in his life before, whom he neither
> loved nor hated; a man whose only qualification for being
> murdered was that he belonged to the human race.
> Alwyn is proud that he killed successfully. (p 147)

The term "adaptable" is used with irony, implying expediency
and ruthlessness for the purpose of self-gratification. It is suggested that "in the interests of human economy, the head of
adaptable man became a basin of uniform shape" (p[9]). The
head's saving grace, its imagination, may transform that basin
into "*a light-filled tomb/a cathedral dome*" (p[9]). Nevertheless,
an imprisoning "*porous two-way stone*" lies between man and the
natural world and between him and other humans. His chief
focus and preoccupation is himself. In the Prologue, the characters introduce themselves to a chorus of "I. I. I." Alwyn, the
"adaptable" post-Auschwitz man, considers that a person living
in the 20th century "didn't want to make heavy weather of an
occasional murder." (p 110) Alwyn is the son of Lucifer or Satan,
and, like Satan's son in *Paradise Lost*, he is also Death.

Alwyn's choice of carpentry as an occupation during his
university vacations can be seen as an attempt to emulate the

carpenter son of God. Alwyn's name is derived from Ealdwine, 'old friend'. This is an ironical way of viewing Death, though at times he may be seen in the guise of a merciful friend. 'Al' is also an obsolete form of 'all' as in 'Almighty'. It could be said that Alwyn, as Death, 'wins all'. Those like Mrs 'Un'win have no chance of winning. Mrs Unwin, an elderly woman, represents those claimed by Death as a matter of course. As she reflects on Alwyn, she remarks amusingly and ironically, "There was talk that his morals weren't very clean" (p 107).

Alwyn's preoccupations betray his hidden identity. Milton's impression of Death's vast insatiable "Maw" (*Paradise Lost* X 601) is in keeping with Alwyn's dream vision of himself with a "monstrous Head." (p 76) His mother observes that Alwyn "was a man who from birth had been provided with a huge set banquet of people. It had taken some years for his appetite to grow. He was satisfying it now." (p 92) This remark seems at first to be a purely figurative appraisal of an indulged and precocious only son. If Alwyn is Death, however, it has a more sinister significance.

Alwyn encourages us to accept that greed and voracity are inevitable aspects of human nature. He thinks that children's drawings of people are entirely accurate with "hands like starfish poised to sting, and their mouths extravagantly ear to ear, greedy to swallow and vomit what they have swallowed, and to kiss, deeply, like knife-blades." (p 63) It is suggested that man should "learn to stare at himself, at the truth of the strange history of his life upon the earth. [. . .] If he does not learn to stare soon, he will be destroyed for ever." (p 155) The implication is that man fails continually to learn from his errors because he deceives himself:

> giraffes weaving through patterns of forest leaves were never as clever as man weaving through his light and dark patterns of ideologies, safely concealing his nature from the enemy, and, incidentally, from his brothers and himself. (p 148)

Death is personified in two consecutive novels. Although Edward Glace of *Scented Gardens for the Blind* has recognisable human failings and inconsistencies, he is a strange, remote being who represents those distant authorities to whom we have entrusted the task of 'Defence'. In the mid-1960s, the Campaign for Nuclear Disarmament was in full cry. *Scented Gardens for the Blind* is in accord with that protest. The characterisation of Alwyn Maude makes a different point. He is familiar; he is self-indulgent and carefree, a typical young man of his age. In this way, Frame reacts against abrogation of individual responsibility for atrocities by suggesting that, since human nature includes greed and brutality, we are all guilty.

In spite of their differences, there is a clear link between Edward Glace and Alwyn Maude. Greta describes Alwyn as surrounded by "debris of the barriers of human habit that are broken . . . when the heat of the inner sun is so intense that the solid covering melts, flows, bubbles, glues the feet and burns black holes in the hands" (p 85). This recalls the eyes of Edward Glace which "glint like newly deposited tar and need barriers arranged about it to prevent people . . . being branded with great black stains that will not rub off or wash out."[13] These two quotations recall *Paradise Lost* XII 41–42 wherein "a black bituminous gurge/Boils out from underground, the mouth of Hell." Indelible "black stains" are imprinted on bodies by Death. *The Adaptable Man* reports that the bodies of Burke and Wills in the Australian desert are marked by such stains: "A dark-blue stain the colour of ink on an old stamp-pad . . . blotted and dried by the sun, showed between their legs." (p 120) They are described as men "who had clearly concluded and signed their treaty with death." (p 120)

Although *The Adaptable Man* draws no direct quotations from *Paradise Lost*, and has fewer allusions to it than *Scented Gardens for the Blind*, the relationship between Alwyn and Greta is patterned upon the incestuous relationship between Sin and Death in *Paradise Lost*. Greta regards Alwyn as her special possession:

"She was surprised to discover that in her secret dreams the treasure and reward of a son belonged entirely to her." (p 84) She admits to being jealous of Jenny, Alwyn's girlfriend: "Greta envied Jenny. She wanted sometimes to strike her." (p 91) The novel includes an incestuous episode between Greta and Alwyn. Greta conceives a child, probably fathered by her son. Greta's concealed allegorical role is that of Sin, for Sin is both the mother and the mate of Death. Greta reflects on her unborn child: "I can't think that I've sinned. [. . .] He will be a little prince with wrinkled skin." (p 92) She is a modern version of Sin. Unlike Vera in *Scented Gardens for the Blind*, Greta is not troubled by guilt or remorse. Her unborn child, in all likelihood the grandson of Lucifer, might well be called a 'prince'. When told of Greta's pregnancy, Russell exclaims: "*My dear, my dear*—he sounded like a Prince Consort! [. . .] He seemed to have grown shorter. She looked with quick dismay to make certain whether he had acquired a club foot." (pp 191–192) The allusion is to Satan, who is frequently represented in medieval art as stunted and with a cloven or club foot.

Greta, as Sin, invited Aisley to her home. Afflicted by doubt and tuberculosis, he is herded or lured through one of the entrances to hell. He is greeted at the gateway of Clematis Cottage by Greta who, like so many of the devils in medieval illustrations, wields a knotted serpent-like stick. Ironically, the name Clematis Cottage evokes a traditional image of tranquillity. The setting, like that of the typical murder mystery, makes murder and incest the more incongruous.

Greta admits only to the effective poisoning of garden pests— "the red spiders and the blackfly!" (p 72) Her hidden nature reveals itself in her memories of the war, during which time she was a ward sister and "witnessed so many deaths occurring with such violence that they seemed more a part of a festival, a celebration, an explosion of lives in a firework of blood and flesh." (pp 78–79) An unconcealed relish for death and war is found again in a longing to be in situations where she "might once more use the dead (if she could not use the living) as stepping-stones over streams of blood to a new land." (p 91) Her aim seems to accord with that of Russell and Alwyn, with the destruction of humankind as the ultimate goal. The apocalyptic vision of *Scented Gardens for the Blind* is reiterated.

Aisley's resolve to lead a solitary life and Greta's dreams of a new son are not fulfilled. Aisley and Greta, together with neighbour Muriel Baldry, are killed when a chandelier collapses at the Baldrys' dinner party. The Venini chandelier, said to be named after an Italian glass-maker, is probably so named because 'venin' is the toxic element in snake poison. The attempt to produce a wonderful light in the underworld fails. The dozens of bulbs enclose the room in "a prison-grey light" (p 30) before plunging it into total darkness.

No one admits responsibility for the deaths of Muriel Baldry, Greta and Aisley. If allegory were not involved, this would be another unsatisfactory episode in the mystery. There is one undoubted culprit: electricity, sign of progress in Little Burgelstatham. Humankind has pressed ahead with technological development which may lead to the collapse of an over-taxed ecology. Muriel, the wealthy modern consumer, is destroyed; so too is Greta, embodying Sin, which in our amoral age is neither understood nor relevant. Aisley had planned to return to ancient Christian ideals, though he knew these would have little relevance in the 20th century. His demise suggests that the inhabitants of our world are beyond redemption. The fall of the chandelier signals the extinguishing of the Light of Christianity in a "dark" age. Everyone is guilty of contributing to the darkness.

A survivor of the collapse, Vic Baldry, is paralysed and must view the world through a mirror. The novel concludes with the question, "don't we all live in mirrors, for ever?" (p 270), implying that today's survivors are two-dimensional. Depth is missing: only reflections and fragments of individuals are left. People are alienated from themselves, from one another and from the earth. Their willingness to detach themselves from the earth is evidenced by the intense activity at London Airport where Russell, as an ageing Satan, spends many hours watching the new arrivals to his domain, and Death, child of this modern age, ranges freely abroad.

In this fine parody of the 'bestseller', the witch-novelist has indeed provided unpalatable fare. For readers unaware of its allegorical allusions and relationships, the novel is a frustrating murder mystery which allows Alwyn Maude to be a proud culprit who is never brought to justice for a gratuitous murder. Once the allegorical aspect has been seen, the novel becomes a highly original blend of the comical, the bizarre and the profound.

Darkness is a motif in Frame's next novel also. But she sets aside all reference to the satanic and holy families. Returning to a New Zealand setting, she makes a study of a solitary woman, an artist adept at shading.

The Adaptable Man was first published by Pegasus in Christchurch, Braziller in New York and W H Allen in London, 1965. Page numbers in this chapter refer to the Pegasus Press edition.

1 Janet Frame, *The Envoy from Mirror City*, p 147.

2 *Ibid*, p 135.

3 The numbering begins on page 10. Earlier pages are unnumbered.

4 This description of London is reminiscent of the later description of Baltimore in *Living in the Maniototo*, p 79: "the city had one murder every day and many more robberies and muggings with violence".

5 The Brothers Grimm, *The Penguin Complete Grimms' Tales*, from "Godfather Death", p 153.

6 *Ibid*, from "The Devil's Grimy Brother", p 351.

7 *Ibid*, from "Frau Trude", p 152.

8 The evocation is purely visual and phonetic, since etymologically 'Maude' is a contracted form of 'Magdalena'.

9 See *The Saints*, edited by John Coulson and *The Oxford Dictionary of Saints*, second edition. The body of St Cuthbert was exhumed in 699, 1104 and again during the Reformation. On each occasion there was wonderment at its lifelike condition.

10 From "The Wanderer", *Anglo-Saxon Poetry*, p 73.

11   See, for instance, "Jüngstes Gericht", Kat-Nr57, *Stadtmuseum Münster Catalogue*, p 125. The original of this medieval painting, depicting two women being drawn into monstrous jaws by a devil, is in the city museum in Münster.

12   *'The Book of Beasts' being A Translation from A Latin Bestiary of the Twelfth Century*, edited by T H White, p 54.

13   Janet Frame, *Scented Gardens for the Blind*, p 212.

A State of Siege

Shading and shadows form a recurrent motif in *A State of Siege*. The novel conveys an artist's world of contrasting colours and shapes revealed by light and defined by shadow. Fifty-three-year-old Malfred Signal has retired early from teaching art to schoolgirls. She aims to embrace "the New View" (p 24) and to "forget the years of rigid shading, obsessional outlining and representation of objects" (p 239). She would like to place the past behind her without disturbing its shadows. As she contemplates 'autumn-cleaning', she envisages "a kind of dry-cleaning where one does not expose the material to boisterous washday treatment, including hanging out the past in broad daylight, but to a gentle, careful removal of stains" (p 172). She does not ever recognise that her shadows are associated with guilt or self-deception.

A State of Siege is intense and narrowly focused; it is concerned with just one character. An authorial (or eye-of-god) narrator has access to Malfred's thoughts and memories. A third-person narration, the work slips into first-person mode in a sequence of five chapters out of a total of 27. From this perspective Malfred recounts her dreams, offering one version of the 'truth'; the authorial narrator offers a significantly different version.

The novel is divided into three roughly equal sections: "The Knocking", "Darkness" and "The Stone". These headings as well as the title proclaim the likelihood of a symbolic or allegorical work. The plot is uncomplicated. Malfred leaves her South Island home to retire to the island of Karemoana in the Hauraki Gulf. Since she has devoted 30 years to teaching and, more recently, to nursing a dying mother, Malfred envisages freedom. She moves into an isolated bach with a fine view. Five nights later, there is thunderous knocking on the doors and the power is switched off at the front porch meter box. After six hours of intermittent knocking, a window is shattered. A stone is found on the floor, wrapped in newspaper bearing the crayoned words "*Help Help*" (p 244). Malfred is found dead three mornings later.

The source of the knocking creates and maintains a mystery that, at the realistic level, will not be solved. The very fact that an "element" (p 41) is blamed continues to prompt questioning. Within an allegorical dimension, the knocking can be identified in two distinct and different ways which are not at variance. The element can be viewed as Death, knocking on the door, the long night of siege being the process by which Malfred is deprived of her life. I will explore this line of development after examining the second, more complex alternative: the element can also be regarded as an elemental or natural force associated with the need for love and procreation. It is 'the heart' in a metaphorical sense: "the heart has laws, sometimes conflicting, to be kept. And the mind has laws. And I never worked out a system in which all laws could be respected." (pp 70–71) Malfred's "mind" and "heart" have long been at odds with each other. It is the mind that endures the long night of siege. The heart's capacity for love has been transformed into something negative and chaotic.

At first, Malfred assumes that the knocking is caused by the wind. She wonders whether her "lovers", "the sea, the sky, the trees" (p 63), have turned against her: "Yet I'm afraid there may be a point reached in chaos, a climax of chaos, that will emit life, like fumes of the storm" (p 63). These images suggest an act of love; but the ferocity of the storm may transform an act of love into an act of violation. In *Faces in the Water*, love "seeps and fumes through the wall like a mephitic presence"[1] because it is confined. Similarly, in *A State of Siege*, a heart that has been imprisoned exerts a destructive power. The knocking continues after the wind has died down.

> But now the walls, the roof, the windows were silent, <u>unresisting</u>, with nothing to resist. Only Malfred's skin, taut against her flesh, took over the role played by wood, glass, iron, as <u>defensive inviolable membrane</u>. The wind struck no further blows; but the knocking of the fists began to bruise her skin and she began to feel some confusion about whether the visitor <u>demanded entry or exit</u>; whether, indeed, it were visitor or guest.
> (p 79, emphases mine)

The pressure of something from outside wanting entry is paralleled by a pressure from inside Malfred demanding recognition and release. The outside force is the mirror image of the inside force. This is why there is confusion as to whether the element "demanded entry or exit". The language associated with sexual violation from outside is ambivalent, reflecting an inner impulse to overcome or to violate the constraints imposed by the mind.

Likening the human body to a building, house or room is a recurrent metaphor in Frame's work. In *A State of Siege*, the bach's white paint and disrepair correspond to the ageing maiden Malfred. The comparison between people and baches is applied to other dwellings and dwellers: "many of the people walking in the street had grown to look like the summer baches: there was an appearance of rust in their skin and eyes; an unoccupied look on their faces." (p 56)

In suggesting that the bach was occupied by a previous owner whose circumstances were very like Malfred's, Frame universalises the exile of the solitary woman. Before the knocking begins, Malfred dreams of a visitor or visitation. She quotes from Elizabeth Barrett: "'a mystic Shape did move/Behind me, and drew me backward by the hair'". In response to the question, "'Guess now who holds thee?'", the answer is "'Not Death, but Love'" (p 45) Malfred's dream is shared by other women similarly situated: "How everlasting was the dream in the human mind that some agent, some time that was never too late, would bring the permanent longed-for release from imprisonment!" (p 45) In longing for release, Malfred is like Zoe Bryce in *The Edge of the Alphabet*, and the greying Miss Walters in *Scented Gardens for the Blind* who spoke sadly as she concluded the poem "Someone" with the line, "'And no one came knocking at my wee small door' . . . turning to stare at the schoolroom door as if she expected a visitor."[2]

Footsteps, laughter, the shadow of a human form on the curtain—all suggest a human prowler outside Malfred's bach. But when she sets herself the task of identifying the prowler, she does not peep through chinks in the curtains. Instead, she searches through her memories. The novel flashes back through past events involving her mother, her sister and her former friend Wilfred Anderson, to find "what it is I wish to be saved from." (p 179) When she falls asleep, her mind continues the search from within her own 'dream-room' located "'two inches behind the eyes'", which has "for forty years" (p 8) been kept locked.

In the dream-room, Malfred asks:

> What is it then that besieges me? Who is it?
> Father?
> Mother?
> Lucy?
> Graham?
> Roland?
> Wilfred?
> The Old Girls, the Art Society, myself?
> What is it, who is it? (p 180)

"Light" is the first to beat upon the door, accusing Malfred of championing shadows. The inclusion of personified Light among the visitors encourages an allegorical view of the book. Malfred is terrified to find the room without light and therefore without shade or shadows. The importance of concealment is thus reiterated. Light is kept out. Her father enters without opening the door. Her mother, sister and husband, brother and wife are also visitors to the dream-room. Malfred acknowledges resentment towards both parents, and an intense resentment towards her sister and brother who took it for granted that "the unmarried eldest daughter cares for the aging parents." (p 214) Resentment towards these family members is overt, understandable and excusable; it is not a source of hidden retribution and inner conflict.

Having decided that family members do not besiege her, Malfred's mind returns to "an old soldier home from the wars." (p 216) From the very start, Wilfred was associated with the knocking, revealing a 25-year-old dream or nightmare that he might return from the war, arriving at any hour of the day or night. "No one would want to visit me at this hour on such a night. That is, no one but—" (p 64). She believes that "it is only those 'legendary old soldiers home from the wars' who knock at doors in the middle of the night" (p 148). She admits that "She had been thinking that perhaps the prowler was Wilfred . . . returned from the dead." (p 125, Frame's ellipsis)

When Wilfred enters the dream-room, Malfred seems uncertain as to his identity: "I might be deceived into supposing that he is Wilfred; but immediately when I think of Wilfred, I must search in my mind for any remains of him." (p 203) Her subsequent determination never to let him in, no matter how hard he knocks, and the fact that her mind keeps returning to the old soldier indicate that Wilfred occasions an intense reaction—one not in keeping with a need to search her mind for traces of him. Malfred reflects that "when a person is taken from the hazardous weather of being into the shelter of memory, he enters on the terms of memory alone, that is, as prey that will be devoured in the end. Fattened and garnished like Hansel and Gretel" (p 203). Memory and the dream-room may consume or transform the images of Wilfred, creating an account that is far from reliable: "I've felt pain and hate many times but my nature is its own sur-

geon and has removed my discomfort almost immediately"
(p 149).

The relationship between Malfred and Wilfred is described,
initially, by the authorial narrator. The friendship concludes
with Wilfred's departure overseas with the troops, a month after
an incident which may well have embarrassed Wilfred and
which, in all likelihood, left Malfred with feelings of guilt and
shame. In the luxuriant setting of a fernhouse, Wilfred kisses
Malfred:

> And then, when Wilfred put his hand inside her dress she felt a
> damp steam, like sweating fern, rise from between her breasts.
> And then she jerked her head back and began to cry, and it
> seemed that all her gentleness flowed away with her tears, for she
> felt callous, aged, experienced, and she did not care when
> Wilfred, a deep flush spreading under his skin, said, "Excuse
> me," and went behind a wet, black-barked treefern, and she
> thought as they linked arms, easily now, and walked out of the
> fernhouse that the white specks and spatters on the fern looked
> like a new kind of mildew, a disease that the ferns had caught
> through being there, in the fernhouse, at that moment. (p 138)

If we bring together the embarrassment, the intensity of the
moment, the need to retire behind the treefern, and the impression that the "kind of mildew" is "new", it seems likely that the
"white specks and spatters" are semen.

The dream-room account of the episode is quite different: "for
we made love in the fernhouse, and I did not as I need to remember that I did, turn Wilfred away or mock him but I loved him
with my body and with my thoughts." (pp 205–206) Her account of the love-making is imprecise: "It is the elements—
earth, air, fire, water—each time with a particular element in as-
cendance" (p 206). But it is likely that the elemental and natural
desire of the young couple was not consummated in the
fernhouse. The authorial narrator's detailed report has far more
credibility. The elemental force that Malfred rejected in Wilfred

and suppressed in herself may be the very "element" that has been loosed or "unbound" to make an "assault" (p 46) so many years later.

Malfred is like those New Zealand women who, in the first half of this century, would have been instilled with the belief that loss of virginity before marriage would result in loss of the lover's respect. This understanding helps to explain Wilfred's change of tone later in the dream-version, as he says, "words bursting like blisters from his lips, 'You bastard, you whore, you . . . '" (p 208, Frame's ellipsis). The earlier, authorial narration of Malfred's turning from the kiss suggests that, like Zoe Bryce in *The Edge of the Alphabet* and many others of her generation, she feared that a kiss ("'Give me your tongue,' he said", p 138) might cause pregnancy: "the childhood fantasy that kisses make babies"[3] endured into adulthood in those days when women were kept in ignorance, and when many communities were just as "provincial, prejudiced, puritanical" (p 47) as Matuatangi.

Malfred's regret at her barrenness is profound. She wonders what her body is for: "a spare part kept to replace nothing." (p 28) Her body continues to hope for fulfilment:

> All that work! Month after month getting ready for the great moment! It was mad, of course, this hope the body seemed to have until it died; it would not listen to reason. Yet, in a way, its reasoning was deeper, held fast to deeper laws than the reason of the mind. Malfred's body, even in its fifty-third year, had still not given up hope. (p 77)

Instead of chastising herself for ruining the relationship with Wilfred through her own fear, confusion and ignorance, she hardens herself against the very memory of him. She pretends that a photograph of a young soldier belonged to the previous bach owner. She finds something "indefinably unpleasant" about him, in a photo that is "specked with mildew." (p 150) The attitude of distaste extends to an observation of an old soldier whom she encounters in her dream. He picks up and chews discarded

cigarette butts. His subsequent action replicates, in bizarre caricature, the action of Wilfred behind the treefern in the
fernhouse:

> and then, suddenly, this old soldier home from the wars begins
> to work his mouth like the preparation of guns to fire a volley,
> and in a swift movement he thrusts his head forward, jetting his
> butt, globed with spit, to the ground at my feet. (p 224)

Wilfred and the old soldier are the same person. The two are
specifically linked in an intricate and riddling section of the
novel. In her dream, Malfred reflects that "Wilfred had a
relation, a baronet in England". She asks, "Was the old soldier
home from wars a baronet?" (p 226) On the following page she
wonders, "Has my shadow ... been choked by baronets with
bun? Baronets. Wilfred's relation. I feel now that I hate Wilfred.
How dare he ... with his lack of hygiene ... spitting his
returned overseas germs on the shining Auckland wharf!" (p 227)
A poem by Lewis Carroll[4], mocking human arrogance and folly,
refers to little birds "choking baronets with bun" (p 223); in *A
State of Siege* the image recurs no fewer than nine times. According to a popular euphemism of the day, pre-marital sex might
result in a 'bun in the oven'. Malfred's self-deception is ironic.
Condemnation of Wilfred as a baronet who takes liberties, or as
an unhygienic old soldier, allows her to overlay with shadow the
enduring grievance of her heart and body. The names "Malfred"
and "Wilfred" convey antithetic ideas: a repressive, judgemental
mind, conscious of evil ('mal' meaning 'ill' or 'evil') is in opposition to heart and body seeking to express its libido ('wil' meaning 'will' or 'desire').

Instead of fulfilment of a "dream in the human mind" that
"Not Death, but Love" (p 45) might intervene, there is an assault
by an elemental force that is love's subverted, destructive
opposite. Malfred also encounters "Death". She moves into a
bach described as a "Deceased estate" (p 42) where she is "alone,
in charge, and at rest." (p 46) The words "at rest", so familiar on

tombstones, have an ominous ring. The imprisonment of minis-
tering to her mother has been like a period of hibernation; in
contemplating her awakening, Malfred asks, "was it the release
that so many people hoped for at their own death, after a lifetime
of sleep?" (p 51)

The coming of death is foreshadowed as the bach is twice
plunged into darkness. It is foreshadowed also by the isolation,
"the dead phone" (p 154), and by an intense silence. Malfred
speaks of "an ache in her breast" and a "silence" that had "fallen
like an irremovable weight upon her body" (p 158). She struggles
to identify the silence—"death, tiredness, soundlessness." (p 161)
A sense of weight and silence often accompanies cardiac arrest or
a fainting fit. When she believes that she should have taken some
action during the silence without knowing what it might have
been, one can only guess that her body was tempted to descend
further into silence and darkness—that is, into death. The text
offers two even clearer indications of cardiac arrest.

> She lay without moving, her heart thudding against her breast,
> hitting and hurting, as if it were a shape of cast iron. Pain came
> in with her suddenly-drawn breath, and stayed, moving down
> her left arm, extending itself like an iron rod. She could feel the
> pressure of it. (p 80)

> Malfred felt a sudden pain over her heart. Her face went pale;
> she could feel the blood going elsewhere, like people making for
> the door when an alarm bell rings. (pp 233–234)

The two structuring ideas come together in the novel's reso-
lution. The heart is attacked by Death; it has also been in
conflict with the 'mind' for 25 years. When the heart suffers,
Malfred's mind protests that she "need not be made a scapegoat
for the knocking, breaking and entering, escaping, the final
encircling freedom!" (p 240) Traditionally, a scapegoat was
released to the wilderness when the sins of a whole people had
been laid upon it (*Leviticus* 16:21). According to the judgement

of Malfred's mind, the elemental desire of the heart is shameful, but the fact that the mind forsook an opportunity to forge a love relationship rather than a "false and formal" (p 136) friendship is, to the heart, reason for shame.

The anticipated "South Pacific paradise" (p 3) proves to be "a derelict, dead island" (p 152), a hell. Here, Malfred is "alone, in luminous metal weather, where a touch of the finger along the sky burns like the touch on hot blue steel." (p 242) But, as hell, the island is not to be compared with the hellish 'civilised' worlds of *Living in the Maniototo* or *The Adaptable Man*. The island is a representation of Malfred herself. Though she would like to believe that "the human heart has no boundaries" (p 147), her own heart is, indeed, confined. A ring of fire is formed by the summer "'blaze'" (p 120) of pohutukawa trees. "'Hell is *your* comparison'", she tells the priest in an imaginary phone call. "'Both sea and fire may be necessary barriers, protection for the derelict souls.'" (p 147)

Malfred suffers torment in which her whole being can be viewed as "a strange land": "the sky in the strange land lit with coals from a fire shovel fed with a human heart, and the night in the strange land its perfect black shadow." (p 233) The suffering of the heart has created burning coals that fuel the fire and create shadow within a personal hell. She continues, to the very last, to take refuge in shadows, finding, when finally she enters the room behind the eyes during wakefulness, that she is in a broom cupboard where there is one old fire-shovel, the very shovel that successive generations of her pupils have had to draw, with "its special magnificent shadow unseen, unknown, as beautiful, Malfred thought, even now, as any lonely flower in a desert." (p 232) The dream-room encloses no more than she has invested. She does not ever fulfil her intention to explore "beyond the object, beyond its shadow, to the ring of fire" (p 239).

The window of the bach is shattered by a stone wrapped in newspaper which "reminded her of the scrap of paper in the pocket of the old soldier" (p 244). With the breaking of the barrier, the "climax of chaos" (p 63) emits not life, but death. "A sense of collapse seemed to overcome the house" (p 244). The newspaper bears the words "*Help Help*" (p 244) in red crayon—crayons are part of Malfred's art equipment. The words are Malfred's own cry. She cries "Help, Help" (p 183) when she must face visitors to the dream-room which has become like a tomb; in alarm, she asks, "even the dead have shadows—surely?" (p 183) But, of course, they do not. She suggests that "Help, Help! Save me, save me" (p 185) might well be the meaning of a baby's cry as it is thrust from the womb into the world: "perhaps I did cry it and no one heard it because no one knew my language; they thought my cry was the cry of life!" (p 185) Instead, it is the heart's own cry when death seems inevitable or imminent. Such a cry recurs throughout Frame's work.

The "news" in which the stone is wrapped is "not", Malfred finds, "in any language she had learned" (p 244). This may be because it is the message of her own heart and soul. As Mark Williams observes, "The nonsense words speak Malfred's unconscious."[5] At first, the 31-lined verse (pp 244-245) seems to be composed of nonsense. But it is not "nonsense", as Williams acknowledges when he notes, "The language is at every syllable controlled."[6] The syllables comprise portmanteau words, actual words, obsolete words, and deliberately misspelt words like the "icy spelling"[7] in *The Rainbirds* which reveals truth more accurately than correct spelling. Malfred's mind, unaccustomed as it is to communicating with her heart, cannot comprehend the message.

The verse suggests the communication of birds as they gather before migration: "carmew", "strilling trone", "who and done"; "barncolum" is a more visual image, suggesting columns of birds along power lines waiting to depart. The little birds in Lewis Carroll's poem[8] from which Malfred quotes cry, "Thanks . . . 'tis thrilling/Take, O take this shilling" (p 223); "tench in pem strilling trone" (p 245) is a portmanteau version of the same lines.

Sounds and images suggest the gathering of birds like the "merle" or blackbird in "ambertime" or autumn, amber referring to the rich browns of the season. The "wingering brime" may be a *kenning* referring to the birds' medium, the air. The word "brime" means in Old English 'surf' or 'flood'. "Wingering" is from Middle English *wengen*, to have the power or means of flight.[9] The cooing, chirping birds prepare to rise in "cloudprime"—as a single cloud. When the flock rises, the wings make the sound "whone, whone".

The rising cloud of birds will leave behind the pain of earthly life, which is suggested by language of aggression and conflict: "kill-crime", "fuming", "illth" and portmanteau words like "rones, deash, done to fleath" (flesh, bones, death, done to death). The bird-cloud will also leave behind memory of guilt and blame, transgression and judgement implied by "per-demtory" (peremptory), "blame", "crime", "evil", "perburning" (purging and burning). The word "torch" occurs three times, reminding us of Malfred's torchbeam that discovered a "wound" in the ceiling, an image foreshadowing the penetration by the stone. The misery of Malfred's past life is condensed into the lines of the verse, but the misery of Malfred the "sorrowbride" is transcended by the concluding words which have echoed throughout the poem:

> *O in ambertime*
> *cloudprime*
> *who and done*
> *whone, whone.* (p 245)

The release of the soul, implied by Malfred's verse, is anticipated by her belief in "a final encircling freedom." (p 240) Becoming one with a flight of birds is also foreshadowed in a dream of death in which she finds herself without a shadow. She asks, "Has my shadow shrunk, changed to a sea gull and flown away . . . ?" (p 227) The poem is Malfred's final act of creativity. Her conscious mind is unable to "name" (p 245) the stone, for 'nam-ing' must come from the heart and soul. With Malfred's death, conflict is resolved, calm is restored and shadows are dispelled: "Outside, the sun, enriching the day, spilled its cleaned grains of light, and the sea lay calm at last." (p 246)

A State of Siege is a tightly patterned work. Images that have seemed 'odd' or 'surprising' to critics[10] fulfil a distinct purpose within that pattern. The novel is deliberately cryptic; language that conceals befits a novel concerned with repression. Frame has conveyed allegorically an inner conflict which had been observed by Freud. R D Laing comments: "Freud insisted that our civili-sation is a repressive one. There is conflict between the demands of conformity and the demands of our instinctive energies, explicitly sexual."[11] Frame does not allude to a prior text but builds on "another simultaneous structure . . . of ideas", to hark back to Frye's definition of allegory[12]. In this novel, there is a framework of ideas in conflict: heart and mind, life (with its need for love) and death.

The allegorical aspect is couched within a realistic narrative, a credibly sustained account of a woman harassed by an unidentified prowler. The authorial narrator ensures a distancing that allows readers to view Malfred's reaction to terror and isola-tion objectively. The narrator offers ideas in a manner that invites allegorical reading: "how many small minds, and islands, like Karemoana, had struggled for centuries to resist the invad-ers, whether they were forces of love, hate, knowledge, aware-ness?" (p 49) In spite of the seriousness of Malfred's plight, the novel is animated by a sense of humour, albeit black humour, which sees death as a liberation from the imprisonment of the brown suit, brooch at the throat, plaits wound close to the head and "spine like a rod." (p 225) Instead of opening her "front door upon a New View of the world" (p 227), Malfred may enjoy a 'bird's-eye view' in the "final encircling freedom" (p 240) of death.

A State of Siege was first published by Braziller in New York, 1966. Page numbers refer to the Angus & Robertson edition published in Melbourne, 1982.

1   Janet Frame, *Faces in the Water*, p 201.

2   Janet Frame, *Scented Gardens for the Blind*, p 53.

3   Janet Frame, *The Edge of the Alphabet*, p 155.

4   Lewis Carroll, "Little Birds Are Playing", *The Oxford Book of Light Verse*, chosen by W H Auden, pp 458-459.

5   Mark Williams, *Leaving the Highway*, p 42. Williams refutes earlier interpretations of the poem like that by Alex Calder (see note 10) which assume that the poem is printed on the newspaper. Williams makes the point that the poem is Malfred's interpretation of the 'news'.

6   *Ibid*, p 43.

7   Janet Frame, *The Rainbirds*, p 135.

8   Lewis Carroll, *op cit*.

9   The Oxford English Dictionary, Vol XII.

10   See Alex Calder, "The Closure of Sense: Janet Frame, Language, and the Body", *Antic* III (November 1987), p 101. "Of these three moments in which a surface is or is about to be punctured, the oddest is certainly the image of the hospital patient with the extra hole in her body." See also Monique Malterre, "Myths and Esoterics: A Tentative Interpretation of *A State of Siege*", *Bird, Hawk, Bogie*, p 92. Malterre quotes from the novel, "the sky burns hot like blue steel" (p 242), and remarks that the word "burns" is "here surprisingly associated with the blue of the sky".

11   R D Laing, *The Divided Self*, p 11.

12   Northrop Frye, cited by Samuel Levin in "Allegorical Language", *op cit*, p 23.

9

The Rainbirds

The plot of *The Rainbirds* is bizarre. Credibility is strained, not by the surreal, nor by excursions into fantasy, but by events, presented realistically, which are simply unlikely. One is reminded of Aristotle's axiom that, in epic and drama, "A likely impossibility is always preferable to an unconvincing possibility."[1] It is intriguing to relate this ancient judgement to the blatant disregard for mimesis in postmodern literature. Within the postmodern mode, language can make real or "likely" any number of impossibilities. A character may vanish leaving two fading footprints, or the letters of many alphabets may descend as rain. In contrast to this deliberate flouting of 'reality', the plot of *The Rainbirds* is an "unconvincing possibility".

After having been pronounced dead, and with all his funeral arrangements in place, Godfrey Rainbird revives. He is discharged from hospital the next day. On reporting to his Tourist Office job after a week's absence, he is dismissed in the interests of the travelling public who might be alarmed at being served by a former corpse. He is later persecuted for working at home. His wife Beatrice takes comfort in drink. Sonny Rainbird is taken into welfare custody for injuring a boy who has taunted him about his strange father. Teena Rainbird is removed to the care of an aunt. Beatrice is found dead one morning with her throat cut. Ten years later the graves of Godfrey and Beatrice Rainbird are a tourist attraction.

Although the plot of this third-person narrative is surely not to be taken seriously, it seems less than ideal for comedy. Parody or satire is more likely. *The Rainbirds*, like other novels by Frame, criticises the valuing of 'things' ahead of people. There is reference to Godfrey's "pet motor-mower" with its "sweet black oiled parts" (p 78). In reflecting on those matters of concern to him, Godfrey lists wife and family among paint-pots, lawn, tools and toolbench. The pleasure inherent in house and possessions, including a "chromium-suited dark-moustached vacuum cleaner" (p 127), mocks the quality of human affection while suggesting the passion with which people relate to things.

The supreme object of Frame's satire is the "topsy turvy language of lies" (p 124) that fails to express adequately the truth of any situation. Language can be used with ease to prove "Fair's fair" (p 116) when, as Godfrey knows, "Fair's not Fair." (p 119) Words conceal the real reason for Godfrey's dismissal from the Tourist Office. When Mr Galbraith the boss speaks, his words are at variance with his thoughts:

> We have to remember that our image is a public image. [. . .]
> No one, Mr Rainbird, no one can be sorrier about this than I am
> . . . It's not my decision, it came from higher up. He waved his
> hand upward more in the direction of God than of Wellington.
>
> (p 117)

Mr Galbraith thinks but does not say, "It's a crime to do the poor man out of a job simply because he died" (p 118). Godfrey's treatment arouses indignation if we think of him as a living being. If, however, he can be perceived as a spectre ("They said Daddy's a ghost", p 94), Mr Galbraith's remark becomes amusingly ironic. It allows us to take a more dispassionate view of the events and to consider the deception of language. One may wonder, with Godfrey, "why he had ever trusted so obvious a deceiver as language." (p 167)

Godfrey learns to "see the word and its lining" (p 135). The clarity of vision that is his legacy from "the country of the dead" (p 121) transforms words from their usual spelling into "icy spelling" (p 135). Rainbird becomes "Brainrid, an inconsectious and killed rememb of our faft" (p 137) (a conscientious and skilled member of our staff). His "re-re-fences" (references) will help to secure "plot-men-mey" (employment) we "ar-ruse [assure] you." (p 135) Ruses and plots to dispense with Godfrey reflect the situation more truthfully than references and assurances.

Although the subject-matter is morbid, the first 20 chapters (out of 35) are often enlivened by ironic humour and a sense of the ridiculous. Godfrey's amazing revival seems less important than its timing: "Ten o'clock Tuesday morning. Morning tea-time. An inconvenient time in any institution." (p 36) In part, the novel depicts the comical progress of a displaced corpse or spectre. Nothing is the same after Godfrey's revival. Even his clothes are missing—Beatrice has donated them to Corso.

—. . . My new suit, and those new shoes?
—Not your shoes. The suit, yes—well you'd been *in* it, Godfrey!
—The coat as well as the trousers?
—The whole suit. (p 50)

Wherever he goes, Godfrey evokes "shock and fear" (p 150). Even his children are frightened every time he looks at them. On one occasion, it seems "as if his head were floating while he walked" (p 113). His appearance is skeletal with "his arms (how thin they had grown!) reaching about like cranes for his clothes" (p 109).

Moreover, his death is not the result of mis-diagnosis:

—. . . You've been *dead!*
—But only figuratively speaking.
She recoiled from him as if he were a corpse.—*Dead!*
—You mean *dead?*
—*Pronounced dead.* (p 49)

The literal meaning of the text is here stated emphatically, even though a 'pronouncement' is not always to be trusted. Since Godfrey dies and returns to life 'on the third day'—the accident took place on a Sunday evening and he revives the following Tuesday morning—his resurrection may be a parody of Christ's resurrection. Godfrey's sister is perhaps comparing him with Christ when she wonders whether the experience "has left a mark on him somewhere" (p 73).

As the novel develops, there are recurrent references to "the city" and its "luminous light" (p 74). Godfrey spends many hours gazing across the harbour to Dunedin, which is "shining with an unreal effect of distance" (p 178) or with its "secret inaccessible light" (p 164). These are allusions to "the new Jerusalem", a city with its own light: "And the city has no need of the sun, neither of the moon, to shine in it" (*Revelations* 21:23). In the new Jerusalem, "light *was* like unto a stone most precious, even like a jasper stone, clear as crystal" (*Revelations* 21:11). The text of *The Rainbirds* alludes to the resurrection of the dead announced in *Revelations* 20:13. Whereas *The Adaptable Man* considers how Christ might react if he were to live in the 20th century, *The Rainbirds* considers how a community might regard a resurrected man if he were to remain on earth after his death. It is resurrection as an idea that is important. Reference is made to two biblical precedents, each of which gives rise to certain expectations. Citizens are surely thinking of Christ when they judge Godfrey severely: "The experience he's had might have ennobled another man, made him stand ten feet tall in charity but it's shrunken him" (p 196). For his own part, Godfrey anticipates that he will come to the promised holy city wherein the righteous dead who have been raised in the body "shall reign" (*Revelations* 20:6) with Christ.

Godfrey is frustrated at first to observe that the view of the city has not changed:

Why did the hills and the sky and the harbour continue as if nothing had happened? He felt an impulse to reach his fist across the harbour, seize the city, shake it, shake it, crying,—Don't you *know* what happened? Why don't you give a *sign?* (p 97)

Eventually, Godfrey is called to the city along with Sonny and Beatrice: "They came to the city." (pp 196, 198) The resurrected dead will be "judged every man according to their works" (*Revelations* 20:13). Godfrey is judged by the Children's Court to be unfit to bring up Sonny. Ironically, his tendency to sit all day looking at "some unreal city" (p 196) is used as evidence to persuade the court that he is a negligent father. Through the visit to the city, Godfrey and Beatrice lose what is most important to them. Sonny's removal leads neighbours and authorities to demand Teena's removal as well.

The Rainbirds does have an allegorical framework: "This Biblical happening in Dunedin" (p 164) in which a man "was killed" (p 102) and resurrected. In his reception, behaviour and attitude, Godfrey is the antithesis of Christ. Expectations aroused by the image of "the city" are also subverted. The concept of resurrection is questioned, together with the Christadelphian belief in "heaven on earth"[2]. Beatrice, too, aspires to a paradise, though not a celestial city but a beach place: "— Islands and shells and seaweed and crabs and pipis and everything." (p 195) But Beatrice has escaped into a dream induced by alcohol. Dreams have undermined the couple's capacity to face the responsibilities of the present.

After the departure of his own children, a so-called "chosen tribe" (p 201) of children gathers about Godfrey. Whereas Christ applauds the unquestioning faith of children ("these little ones which believe in me", *Matthew* 18:6) and enjoins all to "become as little children" in order to enter "the kingdom of heaven" (*Matthew* 18:3), Godfrey's "chosen tribe" is intensely critical. His "winning of the children" (p 203) is equivocal. Although they come to observe and question, they are frequently disrespectful. But they are perceptive, in contrast to their parents who are influenced by rumour and their own imaginings. The adults, without evidence, believe Godfrey to be paralysed (p 185), "a malingerer" (p 185), "a poor victim" (p 196) and "a crank [. . .] masquerading as a cripple, luring all the children" (p 203). The children reject all of these conflicting judgements. In Frame's novels, children usually speak the truth: " —You're mad, aren't you? They said to him.—Mad, mad." (p 203)

Godfrey's behaviour supplies abundant evidence for a diagnosis of clinical madness. At times he sits all day, scarcely moving. He is withdrawn; Beatrice grows "bewildered and angry at his absorption." (p 194) Although he may become excited, he is generally silent during family conversations. He does not farewell his daughter at the airport, but hears the departing plane as he pursues "his constant electrical rhythm" (p 200). His madness can be regarded as the outcome of both rejection and persecution in a society that demands conformity.

If madness is indeed Godfrey's condition, the novel's improbable ending assumes a terrible credibility. The children of an insane father and a mother who drinks might well be removed from parental custody. Furthermore, the most likely explanation for Beatrice's mysterious death is that Godfrey murders her. He expresses no awareness of his guilt but, for the insane, the link between cause and effect is often severed. There may well be a connection between the death and Godfrey's despair at his impotence. After his return from hospital, Beatrice thinks of him as "a corpse at my side" (p 134). She finds that she can no longer warm him.

> His blood stayed like a sunken stone; it would not move around his body in a surge of excitement in a wild self-forgetting excursion to the picnic places; he stayed cold, limp, helpless as a little worm. (p 132)

Godfrey's anguish is clear when Beatrice comments on his purchase of an electric blanket:

— Have you bought this because you think it may help us with the bed warm? I mean artificially warm?

He could have rowed across and strangled her with his Down-Under Do-It-Yourself Motor-Mower's Boat-Rower's hands.

(pp 133–134)

The murder of Beatrice, by plunging a knife into her throat, could be the ultimate expression of Godfrey's frustration. It has the effect of an orgasmic release. Godfrey hears Beatrice "crying out in her sleep". For his own part, "he felt immediately weary" and senses "warmth flowing into his body" (p 205).

Beatrice had already suffered a death, with her severance from Sonny and Teena, the loss of Godfrey as she had once known him and the loss of her role as wife and mother. Her murder is foreshadowed by the image of the aircraft which carries Teena to her aunt in Auckland: "Then the overpowering summer sun seemed to suck the plane up into the sky and it drove forward shining like a sharpened silver knife-blade and was gone." (p 200) The world has conspired to alienate the Rainbirds.[3] At night their roof is pounded with stones. By day the sun is "hot against the window pane searching to enter" (p 205).

If madness is Godfrey's condition after so many injustices, it is not surprising that his attitude towards Christian dogma is contradictory. On the one hand, he has nursed a secret longing to come to "the city". On the other, his response to Christ's resurrection is cynical. He refers to it as "the one advertising promotion of everlasting interest" (p 179) and reflects irreverently upon Easter: "Alternate wails and cheers from the churches: He is dead. He is risen" (p 98). Godfrey sees any refutation of the fact of death as an expression of human fear, an attempt to "camouflage . . . the pit" (p 168). Such an understanding lies at the heart of the novel's negative vision. Godfrey questions the motivation for belief in resurrection, seeing it as an attempt to avoid the dreaded truth of death in which the "earth continues to press, waiting for the decay of the body, the withering of the flesh, with the pages of skin made more fragile . . . and then perhaps an eye explodes in the darkness" (p 54).

Godfrey's accident occurs on a tract of reclaimed land. As the division between sea and land is especially unclear on reclaimed land, the image suggests the intermingling of life and death, their joint occupation of a single territory. Reclamation implies a certain impertinence. The attempt to keep the sea out by boulders or walls, like the attempt to keep death out, can be only temporary. People are like birds "crowding to find and keep their place upon a small square of reclaimed land." (p 203) Godfrey will never escape from his certain knowledge that death is an integral part of life: "one moment it would wear the appearance of life, the next moment of itself, then of love, hate, ranging freely in the mind and body as if there were no wall separating them, nor had there ever been" (p 79). By contrast, most people use their minds as "evasive lanterns" (p 52) to illuminate only what they can bear to see. Godfrey becomes unacceptable as worker, neighbour or citizen because his "death had upheaved layers of life that no one desired to remember; the deepest layer of life—the blanket of death." (p 157)

The name Godfrey, which means 'God's peace', is ironical, for Godfrey neither rests nor lives 'in peace'. The homophone 'free' is also significant. " — Godfrey, you're so far away. He'd been set free." (p 165) Although he becomes increasingly constrained physically, Godfrey's imagination has been freed. He discovers that views of the external world are of little consequence. They merely hinder an inner vision. His experience confirms a conviction that is central to Frame's vision: "only a trained, constantly used imagination had hope of 'facing' the terrors of being and not being." (p 59) But Godfrey's world has, hitherto, been limited by devotion to, and maintenance of, the house and quarter-acre section. For the first time, he becomes aware of "outposts and corners and inaccessible places" (p 59) within himself, demanding a new kind of effort and attention. He learns to embark on excursions into his own interior. It becomes clear to him that "at some time in a man's life the agreed boundary becomes the place not for repelling but entering admitting the unknown." (p 168)

Alex Calder writes of finishing *A State of Siege* and then returning immediately to the first page.[4] But the plot of *The Rainbirds* requires forbearance on the reader's part, as do the long passages of introspection as Godfrey mulls over the same obsessive thoughts. The book, which in the early chapters is surprisingly playful, becomes increasingly morbid as it is discovered that Godfrey is neither ghost nor corpse nor spectre; having died, he lives again in his body. The experience has transformed his appearance and his mind. His paradoxical living death is to be taken seriously.

The concluding chapter, set many years later, suggests that Godfrey and Beatrice Rainbird have long since been buried in Anderson's Bay cemetery. Godfrey was condemned by hearsay and rumour before his burial and is revered on equally unreliable information afterwards. The novel calls for questioning religious concepts that we have been *"led to believe"* (p 159). Having been led to believe in a heaven, paradise or a celestial city after death, Godfrey and Beatrice find, in life, paradise is the family grave overlooking the sea. Beatrice had tended this grave during many weekends. In summer, its warm yellow and gold blooms give way to a mass of red lilies. The gold flowers recall Beatrice's "golden hair" (p 47) and the red lilies her "lilies of blood." (p 205) In making a garden on a grave, Beatrice has created a small earthly paradise in the agonising knowledge and acknowledgement of death. The image echoes and subverts the splendour of Dante's golden-haired Beatrice and the Earthly Paradise in which she makes her appearance. The book concludes with the suggestion that the ability to create a paradise resides in the human imagination:

if you go there in winter you will have no help with your dreams, you will have to experience for yourself the agony of creating within yourself the flowers that you know will blossom there in summer. (p 206)

The Rainbirds was first published by W H Allen, London, 1968. Page numbers refer to the Pegasus Press edition, Christchurch, 1969. Published in North America as *Yellow Flowers in the Antipodean Room* by Braziller, New York, 1969.

1   Aristotle, cited by Richard Levin in *Tragedy: Plays, Theory and Criticism*, p 143.

2   Janet Frame, *To the Is-land*, p 123. "When I came home singing, "There's a friend for little children" with its promise of heaven, I found that Mother disapproved because heaven on earth was the Christadelphian belief, not heaven in the sky. [. . .] At the Resurrection, Mother said, all would be as they were just before they died and would then be judged as worthy or unworthy, and if they were found unworthy, they would be struck dead again for ever. . . ."

3   The name "Rainbird" recalls "the naughty bird" at risk out in the rain. The Rainbird family is destroyed by the hawks of a conformist society.

> *Come in you naughty bird*
> *the rain is pouring down*
> (*Owls Do Cry*, p 150).

4   Alex Calder, "The Closure of Sense: Janet Frame, Language, and the Body", *Antic* III (November 1987), p 94.

I 0

Intensive Care

The title *Intensive Care* focuses on the endeavour to save life. With the knowledge we now have of Frame, we should suspect irony. The narrative has the appearance of a family saga spanning three generations of Livingstones and continuing beyond their demise into a future era. Accidents, illnesses, love affairs, family resentments maintain a steady interest in events that, overall, progress chronologically but include many flashbacks. The language is often cryptic and this seems, at first, to relate to the need to hide a particularly shameful situation within the Livingstone family. Criticism of the novel has tended to ignore the subtle aspects of its first two sections and to concentrate on the "anti-utopian vision of the future"[1] offered in the third and final section.

Tom Livingstone, his daughters, his grandson and those who will live in his neighbourhood at some future time display patterns of cruel behaviour. The narrative is concerned with "the development of brutalising instincts"[2] during one man's life, and the effects of his conduct on others. The work foregrounds the question 'why'? After her marriage, Tom's daughter becomes Naomi Whyborn, encouraging us to ask why she should be born to suffer the pain and violation which are her destiny. The setting for most of the novel is Waipori City, a place with the geographical location of Dunedin; the name evokes the English homophones 'why' and, perhaps, 'poor'. In Maori, *waipouri* means 'sad or dark water' or 'dark memory'[3].

The sickly-sweet title of Part One, "Kindness Itself Happiness Itself and Delphiniums", is surely ironical. Tom Livingstone is the central character. The focus of Part Two, "A Kind of Moss, a Sudden Cry", is on Tom's brother Leonard, his daughter Pearl and his grandson Colin. Part Three, entitled "Pear Blossom to Feed the Nightmare", is set in the future. The members of the Livingstone family have died, though Tom's pear tree and a descendant of his cat survive. Milly Galbraith, who lives next-door to Tom's old property, now becomes the central character.

Parts One and Two are third-person narratives. Part Three is shared among three first-person narrators. However, the whole novel is interspersed with poetry and prose in the first person. The speaker/writer is most often Tom's daughter Naomi. But sometimes, it is his other daughter, Pearl, or his "first and only love" (p 14) Ciss Everest, or Pearl's husband, Henry, or Milly Galbraith's friend Sandy Monk. Sudden changes of perspective, at times confusing to the reader, foreshadow the postmodern freedom that Frame enjoys in her later novels.

While equivocal language makes many of the book's happenings uncertain, some events are not in doubt. Tom was married and sent off to World War I at 18. There he learnt to kill; he "trampled the body of the dead dead dead/enemy enemy into the mud!" (p 10) He was gassed and wounded, and then nursed back to health by Ciss Everest with whom he fell in love. After the war, he returned to his wife in Waipori City where he became the father of two daughters. The novel opens with the 65-year-old Tom who, after the death of his wife, returns to England to find Ciss Everest. By a remarkable coincidence he does so, but learns that she is dying of cancer. She wears a wig, a "transformation" (p 26), because radiation treatment has left her bald. In anger at her changed appearance, her failure to recognise him and the ruination of his dream image, Tom smothers her to death. No criminal action is ever suspected.

According to Naomi and Pearl, Tom relived the war through-out their childhood. On occasion he would don his hideous gas mask or work it like a puppet. He sang war songs, told stories of the war and enacted games of war with his daughters. In his memory and imagination, the war and his love for Ciss Everest became interwoven: "Ciss Everest alias the War", "Miss War, Miss Everest." (p 12) Meanwhile, his wife was "eaten by his own impatience and coldness and his longing for another woman." (p 24) Pearl observes that she and her sister grew up in a house where "Mum and Dad showered unhappiness like climate, not passing weather, on them both" (p 85). We should, therefore, read Naomi's remarks addressed to "Dear First Dad" to mean their exact opposite:

> Alfred who teaches history at a local college is always pestering me to 'write down' something of my early life and again and again I confront him with—my life has been so happy, where is the history of a happy life? Why wasn't I raped as a child? Why didn't you and mother beat me? Why were not Pearl and I brought up in poverty . . . (p 88)

Naomi claims that she and her sister learnt dancing, music and elocution. In response to the question " 'Father may I learn . . .?' " (p 88) she says, "There was no furious raging about money money money and who did we think we were" (p 89). Pearl has already made it clear that learning dancing, singing and elocution were the privileges of "the other children of the neigh-bourhood" (p 86).

Naomi characteristically speaks in riddles or with an irony that reverses the truth. She declares what did *not* happen, but this may be exactly what *did* happen—as we can sometimes discover by comparing her story with Pearl's. For some reason, Naomi is unable to speak openly. The reader is initially unaware that the poetry which opens the novel is spoken by Naomi; it includes images that haunt her—the "sleeping doll", the bonfire and "orgasm" (p 9). Naomi identifies herself for the first time in the fifth chapter, in which she addresses, not the reader, but "Dear First Dad" (p 17). She pretends to have affection for Tom, her father, but there is much to suggest resentment and hatred which she feels compelled to conceal.

Naomi's thoughts, impressions and memories are most often conveyed through poetry that does not yield its meaning easily. Writers of critical commentaries have avoided discussion of more than six lines of the 17 pages of poetry interspersed throughout the novel. When spoken by Naomi, it is characterised by intensity of feeling and a bitterness which is difficult to reconcile with its ostensible themes. The following example is taken from Chapter 26, which is entirely in verse form:

> Dear First Dad, it is Christmas, family-time. <u>Pain</u>
> and Santa, white and red are In,
> getting down to it, distributing upon branches of green pine
>   the gifts
> guaranteed to <u>break</u>, <u>strain</u>, fit, keep warm,
> beautify, <u>startle</u>, <u>harm</u>, amuse. <u>The favour, your favour is</u>
> we never grew out of Christmas . . .
>   [. . .]
>   . . . green crickets swarm
> in the grass
> <u>carolling with their arse</u> as men and women are doing
> on the lupined beach. Our Christmas was
> enjoy, swim, eat, sleep, wake to <u>grief of destruction</u>.
> What was it? <u>We had it</u>. <u>It is gone. Tears</u> then,
> <u>tears</u> . . .
> The annual lesson
> of trying to throw a <u>saltstorm of tears</u> to catch time
> or spreading a sticky mess like cake icing, pretend it is bird
>   lime.
>
> <u>Growing up we grew in</u>
> like <u>unhealthy</u> finger and toenails;
> you cut us to the quick . . .

. . . <u>dec</u>ay is brown
like the earth and the singing cicadas and an old man's or
  woman's
sparse pubic hair and skin
<u>decay-spotte</u>d like the fallen pears. (pp 156-157, my emphases)

The events of Christmas Day convey the "pain" of Christmas.
The reason for the pain is carefully hidden. To "wake to grief of
destruction" suggests an anguish that would not be evoked by
broken toys alone. The lines give insufficient reason for a
"saltstorm of tears". Something is happening that Naomi finds
"unhealthy"; something produces "decay", together with "harm",
"grief", "tears" and a belief that "growing up we grew in".

What is on Naomi's mind can only be guessed at by examining the images she chooses. She speaks of men and women on
the beach "carolling with their arse", a less-than-positive view of
copulation. In referring to an old person's "sparse pubic hair" as
"decay-spotted", she is envisaging the gradual ruin of the genital
area of the body. As if solving a crossword quiz question, we
must try to imagine what is "sticky like cake icing" and like "bird
lime". The words "The favour, your favour is" are followed by a
non-sequitur: "we never grew out of Christmas". Naomi does
not say what kind of favour is being exacted or won. No playing
for time, or tears, can prevent an anticipated, dreaded event. One
option, taken up, it seems, after the dreaded event has occurred,
is to pretend the "sticky mess" is something else. Bird lime was
commonly used during the Depression years to trap the feet of
small birds. Though cake icing takes many forms, pure bird lime
is a sticky white substance which could be likened to human
semen. The ensnared, helpless creatures would be Naomi and her
sister Pearl.

Naomi's reluctance to speak openly is in keeping with the
nature of sexual violation of a girl by her father.

The dilemma of sexual abuse of children has provided a system
of foolproof emotional blackmail: if the victim incriminates the

abuser, she also incriminates herself. The sexual abuse of the child is therefore the best-kept secret of the world.[4]

One can re-read with new alertness the passages of prose as well as poetry which Naomi narrates. "Why wasn't I raped as a child?" (p 88) acquires new significance. In another direct reference to sexual abuse, Tom is challenged by Peg Warren, whom he plans to marry.

> 'You mean . . . no bed . . . no love-a-dove? What have we been leading up to these afternoons on the sofa I'd like to know.'
> 'I've a father's responsibility,' Tom said confusedly.
> 'Father's responsibility my foot. Your girls are out of it . . . [. . .] Anyway what have they got to do with bed? Surely you didn't love-a-dove them?
> Tom reddened. 'I'll have none of that talk in my home.' (p 68, Frame's ellipses in first line)

Tom avoids a direct denial of the charge. He reacts visibly and involuntarily.

Naomi again disguises the truth by negating it when she asks, "why were we not subjected to subtle cruelties that I could describe in detail?" (p 88) She does indeed describe subtle cruelties in such detail as to affirm what is being denied. In the hope that he would invite her to the school dance, Naomi at the age of 14 invited a believable Donald Parker to attend the Livingstone's Guy Fawkes bonfire. He was "not handsome, his cheeks being too ruddy and his eyes too small and his hair too much like straw, but he was clever and I admired his cleverness and his eyes were shy and gentle when he said hello to me." (p 92) Tom had made a guy. After a 'performance' in which Naomi is compelled to bayonet the guy, it is placed on top of the bonfire. Once alight, the fire reveals the guy to be a crude representation of Donald Parker; he is, in a sense, burnt in effigy: "it was only my imagination that Donald's face lost its rosy blush and became as pale as the face of a dead man, and I did not cling to him, sobbing, digging my fingers fiercely into his wet shirt-covered flesh" (p 97). Naomi does not go to the dance with Donald. "I knew I had to be loyal to you, dear First Dad" (p 98). Among fathers who abuse daughters sexually, it is commonplace for them to display excessive jealousy towards boyfriends.

> For some the father becomes very possessive and attentive but the restrictiveness of this may not become apparent to the girl until adolescence. Then she will not be able to go away on school trips or to the school dance unless her father is able to remain close by.[5]

One critic has described the Donald Parker episode as "hallucinatory".[6] However, it is more likely that a minutely recalled event is interspersed with obvious fictions to make the entire happening seem fictitious. As Tom watches the effigy of Donald burning, he is "still" wearing the gas mask. "Then you took it off. Your face was kind, so kind." (p 97) It is unlikely that Tom's expression was "kind" at that moment. By his own admission, he donned the mask to frighten his family. "I showed it to my wife and two daughters, by God I showed it to them, and it scared them all" (p 25). The words "kind", "kindly" and "smiled" form an ironic refrain: " 'Don't worry,' you said kindly . . . And you laughed in that kindly reassuring way you had, and our happiness brimming over we all smiled, smiled, smiled." (p 95)

As part of an emerging pattern of sexual abuse, the gas mask has a special significance. It is closely linked to Tom's memory of Ciss Everest, for while she nursed him she understood his need to keep the gas mask beneath his pillow or bedrug. The fourth letter to "Dear First Dad" includes an italicised verse:

> *Breathe in the gas mask, father,*
> *or poisonous life like a scorpion*
> *stings your lung.* (p 65)

The verse occurs six more times as a refrain in Naomi's letters, though on subsequent occasions the word "air" replaces "life".

The lines have the ring of an incantation invoking misfortune or serious harm. They are spoken by one who is powerless to retaliate by other means. In "the dark dream", Naomi sees the father as "a terrible child-eater/masked to perform the celebration of death." (p 78) To Naomi, the mask is a death image; she speaks of her own imminent death as a "grey mask" (p 65) that will soon cover her face. Tom's mask has a "grey face". Naomi visualises its "grey cheeks inflating, deflating, closer and closer." (p 27) Masks allow constraints and inhibitions to be put aside, but the mask here also brings together the passion for Ciss and the violation of Naomi and Pearl; the "celebration of death" becomes synonymous with a sexual experience.

To communicate what is unmentionable requires a new language. Naomi tries the strange signs found among the letters in the John Bull printing set: "*******!!!!@@@¢¢¢¢¢¢¢ . . ." (p 118) She continues in this vein for some eight lines. Generally, both Pearl and Naomi hide their experiences in the equivocal language of metaphor. When Naomi prints the words "how/now brown Kewpie doll extraordinary" (p 118), she is alluding to herself. The word "doll" frequently means 'girl' or 'woman' in this novel; Tom labels the ailing Ciss Everest the "Cancer Doll" (p 22), referring to her as "doll" 14 times. Naomi reports that the "love-sleep" followed a Christmas meal "in the embrace of toys" (one a Kewpie doll) which are "deformed and blind and dead." (p 118) All three adjectives describe the way Naomi regards herself. After her 'blindness' as a young child, "a spring morning will uncover the eyes" (p 134). A recurrent pattern of imagery involves a reluctance to see winter giving way to spring. Naomi cries, "Bring back the petrifying hand of snow!" (p 107) The transition from winter to spring parallels Naomi's emergence from ignorance to the intense pain of knowing.

Naomi says to "Dear First Dad", "you gave us knowledge" (p 49). The statement, placed among crossword quiz questions, is quickly followed by a description of 19 different kinds of physical pain. But, as Oedipus discovered, physical pain cannot destroy thought indefinitely. Naomi speaks of "the pain of grief brought to birth by thinking" (p 50). As a result of her experiences, Naomi rejects her physical being. She is obsessed by a death-wish, imagining herself in the grave or entering the door of death[7]. She indicates that she is suffering from cancer and dreams that the surgeon brings her the various parts he has removed:

> . . . raw, dead, ugly objects to be flushed away, I thought, with the lid shut.
>
> 'Here's your me', he said.
>
> That made me smile. My me!
>
> 'It's easier,' he said, if I treat you as a flower and name the returned parts of you as petal, stalk and so on.' [. . .]
>
> . . . I think I refused to accept my 'me' because it was a stranger in its separate becoming; it was raw, dead, ugly—cat's meat.
>
> (pp 48–49)

The flower from which "petal, stalk and so on" have been removed may refer to 'deflowering', the taking of a woman's virginity. The "stranger in its separate becoming" could refer, not only to Naomi's sense of the theft of her own integrity, but also to an aborted foetus. An abortion or miscarriage would be in keeping with the "crisscross webbed womb pains" (p 50) that appear in the catalogue of pain. In addition, there is suddenly a reason for the earlier complaint addressed to "Dear First Dad" that "up Central", the valleys were "bleeding with raspberries and the river bleeding green with melting ice" and the raspberries were "haemorrhaging" (p 17) into a bucket.

There is a literary model for an incestuous relationship between father and daughter in *Paradise Lost*. From the union between Satan and his daughter Sin, Death is born. Frame, for the third time, draws on the relationships within the satanic family, adapting them freely to suit her own purpose and interweaving the story of the fall. The 'knowledge' gleaned in *Intensive Care* by not one but two daughters as children and adolescents is carnal knowledge. Once again, *Paradise Lost* provides an allegorical framework for the fiction.

Tom's allegorical role is that of Satan. He was once an entertainer at smoke concerts, and his job before retirement was furnaceman at the cement works. His furnace lay "at the lower intestine, so to speak, and to reach it Tom had to climb a steep iron staircase." (p 38) There are no indisputable allusions to *Paradise Lost*, but Tom's workplace is comparable to Milton's description of hell from its open gates:

> So wide they stood, and like a Furnace mouth
> Cast forth redounding smoke and ruddy flame.
>
> (*Paradise Lost* II 888–889)

Tom cared for an "ever-burning Flame that swayed and danced as it consumed the foul gases" (p 38). In satanic manner, he looked at the Flame "as a father might look in at a sleeping child or a lover upon the woman he loved." (p 41) Tom is the "expert translator of the Flame" (p 56); his passion for Ciss Everest is kept alive to be translated into evil behaviour and into self-torment. Milton says of Satan, "within him Hell/He brings" (*Paradise Lost* IV 20–21). This description fits Tom also. He is "tormented inadequate husband to Eleanor" (p 23). There is frequent reference to his guilt. As a "guilty old soldier" (p 69), he differs from the amoral characters who signify death in this and other novels by Frame.

For Satan, life, as a gift of God, would be anathema; this is why Naomi mockingly urges Tom to "Breathe in the gas mask . . . /or poisonous life . . . /stings your lung." When Satan tempted Eve in the Garden of Eden, he took the form of a serpent. The gas mask has a long serpentine nozzle: "ribbed grey tubing attached to the snout, and windowed eyes." (p 115) As Tom creeps into Ciss Everest's hospital ward, his behaviour follows a pattern in which he is probably well practised: "He planned to surprise her, to creep into the ward one day when no one else was there and confront her" (p 29). "Dear First Dad" alludes, in part, to Satan, the "Father of Lies"[8]. In ensnaring his daughters through games, Tom was using words as hooks; the words "First speech a hook" (p 80) could link Tom with the serpent who seduced Eve with words.

Tom's human role is Adam, the first father.

> Deep below our violences
> Quite still, lie our First Dad, his watch
> And many little maids . . .

So writes Auden in 1953 in "Winds", in which he considers humankind's violent nature. Had God chosen some different creature ("teleost" or "arthropod") to place on earth, "Would our death also have come?"[9] In *Intensive Care*, Frame observes the nature of man in order to reveal those tendencies which cause us to fall again and again.

The assaults on Naomi are described metaphorically as a "flame-coloured summer War." (p 28) A garden is depicted luridly, with overgrown, swollen plants. It becomes a grotesque Garden of Eden. The "shining forests" are said to be "crowned with brilliantly patterned snakes" (p 28). For Naomi, all wars have become one war. Reference to a "feminine war" with its "softness and warmth" is followed by images expressing revulsion and a sense of discord: "decay", "scavengers", "hungry mindless life", "corrupting guests", "mouthing maggots", "the new triangle wedging its unwanted difference into geometrical harmony", "the natural scene invaded by men's hate" (p 28).

In another veiled allusion to the "fall", Naomi thinks of "a honey bee"

> with a basket of poisonous fruit under its arm.
> No, it's grandma with apples and pears red and green
> picked from the once-white wild orchard. (p 166)

This riddling verse evokes the Grimms' stories of Snow White tricked by the wicked stepmother and Red Riding Hood tricked by the wolf disguised as Grandma. The real villain is Tom disguised in his gas mask, in an orchard that was once as pure and wild as the Garden of Eden. The fruit is that of the forbidden tree of knowledge. The dreams and stories of early childhood are translated into nightmare. "All dreams lead back to the nightmare garden." (p 12) The child's playground or paradise garden has been transformed into "the nightmare garden."

There is much to suggest that Naomi should be compared to Eve, but not Naomi alone, for Ciss, Pearl, Peg Warren and Milly Galbraith also represent facets of Eve, the original woman. Three women in Tom's life have violet-coloured eyes. Ciss Everest, Naomi and Peg Warren exchange places or are mistaken for one another. The young Ciss Everest, whose name includes 'Eve', is the innocent Eve; Naomi is the Eve who is misled into a 'fall'; the aged Ciss and the dying Naomi become one and the same woman. "He watched Ciss Everest's face. [. . .] . . . she resembled his own daughter Naomi, she *was* Naomi." (p 24) Naomi dreams of Ciss Everest and says, "I think I disappeared, or perhaps I watched from a height while she took my place in bed and became instantly the dying me" (p 49). There is also a link between Ciss and Peg Warren. Peg finds a photograph of Ciss:

> Peggy stared at the woman with a feeling of recognition—she'd seen those eyes before . . .; the hair too . . . they were as familiar to her as her own face and body in the mirror—
> *they*
> *were*
> *her*
> *own*
> *face and body*
> *in the mirror.* (p 116)

The three women form a composite woman before and after the fall. Whereas Naomi and the aged Ciss are the aspect of Eve that is damaged and destroyed, Peg is an aspect which has survived all the blows that time, men and the devil can bestow.

Peg is the bold fallen woman, a modern embodiment of 'Sin'.

She is self-seeking, manipulative and free from pangs of conscience. She is "Furcoat Peg" (p 81) who gave the Americans a good time during World War II. According to Tom's brother Leonard, she is "supposed to go out with just about every man this side of Wellington, and beyond" (p 55). With Peg's help, Tom becomes "a dirty old man" (p 84). Her seduction of Tom includes, on each occasion, a bottle of gin, which Peg calls "a leg-opener" (p 54). She finds Tom "nice and wicked" (p 68): "Oh you wicked old . . . wicked old . . . not there silly, stop it . . . you wicked old." (p 69, Frame's ellipses) It is surely Sin who asks "who cares about innocence?" and continues

> It's only a taste
> found and lost
> like my mustard waste
> and your poisonous past. (p 65)

Tom's past can readily be described as "poisonous". The "mustard waste" refers to mustard gas, the horrors of which surely belong to the province of Sin, whom Satan enjoined to exercise dominion "on the Earth" and "in the Air" (*Paradise Lost* X 399–400).

Pearl embodies a further aspect of Sin. As her name implies, she was once pure and innocent like Sin, who lived among the angels before Lucifer and his followers were expelled from heaven. Tom's fall from heaven is perhaps alluded to in the verse that speaks of his flight as a child "from the roof/on brown paper wings" (p 64). Milton's "Sin" is described as "Voluminous and vast" (*Paradise Lost* II 652). During the birth of "Death", her entrails were "Distorted, all my nether shape thus grew/ Transform'd" (*Paradise Lost* II 784–785). Whether or not Pearl's son Colin was fathered by Tom is not indicated. However, since the birth of Colin, Pearl has grown "fat and fatter and fatter" (p 80). In spite of frantic activity, she has retained her size, "while Henry and Colin moved like <u>snake-thin</u> deadly shadows in and out of doors" (p 81, emphasis mine). They are reminiscent, perhaps, of the creatures that move in and out of the entrails of Sin in *Paradise Lost*.[10] Pearl harbours an "increasing supply of bitterness" (p 80). Milton's Sin considered that she would be "a bitter Morsel" (*Paradise Lost* II 808).

Colin's "deadly" attributes become apparent later in the novel when he takes "four lives, a conservative tally" (p 56). The murders were planned and imagined in detail before being carried out. It is said that "There was cold enough within him to freeze his flesh and his skin and clothes and the breath coming out of his mouth and all thoughts and all feelings coming out of his mind and heart." (p 153) He and the Colin of the final section, Colin Monk, assume the role of Death in the novel's allegorical dimension.

Colin Torrance, son of Pearl, is afflicted by a passion for another violet-eyed woman. Colin grows up as an indulged only child, receiving from his mother "a suffocating love and concern" (p 80). He has no hesitation in leaving his wife and three young children to sail to Australia with Lorna Kimberley. She is untroubled by any conscience, but when informed by her parents that she must return home at once, she agrees, saying, "Mum and Dad are awfully angry" (p 137), and concluding, "we're really not all that keen on each other, are we?" (p 138) Lorna is as uncommitted to Colin as he has been to his wife. Colin, however, cannot endure the disintegration of his dream. He murders Lorna and both her parents before killing himself. His dream was to meet "a new unpatterned woman upon whom he could impress, with the starvation of a personal never-used printing machine, his own self, or his image of it" (p 84). "Starvation" is an appropriate metaphor to apply to a Death figure; Milton's Death is characterised by insatiable hunger. Colin's dream mocks the belief that man is created in God's image, suggesting that it is man who has an inordinate desire to see himself replicated.

After the dissembling Tom, the concealed bitterness of Pearl and Naomi and the uncompromising boldness of Peg, the interlude between Colin and Lorna forms an anticlimax. There is crisp and amusing dialogue between Tom and Peg, and lively exchanges between Peg and Tom's brother Leonard. These give way to Colin's monologues; his mind traverses the same obsessive thoughts. Tom's keen awareness of good and evil has been replaced by Colin's amoral position. His response to being crossed is very different from Tom's. While the satanic character resorts to deception, mischief and cruelty, Colin finds death the only solution. Instead of the "dreadful Dart" (*Paradise Lost* II 672) carried by Milton's Death, Colin arms himself with a rifle.

With or without a guiding sense of good and evil, man is destructive. The paradoxical name Living/stone suggests coldness, heartlessness and an inability to 'live': "to be a human relative was to be, inevitably, one of the murderers or the murdered" (p 11). Milton's Death "can turn everything at which he looks into stone."[11] According to Milly Galbraith, who lives in a future time, the Livingstones were "a tippykill family of the old days" (p 221).

Part Three, set in the future, requires that the first two parts be viewed from a different perspective. They become, not the saga of one extreme family, but part of the continuing story of man, enacting his ancient and continual fall throughout history, until the day of judgement in a future era. By bringing the population to a judgement day called Human Delineation Day, Part Three turns our attention from individual failings and grievances to focus on the greater horrors of mass extermination.

Colin Monk narrates the opening and closing chapters of this part. Although he excuses himself by saying that the decision has been made by the government, he becomes responsible for judgements which will distinguish between those people considered "animal" and those deemed "human". As guardian of the university computer, Colin Monk takes over the role of Death. His weapon, neither dart nor rifle, is the computer: "I was in charge of a weapon, a delicate axe that would choose and fell people, moral and ethical codes, habits and conventions." (p 176) Colin Monk is concerned with killing expediently. He uses language to justify his actions and to preserve his own good opinion of himself.

The large central section of Part Three is recorded in an exercise book by Milly Galbraith. A mentally handicapped woman of 25, Milly is one of the many who fail to meet the criteria for acceptance as "human", though she is known throughout the neighbourhood as a "treasure" who knits, sews, cleans and helps with children and the elderly. She is described as "*doll-normill*" (p 179) (dull-normal) in a further play on the word 'doll', reminding us of the discrepancy between her individual personality and her treatment as a mere commodity. Colin Monk admits, "I was tallying people as commodities." (p 175) While Tom's abuse of women was concealed, the future amoral era authorises and makes public its range of abuses against both men and women.

Milly keeps a record of the time immediately before Human Delineation Day. She chooses to make subtle alterations to spelling to convey a word's meaning more plainly: "I wanted to use my special spelling to make the words show up for what they really are the cruel deceivers." (p 193) "Wreckawds" (p 210) keep the information that may count against Milly; her father is a "respected citysin" (p 225) accepting and abiding by the new laws; "masheens" (p 206) are seen to be more destructive than constructive; "maw men went to the War" (p 208) suggests that the soldiers were hungry for killing. Because we gain an insight into how Milly perceives the world, we see her less as a retarded person than as one with special ability. " 'It would surprise you', my father said, 'what Milly knows.' " (p 204) The question raised by Auden's poem "Winds" is again relevant: had the world been populated with other beings ("teleost" or "arthropod") whose 'knowing' was more like Milly's and less like Colin Monk's, the communities of the world would surely not be violent.

Milly remains childlike for her lifetime, thus retaining her innocence. In an allegorical context, she is Innocence, the anti-thesis of the succession of fallen women who comprise the figure of Sin in Parts One and Two. In an early appearance, Milly wears "conventional Sunday best, including pearls and white hat and white gloves ... all the Waipori female trimmings of formality, expectation, underlined innocence." (p 182) The nightmare garden of Naomi's childhood is transformed; it becomes a garden comparable to the Garden of Eden sheltered by the Livingstone pear tree, the largest pear tree anyone has ever known. Milly's favourite place is under this tree, "when there are not many places in the world just to be." (p 230) The tree is said to stand "in a wilderness, hung with pears as a chandelier is hung with light" (p 173). The "wilderness" is the world beyond the garden because the pear tree is described, on two other occasions, as standing in a "vegetable garden" (p 178) cultivated by Milly's father and brother. The pear tree has divine significance, being comparable to the Perindeus[12] a tree revered in medieval times as symbolic of God: "it is bigger than everybody and can see more" (p 189). (Frame is drawing on a traditional belief recorded, for instance, in medieval bestiaries. Filled with fables and moral teachings, these were among the most widely read books in their day.)

The shadow of the Perindeus was said to symbolise Christ. Often, within the tree's shadow, Milly's friend Sandy Monk appears, supplying the words she needs. Sometimes he dictates what she writes. Sandy is considered to be a figment of Milly's imagination, but to her his reality is unquestionable. She believes him to be the invisible twin of Colin Monk. Whereas Colin can be viewed as Death, Sandy is a Christ figure, or Life. As the Divine Word, he inspires Milly to write accurately and perceptively. It was Sandy who made the original suggestion that Milly should record events for the benefit of those living in the future "in your own words." (p 197)

In a chapter written from his perspective, Sandy tells us that he is a "hero" (p 196), being the world's first "Reconstructed

Man" (p 196). He explains that surgeons "relit my shadow to make my years burn full and bright and tall in a golden flame." (p 196) Sandy has gold skin which glows in a divine manner, "like sunlight" (p 257). Milly is told:

> 'There are no reconstructed people, Milly.'
> My anger flaired. [sic]
> 'What about your Christ?' (p 249)

Traditionally, the Perindeus offers within its shade safety from the devil disguised as a dragon. Milly is aware of the tree's protective powers; she places herself in danger when she leaves it and walks in the city. Later, the tree is cut down. Though Sandy promises to take care of Milly "forever" (p 257), she is removed on Deciding Day, helping perhaps to fuel "the fires of the dead" (p 264). However, Milly's distinctive personality continues to live through her words with their special spelling preserved in the exercise book. This may have been what Sandy meant when he said to Milly, "whatever happens you need not be afraid, yew[13] will be safe." (p 258) However, Milly expected a different kind of safety. When she is sent away to share the fate of those designated 'animal', she "didn't go as docilely as we thought she would. Seemed to be expecting a miracle." (p 261)

Frame depicts a future world in which God and Christ have been usurped. Memory of tradition and culture is deliberately erased with Sleep Days: "The sleep drug acted as a strip of darkness lying across the country's memory, erasing its identity" (p 265). As in *Scented Gardens for the Blind* and *The Adaptable Man*, the novel concludes with Death in command. Those who accept Waipori City's new régime are compared to mechanical dwarfs displayed in a shop window where they devote themselves to digging for treasure. The dwarfs reflect the behaviour of many citizens—heads down, digging, extracting, reducing natural resources, without appreciating that the real 'treasure' lies within trees like the Livingstone pear tree and within individuals like Milly Galbraith. In Waipori City, people have become as inhuman and clone-like as mechanical toys.

The novel expresses concern at the readiness of the populace to accept what the government has decreed. Ted Galbraith says weakly, "Why are we taking it this way? Why haven't we banded together?" (p 251) Misleading slogans and persuasive language have lulled the community into compliance. Milly is justifiably afraid of "'important words . . . from pages and mouths I know nothing about.'" (p 199)

Potentially, language can enrich life. Words have provided Milly with inspiration from Sandy's friendship. Words can preserve the divinity of a pear tree in blossom and the perfection of "'*the lily of the valley / its little white pear-drop and its green spears.*'" (p 200)

The novel's title is indeed ironic. Although they like to give the impression that they are care-givers, people frequently deliver the opposite. When Colin Monk speaks sanctimoniously of the difficulties faced by policy-makers, he refers to "our clothes, lead-lined" (p 172), an allusion to Dante's *Divine Comedy* where the Hypocrites in Hell are weighed down eternally by lead-lined cloaks[14]. Among the brutal in *Intensive Care* are the rationalising Colin Monk, the obsessive Colin Torrance, and Tom Livingstone, who seems to be an "average New Zealand bloke"[15]. The war is given as the reason for Tom's brutalisation. His daughters are brutalised through his "intensive" and destructive "care". As a young child, Naomi imagines the deaths of her mother and sister so that she alone might enjoy a close relationship with the "first" Dad she remembers, presumably before the abuse took an extreme form and before she was old enough to understand its significance. Pearl's "care" of her son is also destructive; her over-indulgence and possessiveness lead him to become entirely self-centred. Many experiences can contribute to the development of brutal conduct. Frame considers some of them and their long-term effects.

In writing *Intensive Care*, Frame has for the second time cast the "Bird Hawk Bogie" myth into allegorical form. The singing birds are Naomi the poet and Milly, the writer of a special diary. Both are silenced by predators. The crime against Naomi can be seen as one of many examples of brutality and perversion that will accumulate over time, contributing to the politically sanctioned abuse inflicted on humans collectively. The bogie unleashed by the Human Delineation Day atrocities will eventually destroy the predators. Colin Monk concludes his account with the admission, "I do not know what will happen to me. My wife and children are dead." (p 226)

Frame's original myth is interwoven with the biblical myth of man's fall. In examining 'why' the bird must be destroyed and 'why' man must continue to fall, *Intensive Care* shows a family's transmission of evil characteristics from one generation to the next. The Livingstone family saga, which comes to be seen as the human family saga, is modelled on Satan's family saga. Only through this horrific extended analogy can Frame account for the "tippykill" (p 221) barbarism of human conduct.

Intensive Care was first published by Braziller in New York and Doubleday Canada in Toronto, 1970. Page numbers refer to the Century Hutchinson edition, Auckland, 1987.

1   Victor Dupont, "Janet Frame's Brave New World: *Intensive Care*", *Bird, Hawk, Bogie,* p 104.

2   Patrick Evans, *Janet Frame* p 175: "Janet Frame traces the development of brutalizing instincts during the life of one man". And, p 176: "The experience of Tom Livingstone dominates *Intensive Care* since it is intended to be paradigmatic for his descendants".

3   "Waipori" does not exist in Maori. There is an Otago township named Waipori, probably a misspelling of Waipouri. In English, the syllable 'pori' could be linked with 'porism', meaning 'a corollary', evoking the meaning 'Why these consequences or results?'

4   F Rush, "The Freudian Cover-up", *Chrysalis* I (1977). Cited by Miriam Saphira in *The Sexual Abuse of Children,* p 36.

5   Saphira, *ibid,* p 20.

6   Evans, *op cit,* p 171.

7   Saphira, *op cit,* p 26. Girls in Naomi's situation suffer a self-destructive depression. Saphira writes: "At puberty or within eighteen months of the

menarche, the developing girl realises the full impact of the previous sexual assault. . . . this is a major crisis period as the girl tries to resolve the anger, guilt and hostility she feels towards herself. Suicide attempts are common."

8 *John* 8:44. The devil is called "a liar and the father of it."

9 W H Auden, "Winds", *Selected Poems*, p 202.

10 Milton, *Paradise Lost* II 798–801:

> . . . when they list, into the womb
> that bred them they return . . .
> . . . then bursting forth
> Afresh . . .

These creatures are distinct from Milton's character Death. But any offspring born of Sin can assume the role of Death. See *James* 1:15, "Then when lust hath conceived, it bringeth forth sin: and sin . . . bringeth forth death."

11 Milton, *Complete Poems and Major Prose*, p 413: *Paradise Lost*, editorial footnote to line 297.

12 T H White, *The Book of Beasts*, edited by T H White, pp 159-161.

13 Ironically, Milly will be 'cut down' as easily as any yew (or pear) tree.

14 Dante, *The Divine Comedy, I: Hell* C23 63-64.

15 Ian Reid, "The Dark, the Dull and the Dirty", *Australian Book Review*, Autumn 1972, p 258. Reid reviews *Intensive Care* and four other works by New Zealand writers. He finds Frame's novel "dark" and implies that he considers it dull by describing different aspects as "unshapely", "banal" and "of little interest".

I I

Daughter Buffalo

In *Daughter Buffalo* Janet Frame again uses the recurrent event of the fall in an allegorical progression. The fall has occurred whenever "new knowledge" (p 137) has destroyed a way of life in harmony with the seasons, the land and its animals. The novel embodies a second allegorical progression which is also familiar in the Frame canon—a *catabasis* or descent.

Turnlung, an elderly writer from a distant land, enters New York, a living hell and the "country of death" (pp 21, 27, 89). The Epilogue indicates that he returns to his native land. He is like a legendary hero embarked on a quest: "I believe in making the journey, the search, the discovery." (p 106) His discovery is very different from that of Thora Pattern or Toby Withers in *The Edge of the Alphabet*, or of Istina Mavet in *Faces in the Water*. In "the country where death appears to be more important than life" (p 28), Turnlung meets a young doctor named Talbot Edelman, a "student of death" (p 5). He finds Edelman to be his own negative counterpart. The two are likened to comrades who are "a mirror image of each other, affirming each other, a perfect exchange of shadow and substance." (p 141) From one perspective, Edelman is the shadow, the embodiment of death. Having descended into the "country of death", Turnlung confronts his own shadow, his own death.

A study of the novel's *catabasis* will introduce the setting and the two characters. Turnlung visits "the country of death" in the hope that death may disclose some of its secrets. But he admits: "One of my old friends ... is always prepared to remind me, slyly, that as far as he knows I have never left my native land, 'except in imagination'." (p 209) The native land is not named, but it is recognisable as New Zealand; there is reference to its small population and volcanoes, and to a unique event in geological history which occurred in New Zealand in 1886: "the lava burial of my country's Pink and White Terraces which few in my generation had seen but which everyone spoke of with wonder and a sense of loss."[1] (p 41) Once again, Frame arranges a fiction within a fiction. Turnlung is the elderly writer-creator.

Turnlung's destination, albeit imaginary, is New York, which is compared to a hell and to a prison. The air is poisonous and the whole city is likened to a gas chamber:

> There was no sky. The eastern cloud-lid fitted exactly around the rim of the city's horizon, with the pressure rising within, and the bursting point close. (p 195)

The sky is a "pseudo-sky ... striped with yellow, with a fume-cloud like a poisonous puff-ball" (p 195). The stripes recall *The Rime of the Ancient Mariner* in which the sun peered "As if through a dungeon grate"[2]. The grate-like stripes and the fumes also suggest the gas chambers of Auschwitz, where gas entered cells from overhead. Indeed, the inhabitants of this "country of death" have, at times, "the look of the damned" (p 154).

The purity or pollution of the air is of special significance in a work whose main character is named Turnlung. At birth the lungs begin to function. At death, breathing ceases: "all the messages from the country of death convince us that our final role must again be that of turncoat—turnheart, turnlung." (p 27) The name Turnlung both signals an allegorical character and provides a constant reminder that man is mortal. The acknowledgement that he is ageing and dying may allow him to live more fully. Turnlung embodies the concept of mortal life.

Edelman's name is also allegorical. It is German for 'nobleman'. Since Frame regards the typical man of this century as a destroyer, it is no surprise to find that Edelman, an arrogant 'Everyman', personifies Death. He is a modern exploiter and consumer who belongs to "the generation which expected to receive more than it gave." (p 143) The characterisation of Edelman is part of an evolving statement in Frame's work. He differs from her other personifications of Death in that he does not admit, even to himself, that he is a killer. As a doctor, he is never found guilty of murder, though people in his 'care' die[3]. He wields deadly instruments. He has "control of the crossbow or its equivalent" (p 207). The "crossbow" is one of the novel's several references to *The Rime of the Ancient Mariner*. The gratuitous killing by the Ancient Mariner is a paradigm for many acts of homicide perpetrated by those who, like Edelman, decide on the treatment of others. The city of New York is "as haunted by death and guilt as the Ancient Mariner, though here the mariner is young, he is the young Marine who has recently killed." (p 32) Turnlung speaks of Edelman as "the 'typical American'" (p 210).

Turnlung's journey is to the "'antipodes' or the other pole of the self".[4] It involves a confrontation with Death. As we learnt in *The Rainbirds*, "life and death are actually one piece; they are inseparable, complementary as it were, just like the land and the sea."[5] Edelman narrates the following:

> And what was all this lofty talk of death? I asked myself, when, if the truth were known . . .
>
> 'It's never known,' Turnlung said, answering a remark I had not even voiced. (p 112)

The relationship between the two men is peculiar, communication being possible without speech. Furthermore, both men are the book's first-person narrators. Turnlung presents the Prologue, Edelman Part One and Turnlung Part Two (except for its concluding chapter, which is offered by one of his friends). The narration alternates between Edelman and Turnlung throughout Part Three and Part Four. Turnlung supplies the Epilogue. The two characters seem to be one man.

At a realistic level, Turnlung and Edelman are united in a homosexual relationship. Figuratively, in the Prologue[6], Turnlung refers to himself and "Death", saying, "we shall be lovers tuned at last". The literal act of love is at the same time a figurative enactment of the orgasmic release of tension that may eventually accompany the moment of death. It is through love that Turnlung completes his death education. He speaks of those "who completed my death education by loving me" (p 183).

As a destroyer, Edelman admits that the place where he *takes* lives might be *my* sanctuary" (p 15). It is, for example, a place "where the marshbirds go/to tangle with the wild rushes" (p 180). Turnlung, by contrast, finds sanctuary in the act of giving, in the form of warmth, enthusiasm, attentiveness and compassion. Turnlung's final gift is the novel *Daughter Buffalo*. There is sanctuary to be found in the work of art, whether of paint-and-canvas or of words. Paintings provide a sanctuary for Edelman's father. It is the special function of art to contain "opposing impulses" (p 159), holding them in balance. A painting entitled "Noon" (p 158) provides an example, depicting a timeless, shadowless moment uniting anger and joy, sea and land, life and death. The giving and the taking unite as they will at the moment when a life is completed; Turnlung believes that "to die is to be complete" (p 179). At the end of the novel, Turnlung anticipates the sanctuary of his own death.

The book proposes that the formation of inhuman attitudes may be related to the quality of our "death education" (p 183). Differences in death education have been largely responsible for determining the character of each of the protagonists, Turnlung as Life and Edelman as Death, Turnlung as the man of the past, Edelman as the man of the future. Turnlung speaks of a place where the remains of animals could be found lying on the land "untouched as earth-hosts to the mushrooms growing up through the skulls and the buttercups blooming in the rib-cages." (p 35) The dead cat that he found as a boy was lying "under the flowering currant bush where honeybees swarmed about clusters of tiny bell-like flowers" (pp 35–36). Such knowledge of death developed Turnlung's understanding of a natural harmony between the earth and its creatures, in both life and death.

In New York, death is concealed "safely within the delusional dream of the dollar-people." (p 29) The Funeral Homes, the Dogs' Heaven, the Hosts waiting to greet the bereaved—all surround death with fantasy and all belong to money-making enterprises. Hospital deaths are "marvels of cleanliness, conceal-ments and dispatch." (p 79) Those who die in the streets are removed in much the same way as dogs' excrement—both are "scooped up" (p 81). Deaths in great numbers are conveyed through the media—"unformed, ill-matured, ungrieved-over deaths ... and a scarcity of feelings to match them" (p 42). Whether or not a man learns to value other people and to revere life may well be determined by his death education. Turnlung has, from boyhood, experienced the deaths of family members and friends. Such an education is essential if a man is to develop his own capacity for emotion.

Edelman complains of his lack of death education. He resents "the way I had been deprived of experience of death almost as I would have resented being deprived of love." (p 10) His scientific research into death is no compensation. His girlfriend Lenore denies that he has human status, alleging that his studies have "tampered with, contaminated" (p 130) his life.

The descent to Turnlung's own 'antipodes' achieves two results. First, it establishes that ageing and death are continu-ously integral to life; it follows that this knowledge should shape the way our lives are lived. Second, the meeting and interaction with Edelman allows Frame to expose man's expediency. Turnlung's boyhood included customs which seem both natural and humane. The manner in which families provide for elderly people reflects the extent of their humanity. Turnlung's grand-father was a member of the family household, a familiar situation in an era now past. When the grandfather died, "his bed and his room and his chair, the spaces he occupied about the house and in the garden were hungry for him" (p 36). Edelman's grand-father, by contrast, lived in a nursing-home. A crisis occurred when it was to close down: he was not reunited with his family but sent to a different institution on the Canadian border. His need for human warmth or the closeness of family was ignored.

It might seem that New Zealand practices are commended in contrast to those found in New York. But New Zealand is simply an "unfinished land" (p 149). Children's playgrounds are described as "not yet paved with plastic turf" (p 149, emphasis mine). Turnlung's boyhood lifestyle has already been trans-formed. His Aunt Kate is cared for in a private hospital rather than a private home. The community can offer no satisfactory home for a "'backward'" man like Rory Flett. There is only a

> place in the country . . . in a group of low wooden buildings painted the colour of a railway station, with long seats in the sitting room like seats on a railway platform . . . (p 46)

The evidence suggests that New Zealand is well on the way to becoming as lifeless and inhuman as any other modern place.

Turnlung sees his home town as a sarcophagus. Many build-ings are constructed of the local limestone. The townsfolk seem to have absorbed the stone into themselves—instead of the bodies being absorbed into the stone, as they are in limestone tombs[7]. Turnlung finds the people stone-hearted and rigid in their habits and puritanical standards: "The stone bees flew alive out of the carved walls of Bee Supply Ltd the Best Honey." (p 174)[8] Nonetheless, New Zealanders like to think that their land is comparable to Eden:

> 'I live in a land that's like the Garden of Eden,' he said. 'But it can't be Eden without a snake. We're terrified it may become a true Eden. How we long to remain unharmed!' (p 88)

The hope is mocked with ironic humour. The serpent can take
many forms. Turnlung describes the panic when a black widow
spider escaped, having been transported to New Zealand in a
case of fruit. It "went on a spree to see the sights like any tourist.
I think the troops might have been called out to get it." (p 88) In
spite of the care with which New Zealand shields itself and
nurses its illusions, it is no longer an Eden.

The novel suggests that serpents in one form or another are
everywhere, and that the fall is repeatedly re-enacted. In New
York's Natural History Museum, Edelman and Turnlung visit
Reptile Hall. In the course of this meeting, they are tempted to
acquire new knowledge. Turnlung becomes "like a young man in
love for the first time" (p 91) and Edelman speaks to Turnlung
"as if I *knew* him." (p 90) The two enter a homosexual relationship, anticipating knowledge forbidden by the puritan ethic or
the ethics of the Old Testament. The zoological names of the
creatures in Reptile Hall become, for Turnlung, "a prayer for
living things, *squamata, sauria, serpentes* . . . "(p 148, Frame's
ellipsis). The words recur as a refrain. They mean 'serpents,
reptiles, snakes' and represent the serpent in this allegorical
reenactment of the fall.

"Our act was a rehearsal of time—for me, of the future, for
Turnlung of the past." (p 145) Within the allegorical dimension,
the homosexual act is another sin like that committed in the
Garden of Eden. But for Edelman, the amoral man of the future,
it is simply an act of self-gratification. He sees Turnlung and
himself as "the old and the young Narcissus" and admits that he
"was using Turnlung." (p 144) Immediately following the experience, Turnlung recalls Edelman's invitation to him to share his
apartment:

> 'By the way,' Turnlung said. 'About your invitation to stay . . . '
> I interrupted quickly. 'I find it can't be managed.' (p 145)

Having been deceived by words, Turnlung is rejected. He is,
in effect, cast out into a wilderness where he will lack human

love and care. His response to this or to other 'falls' in his life is to say:

> I bought a waxed apple for thirty-nine cents. Eating it,
> I ate Plaster of Paris. With a dislocated mouth
> I talk to the world and the words come out
> fractured, unset, in spite of their apple-cast.
> I too was broken by the clamber and the fall . . . (p 135)

Turnlung's dream of becoming a member of a 'family' is destroyed: "the first choice fantasy of Turnlung's approaching senility was his being part of the family group from which he had always been an outcast." (p 148) He has been dreaming of "Talbot Edelman, my daughter and I" (p 137).

The daughter is a six-month-old buffalo confined in Central Park Zoo. Turnlung tells Edelman, " 'It's *our* daughter, yours and mine.' " (p 138) Turnlung, moved by the animal's bewilderment, imagines that he adopts and frees her and that he, she and Edelman "will race with the wind on the golden prairie, and follow the moon." (p 137) He envisages a new paradise without alienation among men, beasts and the earth, such as existed before the fall. It is with the fall in mind that he resolves to prevent Daughter Buffalo from "speaking to strangers—the grey wolf and the red fox." (p 136) The link between the fox and Satan has already been noted in relation to Russell in *The Adaptable Man*. Turnlung suggests that his daughter should be taught only "a word here, a word there"; he is determined that "she shall not be tricked or threatened by words" (p 147). He is alluding to the language with which the serpent deceived Eve. But Daughter Buffalo will remain innocent and ignorant. Official outings will be known as "E.V.A./Extravehicular activity, the vehicle being history." (p 136) Turnlung's imagination creates a different direction for the history of the world.

The baby buffalo who has "aged a lot in six months" (p 113) is a perfect image for a lost freedom and a lost harmony between creatures and the earth. She and her mother, in captivity, look

"As if they'd been offered the world, the earth and the sky, and they had to refuse, and couldn't explain the refusal." (p 113) In fact, the buffalo have been disinherited by Western greed, brutality and 'knowledge' in the form of rifles. The image of a vast prairie on which buffalo may gallop without constraint provides an ideal that is in direct contrast to the reiterated images of urban imprisonment. In *The Rime of the Ancient Mariner*, the moon and stars enjoy a freedom to which the Mariner aspires. Turnlung quotes part of Coleridge's commentary: " 'in his loneliness and fixedness [the Mariner] yearneth towards the journeying moon and stars' " (p 32)[9]. Such might be the yearning of imprisoned buffalo and the imprisoned citizens of a modern world.

The novel demonstrates the fulfilment of a biblical prophecy. When the serpent tempted Eve, it promised "in the day ye eat thereof, then your eyes shall be opened, and ye shall be as gods, knowing good and evil." (*Genesis* 3:5, emphasis mine) The tendency for man to "play God" (p 119) is directly related to his fallen condition. The technical knowledge of men like Edelman allows them to wield extraordinary power over their fellows. Edelman is interrogated by Turnlung on the subject of playing God.

> 'And don't you play tricks with genes, chromosomes, medicines, bloodtypes, adding a little something here, subtracting a little, finding the difference, magnifying it, diminishing it? You don't play tricks with mice, giving them a universe, believing them to be men while you play God?'
> 'With genes and so on,' I said, 'there's a risk and a responsibility if you start tampering with them.' (p 119)

Later, Edelman admits to "tampering" with his dog Sally:

> I had changed her, broken her bones, mutilated her, transplanted her, stolen half her quota of breath by collapsing

one lung. [. . .] I tampered with her. That's the word.
Tampered, made corrupting changes. (p 141)

"Tampering" with a powerless creature or person is one way of
playing God. It is Edelman's specialty and is integrated with his
role as Death. "Death will make corrupting changes, will
tamper" (Prologue). Turnlung views the arrogance of Edelman
with ironic enthusiasm:

'I can't help admiring you Americans. You're great killers, death
is your way of life, but you're also great reconstructors of what
you've killed. Only God can do that and get away with it.' (p 87)

Modern man, heralding the man of the future, has an overween-
ing sense of his own power and importance. Edelman attributes
his own power to his wealth—"money, always with us and in
use. [. . .] What control we had over our world!" (p 8)—and to
his profession—"my profession was acknowledged and respected
everywhere" (p 186). He is one who treats his fellows as mere
mice in relation to his own lofty position: "It then occurred to
me that a rat or white mouse could be substituted for Lenore,
without much loss to her or to myself." (p 126) Such reminiscences account for Turnlung's sarcastic verse:

Men are not Gods everyone is saying
when the mice began praying to the men. (p 123)

While Edelman destroys, Turnlung is creative. Having travelled
"in imagination" to the country of death, Turnlung's "golden
trophy" (p 31) is his writing, a manuscript of his "impressions
and memories, with Edelman's version of the time, the events,
the dreams he dreamed" (p 209). Grief is an essential ingredient
in the creation of art. Whereas Edelman seems incapable of sustained feeling, Turnlung explains that

Grief can spin the silk that you must cut to the core, unwind,
plait, removing all traces of the toil and the impossible life, love
and death of the makers, before you set your golden trophy on
display. (p 31)

While silk-worms and artists secrete the gold thread of creativity, New York continues "to secrete the milk of death" (p 102). The city, and perhaps the modern world generally, fosters an inhumanity that may, in time, see the demise of art—and the demise of humankind.[10]

Like a message in a bottle, Turnlung's message may one day be found among the debris left by a throw-away society or a ruined civilisation.

> I am a bottle with a message in it.
> [...]
> Then one day or night when those who knew me have forgotten
>   I existed,
> then someone will find me, my message will get across, (p 34).

Turnlung's perception that his message might not be understood immediately has been borne out by those reviewers who found in the novel "elaborate mazes"[11], "a controlled enigma"[12] and "a rather closed system"[13]; one critic has judged it "probably an artistic failure, but it is not one I have the heart to deplore"[14], while another found the work "as difficult to read as any of Janet Frame's novels, difficult because she is never comfortable"[15]. Unlike those who have revealed diffidence or confusion, Jeanne Delbaere sees it in relation to Frame's other work. The protagonist undertakes a "'journey' to America" which, Delbaere claims,

> is nothing but the inner journey from division to wholeness, from ego to self, which, from Daphne onwards, had been undertaken by the 'mad' characters in Janet Frame's novels. It is a journey inwards to the 'antipodes' or the other pole of the self[16].

The composite Turnlung/Edelman explores the potential strength and failure of humankind. The novel's two allegorical patterns are inter-related; they reveal two truths of the human condition. First, as a fallen creature man must meet death; since he must age, his living is continuously his dying. Second, as a creature composed of "shadow and substance" (p 141) he must fall and continue to fall. In *Intensive Care*, Colin Monk has the final despairing word. But in *Daughter Buffalo*, Turnlung has the final word, reiterating his philosophy: "What matters is that I have what I gave" (p 212). Energy that can be used destructively can also serve a creative purpose. Although it examines death education, inhumanity, ageing and dying, this novel is more optimistic than those preceding it. Turnlung, by finding sanctuary in giving, sanctuary in literary work and sanctuary in death, transcends the dark side of human nature. He also transcends death.

Daughter Buffalo was first published by Braziller, New York and Doubleday Canada, Toronto in 1972. Page numbers here refer to the Century Hutchinson edition, Auckland, 1986.

1   The volcanic eruption of Mt Tarawera which buried the Pink and White Terraces occurred on 10–11 June 1886, in an area south-east of the New Zealand town of Rotorua. The allusion to Mt Tarawera's eruption, like the reference to Mt Taranaki in *Living in the Maniototo*, serves to remind us of our precarious tenure of the earth's surface.

2   S T Coleridge, *Poems and Prose*, p 43, *The Rime of the Ancient Mariner* line 179.

3   The characterisation of Edelman extends the mistrust of the medical profession apparent in earlier works by Frame.

4   Jeanne Delbaere, "Turnlung in the Noon Sun: An Analysis of *Daughter Buffalo*", *Bird, Hawk, Bogie*, p 126. The context of this quotation appears later in this chapter.

5   Annemarie Backmann, "Security and Equality in *The Rainbirds*", *Bird, Hawk, Bogie*, p 100.

6   The two-page Prologue is unnumbered in this edition.

7   In Ancient Greece, limestone outcrops were sometimes hollowed out and used as tombs, in which bodies would gradually disintegrate and be absorbed into the stone.

8   Edelman also is characterised as stone-hearted. The sarcophagus image is reiterated when Edelman dreams that he is entombed and his faculties auctioned. He is anticipating his own death. The stone walls are "like a membrane seen from within; like the tissue perhaps, of the placenta; then

the pink flush would be blood" (p 198–199). His own body is his imprisoning tomb.

9 Coleridge, *op cit*, pp 45–46. The quotation is from Coleridge's commentary on lines 262–271. The "blue sky" is for the moon and stars "their native country and their own natural homes which they enter unannounced, as lords that are certainly expected and yet there is a silent joy at their arrival."

10 This extreme result has been proposed in *Scented Gardens for the Blind* and *Intensive Care*.

11 Lauris Edmond, review of *Daughter Buffalo, Islands* III (1974), p 338.

12 Lydia Wevers, review of *Daughter Buffalo, NZ Bookworld* I (1973), p 21.

13 Patrick Evans, *Janet Frame*, p 194.

14 Dennis McEldowney, review of *Daughter Buffalo, NZ Listener*, 21 May 1973, p 50.

15 Wevers, *op cit*, p 21.

16 Delbaere, "Turnlung in the Noon Sun: An Analysis of *Daughter Buffalo*", *op cit*, p 126.

I2

L i v i n g   i n   t h e   M a n i o t o t o

Maniototo is the name of a high plain in Central Otago, New Zealand. An introductory quotation describes the terrain. Mountain ranges isolate its

> "unforgettable landscapes composed of severe lines and blocks and planes; . . . an extensive surface from which most of the cover has been stripped[1] . . . the Maniototo plain . . . mania, a plain: toto, bloody,"[2]

The description offered here is, however, at variance with the meaning of "Maniototo" in Part III of the novel: "Attending and Avoiding in the Maniototo". The setting for this entire section will be Berkeley, California.

The Maniototo bears a range of figurative implications. It is one of numerous "worlds" or planes created in this novel. The Maniototo forms a paradigm; Frame draws on geographic elements and transforms them. She is giving due warning that the "Berkeley" of Part III may exist only in the imagination. The novel's many imaginary realms include the city of Baltimore, a suburb called Blenheim, a room filled with patterns of light, a battle scene worked in embroidery, and even a sentence, since "Sentences are the smallest bedrooms." (p 73) The novel's settings derive from the New Zealand countryside, an Auckland suburb, industrial Baltimore and suburban Berkeley.

The subject of a second introductory quotation is Peter Wallstead, an imaginary writer[3]: "He lived all his life in the Maniototo. Few people outside the area know of it. Why did he never leave it?" Virtually unknown in his lifetime, Wallstead is acclaimed after his death; a photograph reveals a "sly see-you've-missed-me smile" (p 56), the smile of satisfaction at having pursued his art undisturbed. He has avoided the modern city which will destroy several other artist characters in the course of the novel. A recurring view in Frame's work is that art is wrought through a process of pain, as if suffering were an essential part of its making.[4] Each artistic gain is the result of a 'battle'. While Maniototo means 'plain of blood' in Maori, the Latin meanings combine to suggest 'total madness'. The area is under attack: "there's a scheme to drown the land and the towns."[5] (p 56) Figuratively, the Maniototo may be the creative mind threatened by 'madness' caused by 'progress' or 'civilisation'. As "plain" is written without an initial capital, its significance can be broadened to include the meaning of its homophone "plane". The very mind of Peter Wallstead can be equated with the high plain of the Maniototo, a vast territory of the imagination.

In direct contrast to the plain or plane in which Wallstead was able to 'live' in the fullest sense, the Baltimore apartment of a professional man named Brian is depicted as a dark, over-furnished prison. Numerous locks, bars and chains guard exits and entrances. Brian's young nephew Lonnie, on holiday from New Zealand, complains: "there's no real *outside*. [. . .] And there's no inside either; it's all dark." (p 100) To Lonnie, "*outside*" implies lawns, gardens, hills and bush. In Baltimore there is "no earth left" (p 36) because it has been overlain with concrete or asphalt. One implication is that imagination, too, has been stifled or buried.

The novel's contrasting images and events are manipulated by a narrator-writer named Mavis. She is the unreliable narrator so familiar in 'postmodern' fiction[6]. Mavis is a woman of many names but no fixed identity:

> And I, Mavis Furness, Mavis Barwell, Mavis Halleton, perhaps ... just <u>Alice Thumb</u>, or Ariella, Lokinia, or Maui's sister, or mere Naomi ... <u>Or Violet Pansy Proudlock,</u> <u>ventriloquist</u>.
>
> (pp 11-12, emphases mine)

Knowing an individual by name creates a relatedness, even a bond, but we feel no closeness or commitment to Mavis because nothing about her is certain. Elusive from the start, she seems to direct attention away from herself. "I could go to the centre, but I choose to be here, as an entertainer." (p 13) But where is "here"? The implications of her role and identity emerge gradually.

Being inclined towards playfulness and trickery, Mavis is able to slip into the role of Violet Pansy Proudlock, a puppeteer-ventriloquist: "my real artistry is in daring to enter the speech of another" (p 13). If Violet Pansy Proudlock embodies the writer's skill in giving characters power of speech, Alice Thumb "'having turned' to eavesdropping and gossip" (p 13) embodies the writer's capacity to 'listen in' to their spoken and unspoken thoughts.

Mavis fictionalises and exposes the shaping of fiction. She sees herself as a "host" who creates, from her own substance, fictional characters, all of whom are her "guests" (p 133). They emerge from a space in the mind which she calls the "manifold", containing memories of experiences, feelings, dreams and books. She explains how the writer then draws on the manifold:

> A writer, like a solitary carpenter bee, will hoard scraps from the manifold and then proceed to gnaw obsessively, constructing a long gallery, nesting her very existence within her food. The eater vanishes. The characters in the long gallery emerge. (p 134)

The writer creates the narrative space in which the characters can live. They develop lives of their own as they move into the world of the novel.

Characters, not linked by plot, appear in an incident or

sequence and do not return. They are conjured up and, at the appropriate time, disposed of swiftly and nonchalantly. Mavis has Lance, her second husband, choke to death "for all I know . . . on a remembered idiom" (p 64) and can even suggest that a character might have extracted "a large square of white cloth [. . .] from a portrait of Lawrence [of Arabia]" (p 172).

Like the postmodernists, Mavis is not concerned with credibility. But she differs from them in her concern for the 'wholeness' of the work of art. As a writer, she describes herself as "part of the whole only, hypotenuse" (p 68). The place of the "hypotenuse" is the place of the author. The triangle is a model showing the connection between a writer and the work she creates. The "hypotenuse", "burdened by the weight of opposite and adjacent" (p 70), is the longest side of a right-angled triangle. The novel's form is represented by this simple yet balanced entity. 'Right-angled' implies the 'right' degree of contrast or emphasis. A writer may imaginatively take a stance "adjacent" to any proposition, defining and exploring it in relation to its "opposite".

The principle of opposite and adjacent is established by the end of the first of the book's five parts. Throughout the novel, characters and concepts are placed in triangular juxtaposition, as are the three localities—Blenheim, Baltimore and Berkeley. Their "adjacent" features are plainly indicated. Blenheim[7] and Berkeley "had once been declared 'twin' cities, partly in recognition of their being 'over the bridge' from San Francisco and Auckland city" (p 17). Similarly, Blenheim and Baltimore are shown to be "adjacent" in that each possesses a dead poet[8] whose ghost is seen or heard by the residents. But there are even more dramatic and macabre links. Each of the three places can be seen as both a living city and as an underworld.

The journey of narrator and protagonist Mavis from Blenheim to Baltimore to Berkeley parallels the journey of narrator and protagonist Dante Alighieri from Upper Hell to Lower Hell to Purgatory. Considering *The Divine Comedy* as a prior text unifies

Living in the Maniototo in a startling manner. Blenheim is comparable to the upper levels of Dante's Hell, the region in which those guilty of "Incontinence"[9] are punished. Baltimore is comparable to an adjacent region, Lower Hell, otherwise known as the City of Dis. Grizzly Peak, Berkeley, has as its model Dante's Earthly Paradise on the summit of Mount Purgatory.

Through allusions to *The Divine Comedy*, Mavis demonstrates the folly and tragedy of life in Blenheim and Baltimore[10]. Dante, too, was a social critic. He deemed guilty many dignitaries, especially church authorities. Whereas Dante identified certain 'sinners' by name, relegating them to ignominious penances and postures in hell, Mavis identifies a collective guilt, condemning a modern lifestyle and all who participate in it. The Berkeley episode, however, fulfils a very different purpose. In contrast to Dante, whose *Commedia* affirms his religious ardour, Mavis questions basic tenets of Christian faith by parodying religious figures and concepts. She assumes an ironic detachment, announcing at the outset, "I am here to entertain you." (p 13) And she does.

In Blenheim and Baltimore the evils of modern mass culture become the sins of Hell. In the industrial city, the smog is reminiscent of conditions in Hell where there is "dark wind" (C5 75)[11] and "black air" (C5 89). Blenheim is polluted by "smoke-and-fume-filled Kaka Valley" (p 24) and "the burning of rubber tyres, old carpets, and plastic containers which filled the air with a dark foul smoke." (p 46) In Blenheim, you are "on your way to your 'real' destination." (p 21) Likewise in Dante's cosmos; those who make atonement in Hell may eventually be released to Purgatory. Compared with neighbouring suburbs, Blenheim has "more robberies, car conversions, civil and supreme courtcases, more arson, bounced cheques." (p 21)

When Blenheim is seen as the "Inferno", its "streets of unimaginable death" acquire new significance. They are not simply named after famous battles—"El Alamein Road, Corunna Crescent, Malplaquet Place" (p 23)—in which the deaths are "unimaginable" because the residents are incapable of imagining the death of a multitude; the "'shocking sights'"[12] (p 23) of Blenheim's urban wasteland parallel the shocking sights revealed to Dante in Hell, inhabited by the unimaginable dead.

The building that dominates Blenheim is called "Heavenfield Mall", ironically, a consumers' "paradise" which is "enhanced . . . by the aviary on the second floor where canaries and love-birds sing . . . an arrogant and costly reminder, however, of the lost noise of the sun." (p 23) The "noise of the sun", native birds and cicadas in sunlight, has been "lost", replaced by foreign birds unnaturally confined indoors. The "lost noise of the sun" takes on even greater significance when Heavenfield Mall is located in an underworld.

The typical activities at the mall are expressed with the insistence of a television advertisement: "parents buy buy buy for cash or credit their furniture, electrical appliances, food, a variety of services" (p 23). The frenzied activity becomes ironical when compared with Virgil's calm words addressed to Dante:

See now, my son, the fine and fleeting mock
Of all those goods men wrangle for—(C7 61-62)

Those who "buy buy buy" are the "Prodigal", while "Carnality" is the sin that characterises Lewis, Mavis's first husband who was guilty of "trying to put his hand up young Edith's skirt and even trying to seduce his son." (p 26) Lewis, a stroke victim, has been "struck by lightning that burned great holes in his language and scorched the rest" (p 26). Figurative burning and scorching becomes the more literal burning and scorching of an inhabitant of Hell.

Humour animates the Blenheim episodes. A particular kind of guilt is examined through the character of Mavis's second husband, Lance: "You have been given, you have bought, you have stolen, and you *owe*, even from before your very first breath." (p 44) Mavis explores this existential problem. Lance attempts to expiate his own sense of indebtedness by collecting the bad debts of others. In white bowling hat, gym shoes, shorts and striped blazer—a bizarre mixture of the outfits worn by elderly lawn bowlers and schoolboys attending private school—he stalks those who owe money for the "dining suite . . . glittercoal electric fire . . . uncut moquette mahogany veneer" (p 51). Lance's boss is described as a "joking devil . . . his knees and shins carboned with blue . . . in an officially frost-free district" (p 46). Quite suddenly, we see the "debt-collectors" as devils punishing the guilty, exacting payment for sins committed. Among the fires of Hell, the knees of the devils might well be "carboned with blue".

Lower Hell is the dwelling-place of those whose sins are due, not to "Incontinence", but to permanent evil disposition producing crimes of violence, fraud and malice. This realm is evoked by the poor districts of Baltimore, where inhabitants are guilty of theft, robbery, murder: "the city had one murder every day and many more robberies and muggings with violence" (p 79). Children have the characteristics of young devils. They try to

> set fire to the school by thrusting lit pieces of paper through the keyhole or lighting kerosene in bottles. The children, not yet in their teens, move in waves along the streets, pausing now and again to cluster, scream, fight, laugh. How they laugh! The impurity of their practices intensifies the purity of their enjoyment. (p 32)

Dante's City of Dis is surrounded by a mire or marsh:

> On every side, the vast and reeking mire
> Surrounds this city of the woe-begot (C9 31-32)

Beyond the city of Baltimore lie "the sick marshes of New Jersey with their dead swamp birds and rubber- and gasoline-smelling fumes." (p 91) The ruined environment is conveyed through careful choice and juxtaposition of detail. Mavis observes that Baltimore children, having no countryside in which to run, play among mountains of rags where they scramble "as if in a haystack in a golden countryside" (p 90). Children also like to break off car aerials for switches "as if they lived in a forest where cars were trees branching aerials and blossoming headlights." (p 34) There is irony and pathos in the juxtaposition of the natural and unnatural images, as if the substitution of one for the other were acceptable. Image upon image reveals human-kind's alienation from the earth and forms a lament at the loss of a natural environment.

Mavis believes that she hears the distant howling of wolves in Baltimore. But Baltimore, like Dante's Lower Hell, has no wolves. In both realms, though, "The Sins of the Wolf"[13] abound. These are "Fraud" and "Malice". Wolves symbolise those who would prey on the industry of others. Brother Coleman, for example, claims that for a mere five dollars a month, "God would fulfil all needs, particularly the need for cars, washing machines, new furniture, houses." (p 84) He is like one of the "Hypocrites" whom Dante observes in the chasm of the Eighth Circle. Their cloaks of lead are gilded: "Outwardly they were gilded dazzling-bright" (C23 64). Brother Coleman wears a "gold suit sewn with glitter" (p 88).

While Dante's City of Dis harbours Erinyes or Furies, a Balti-more resident is attacked by a "Blue Fury", comparable to the "White Tornado"[14] of a television advertisement.

> With a fearful look in his eyes he turned toward some apparition beside him.
>
> "Got you," he cried, grasping the air.
>
> There was a flash of light, a smell of laundry and the penetrating fumes of a powerful cleanser, then a neutral nothing-smell, not even the usual substituted forest glade or field of lavender or carnation, and all that remained of Tommy were two faded footprints on the floor. (p 38)

The humour in this moment of crisis derives from the surprising nonchalance attending the disappearance. If we can see the victim, Tommy, as a wraith in Hell, his vanishing becomes unremarkable. But the event has serious implications. Tommy is an artist, a silversmith who sees the earth as a cage, the lines of longitude and latitude its bars. One reading is that, like a stain or a mark on a lavatory pan, Tommy is eliminated. This, figuratively, is the way citizens would like to treat those who offer disquieting insights.

Mavis flies to Berkeley to stay in the home of Irving and Trinity Garrett on Grizzly Peak Road, an appropriate address for a property that may be "a house of the dead." (p 169) This place high above Berkeley "belongs to the trees." (p 214) Troops of deer, wilderness gardens, "tall grasses thick with bees and blossom" (p 214) evoke Dante's Earthly Paradise where, beyond a "sacred wood" (II, C28 2), there are "blossoms pied/ . . . which on that high land grow wild" (II, C28 68–69); there is nectar and "dulcet melody" (II, C29 22) and a tree is seen to burst into blossom. In Berkeley, "hummingbirds never failed to appear, at noon, in a mist of suspended colour and motion." (p 132) Their favourite blossom tree supplies nectar.

Although the two settings are similar in many respects, the allegorical parody depends on opposites. Mavis's role is the opposite of Dante's. He was an advocate for a Christian order transcending human wickedness. In the course of the novel, Mavis adopts several different roles—writer, widow, naïve observer. In the Berkeley episode, she is a writer who plays the part of Devil's Advocate, manipulating her characters in a way that questions ideas intrinsic to Christian belief.

Irving, a town planner, has created a model of his "dream-city" (p 195). This represents a reconstructed Blenheim: "Whatever Blenheim might have been, then, it was, in a sense, to have become Irving's heaven." (p 196) Since Irving's "heaven" corresponds to Upper Hell, Irving must be one guise of that master of disguise, the Devil.

The Garretts' will specifies only one "*deal* coffin" (p 220). "*Deal*" suggests 'devil', often contracted to 'de'il' in the Middle Ages. Irving and Trinity together with their deceased daughter

Adelaide parody the Holy Trinity by representing its opposite. The name 'A-del-aide' suggests 'a devil's aid'; the daughter, who died at 15, was a wolf-child. Just as the Devil is the antithesis of God, so is the female wolf-child the antithesis of the Lamb of God. Following the imagined death of the Garretts, 'Advocate' Mavis becomes heir to their property.

In her new home, Mavis is visited by four guests—Doris and Roger, Zita and Theo. Each has an allegorical identity.

Roger's role is Christ. He is concerned that, in an "Age of Explanation", faith disappears: "The efficiency of our explanations is like that of the insecticide which reduces the insect to a crumbling shell." (p 139) Roger's suspicion that his "given nature is empty as a ventriloquist's dummy" (p 139) mocks Christ's role as God's spokesman on earth. Roger, "the translator of clichés into rules to live by" (p 156), is described as:

> A man who yearns for the desert, for the company of nothing
> may grow <u>thorns</u>, put forth <u>crimson blossom</u>, feast on his own
>   <u>stored blood</u>
> after the blood-rains of each season fall from whatever sky he
>   lives under
> <u>defending the sun's intensity</u>
> its privilege of burning
> its gift of cautery,
> the eschar that may be God. (p 155, emphases mine)

These lines allude to Christ's crown of thorns, the blood from the wounds of Christ ("crimson blossom") and the sacrament ("stored blood"). One of Christ's undertakings is to interpret or defend the purifying quality of the "sun", symbolising here, as it does in *The Divine Comedy*, God's exacting regime.

Like Christ, Roger endures the desert; unlike Christ, however, he does not remain there for 40 days. He is retrieved by his wife after a few hours, having meditated and enlarged his understanding. At the mercy of the heat, Roger and a jackhare share a shadow. He comes to realise what "being at home" means: "Just sharing a space in peace . . . that was life-size and therefore death-size." (p 177) Roger discovers, moreover, that those who share the "gift" (p 185) of their own sensitivity or creativity (or, for that matter, their own shadow) are making payment for their portion of air, sunlight, life. Payment is made by the person who will "pay attention" (p 45) to the natural world, its jackhares and its people.

Zita and Doris are opposites. Twice in *The Purgatorio*, Dante dreams of Leah and Rachel, who exemplify the 'active life' and the 'contemplative life'. These dreams foreshadow Dante's meeting with their counterparts Matilda and Beatrice. Doris represents those who are creative in a practical way. Like Leah, she is fruitful, her children often forming the subject of her thought and conversation.

Zita, golden-haired and childless, is both opposite and comparable (adjacent) to the 'contemplative' Beatrice. Beatrice appears in one of Dante's pageants stepping from a triumph-car drawn by a Gryphon[15], resembling the vehicle which in Corpus Christi festivals bears the host or sacrament in a special urn. She represents, for the purpose of the pageant, "the Holy Host Itself".[16] Zita too assumes the role of "host", but in relation to Theo. She has promised to devote, one could say to 'sacrifice', herself to him; she will become his strength and support as he ages. The words "host" and "guest" have, in the course of time, exchanged meanings, "with a guest as originally a host" (p 133). In relation to Theo, Zita was initially the "guest", for at the age of 17 she was rescued by the 57-year-old Theo. Dependence by one person on another is ultimately destructive. Should Theo become dependent on her, he would drain Zita's energy and creativity.

Mavis's fourth "guest" is Theo Carlton, Theo suggesting 'God' and Carl suggesting 'man'. He can be seen both in the role of God and as a credible human character. Theo has a penchant for rescuing people. He achieves many of his "ambitions only through the lives of others." (p 145) and reveals that "half the

people in the top positions in foreign affairs, internal affairs, agri-
culture and fisheries, had been put there by him" (p 198). Mavis
takes a feminist stance in her depiction of Theo. She parodies the
patriarchal assumptions on which Christian belief rests and the
dogma that God made man in his own image. Theo is loud,
arrogant and vain, being overly conscious of his own appearance.
He says, " 'When I look in the mirror I see my sun-tanned skin,
my glossy white curly hair, my fine athletic body' " (p 144). He
remarks, " 'I have always been proud to be a man, and although I
do have liberal views, I despise unmanliness.' " (p 144) There is
irony in this contradictory remark and in Theo's loss, through
suffering a stroke, of "much of the power to name—the God-
power and poet-power." (p 211)

Dante's 14th-century view accepted a divine hierarchy which
guided humankind and offered a model for human institutions.
The Berkeley episode is likely to provoke opposite theses. One
possible inference is that order within any community begins
with the individual. But when the majority fail to 'sur-vive'
childhood—that is, fail to grow above and beyond childhood
with its implicit reliance on a father—order within a community
is impossible. As Mavis observes, "I used to wonder how people
survived their childhood: I now know that few survive it."
(p 107) We are invited to connect the ills of the modern world
with the immaturity of its inhabitants.

Blenheim and Baltimore are associated with a materialistic
and exploitative way of life. Creativity is associated with the
Berkeley hills and the high plain of the Maniototo, hence the
cryptic name of Part IV: "Attending and Avoiding in the
Maniototo". Berkeley is Mavis's Maniototo, her realm of imagination and her earthly paradise in which, as a writer, she is "com-
muting between 'real life' and 'fiction'" (p 118). She creates a
fiction which allows her to enter imaginatively the lives of four
characters. She admits to spending many hours "working out of
sight downstairs attending to the fictional needs of my guests"
(p 231).

Mavis herself exemplifies the creative individual. Entering her Maniototo has been the culmination of her travels. In the novel's final chapter she returns to Baltimore, to learn of the death of her friend Brian. There is a clear contrast between Mavis with her manuscript, her "golden blanket" (p 218) to keep her warm and alive into the future, and the uncreative, rational Brian, who sought no earthly paradise and who lived and died without trace.

Once the parallel between the modern city and Hell is established, the impact is immediate: it shocks and amuses, showing the familiar world in a bizarre light. The parallels between Frame's text and Dante's require constant comparison and contrast. They belong in a network of contrasts which structures the novel: inner and outer worlds, reality and fiction, paying and owing, attending and avoiding, host and guest, replicas and originals, hell-on-earth and an earthly paradise, living and dying.

The novel underscores life's precariousness, with the death or disappearance of Lewis, Lance, Tommy, Mrs Tyndall and Brian Wilford. As in life, strokes, heart attacks, asphyxiation occur without warning. Even Brian "simply never included death in his plans . . . and he was such an infallible planner!" (p 239) Brian is typical of those who avoid acknowledging the presence of death. By her contrary perspective Mavis mocks Brian. Her ironic stance is comparable to that of the little black fantail, the piwakawaka of Maori mythology who laughed aloud at the half-god Maui's attempt to vanquish the Death Goddess Hine-nui-te-po. Awakened by Piwakawaka's laughter, the Goddess crushed her would-be assailant. We are reminded of this myth when, in Blenheim, a little black fantail accompanies the ghost of the suburb's famous poet. A typically cryptic allegorical image, the black fantail links the creative writer not only with the song-maker of Frame's very first tale, but with the artist's disenchanted view of human arrogance.

Mavis voices her own complex truth, taking care to reject words that are "screens, moveable walls, decorations, unnecessary furniture, and keep only the load-bearing words (the load-bearing birds?) that stop the sky from falling." (p 78) From the whole range of language, she chooses and arranges, in the most effective manner, the "load-bearing words". Through Mavis, Frame is surely affirming once again the capacity of the artists as "the load-bearing birds" to keep the hawks in flight; the poised hawk which signals the truth of death provides the tension and anguish that inform the work of the writer. In this novel, the hawk metaphor broadens in significance: "language in its widest sense is the hawk suspended above eternity" (p 43). Language itself, because it articulates, however inadequately, the concept and hovering truth of death, impels and inspires the writer. Her reward is to discover "living" in a "Maniototo".

Living in the Maniototo was first published by Braziller in New York, 1979. Page numbers in brackets refer to this edition. Spelling has been anglicised. Since The Women's Press, London, re-used the original plates, there is no 'English' version available.

1   Frame acknowledges that her quotation is "from the Encyclopaedia of New Zealand". Its source is *An Encyclopaedia of New Zealand* Volume 2, edited by H McLintock, p 727.

2   The Maori meanings of "Maniototo" do not appear in the *Encyclopaedia* but are presented in this manner in *Wise's New Zealand Guide*, p 219. It is believed that the Maniototo was named 'plain of blood' because the region was the scene of fighting between Maori tribes in the first quarter of the 18th century.

3   There is no New Zealand writer of this name, but Wallstead is reminiscent of Ronald Hugh Morrieson, 1922–1972. Like Wallstead, he was a novelist and a teacher (of music) in a rural community (Taranaki). Morrieson was not well known in his lifetime but his work received acclaim after his death. While she was writing *Living in the Maniototo*, Frame lived in the Taranaki town of Stratford, neighbour to Morrieson's home town, Hawera.

4   For example, *Daughter Buffalo*, p 31. "Grief can spin the silk that you must cut to the core, unwind, plait, removing all traces of the toil and the impossible life, love and death of the makers, before you set your golden trophy on display."

5   Frame is referring to a massive hydro-electricity scheme in an area adjacent to the Maniototo, adopted in 1976 in spite of widespread opposition and a

petition to Parliament. Technical and financial difficulties have plagued the Clyde High Dam ever since; it was not completed until 1992 and is widely regarded as 'total madness'.

6 Postmodernism describes an attitude to life and literature as well as to a mode of writing. Modernist anxiety ("angst") has been replaced by acceptance of the fundamental uncertainties of existence. A world in disarray is beyond remedy. The postmodern writer playfully and ironically conveys disillusionment and loss of innocence. Postmodern texts are characterised by inconsistencies, unreliable narrators and the impression that fact and fiction are equally fictitious. Language is the maker of our world; words are used consciously. There is an awareness that any new text is a reworking of many that have gone before.

7 Blenheim does not refer to the South Island town of that name. Frame calls an imaginary suburb on Auckland's North Shore "Blenheim". It resembles the inland part of the suburb of Glenfield, which is dominated by a shopping complex called Glenfield Mall, parodied by Frame's "Heavenfield Mall".

8 Blenheim's "famous poet" is not named, but it is likely that Frame is referring to the New Zealand poet James K Baxter. He collapsed in the street of an Auckland suburb and died (in 1972) in the home of someone with whom he was not acquainted, who "took him in" (p 22).

9 Dante, *The Divine Comedy, I: Hell*, translated by Dorothy L Sayers, p 101. The translator comments on "*The Circles of Incontinence*": "This and the next three circles are devoted to those who sinned less by deliberate choice of evil than by failure to make resolute choice of the good. Here are the sins of self-indulgence, weakness of will, and easy yielding to appetite—the "Sins of the Leopard"."

10 Specific reference to *The Divine Comedy* occurs on p 174, showing the work to be part of Mavis's reading experience. Thorn trees are compared to "stripped selves, or . . . the trees of the suicides in the Wood of the Second Ring of the Circle of the Violent."

11 Dante, *The Divine Comedy, I: Hell*, p 99. All Dante quotations refer to the Sayers edition. Canto and line numbers are for *Book I: Hell*, unless preceded by II, which refers to *Book II: Purgatory*.

12 Robert Southey, "The Battle of Blenheim", *Poems of Robert Southey*, edited by Maurice Fitzgerald, p 366.

> 'They say it was a shocking sight
> After the field was won;
> For many thousand bodies here
> Lay rotting in the sun;'

Allusion to this poem is one of a series of impressions by which Mavis suggests that battles over the "world's real and unreal estate" (p 225) are futile.

> 'But what good came of it at last?'
> Quoth little Peterkin.
> 'Why that I cannot tell,' said he
> 'But 'twas a famous victory.'

13 Dante, *I: Hell*—see editorial note p 185. The Eighth and Ninth Circles are the circles of fraud and malice, which are known as the "Sins of the Wolf".

14 In the 1970s there was in New Zealand a television advertisement for a household cleaner, said to clean "with the power of liquid lightning". The advertisement showed a container from which a small whirling "White Tornado" arose whenever it was used.

15 The Garretts' house has "a carved door knocker (a griffin)" (p 125).

16 Dante, *II: Purgatory*, p 311. In an editorial note, Sayers writes: "If throughout the whole course of the poem our minds had not been insistently prepared for the coming of Beatrice, the whole symbolism of the Masque . . . would lead us to expect the appearance upon the car of the Holy Host Itself . . . What appears is indeed Beatrice . . . But she is also, in the allegory of the Masque, the Image of the Host."

I 3

The Carpathians

Frame's most recent novel appeared nine years after *Living in the Maniototo*. Its self-conscious manipulation of character and point of view, and its overt disregard for credibility, are among its postmodern features. At the same time *The Carpathians* parodies the biblical myth that has appeared in so many guises in Frame's work. The fall, which is important thematically and as a structural device in *Scented Gardens for the Blind*, *Intensive Care* and *Daughter Buffalo*, receives quite different treatment in *The Carpathians*. Here Frame shapes a new legend, celebrating a woman who willingly tastes new knowledge.

A small invented "legend" (p 11) provides a "threshold text"[1], which is a pattern of action prefiguring the main events in the narrative, like the first brief rendition of a melodic theme in a concerto. In an allegorical novel, the ordeal of the hero or heroine follows the pattern outlined in the threshold text, unfolding an allegorical progression in which "every experience has a greater possible value than the hero can himself detect. [. . .] He may have a choice of guides who will either help or mislead him."[2] Frame's legend parodies the biblical story of the fall by inverting or transforming each step of its progress.

A young woman, chosen by the gods as collector of the memory of her land, journeys . . . to search for the memory; and as in all legends the helpers . . . who are themselves guardians of the

inner world of searches, make or find time to stand at convenient
places—corners, crossroads, shores, boundaries . . . [. . .]

The legend describes how the young woman released the
memory of the land when she picked and tasted the ripe fruit
from a tree growing in the bush: where <u>Eve tasted her and
Adam's tomorrow</u>, the woman of Maharawhenua tasted the
yesterday within the tomorrow . . . (p 11, emphasis mine)

The woman is not lured or deceived by an evil power, but is
"chosen by the gods". Her picking and tasting of the fruit of the
tree does not occasion interrogation and retribution. It is the
culmination of her search which she marks by calling together
the people of the land and recounting "the memory". Eventually,
she disappears, having been transformed into a tree which bears
the Memory Flower and "fruit invisible to most eyes" (p 11). The
biblical Tree of Knowledge has been supplanted by the tree of
the flowering memory. Frame has replaced the biblical story with
a myth that focuses on the creative aspects of knowledge, those
aspects which can contribute to a cultural legacy. The "yesterday
within the tomorrow" suggests that cultural and genealogical
roots can be known and valued and preserved for the future.

The main setting is a New Zealand town named Puamahara
in a region called Maharawhenua[3]. The invented Maori names
mean Memory Land (Maharawhenua) and Memory Flower
(Puamahara). If the Memory Flower forms one "threshold symbol"[4], the Gravity Star forms another. The two concepts comple-
ment each other. They have no literary referent or universally
acknowledged significance, but unfold as concepts within the
novel. The Memory Flower signifies the created work that has
value in its own right and endures from one generation to the
next. The Gravity Star is a force responsible for the many inver-
sions and transformations which characterise *The Carpathians*—
including the inversion of the story of the fall. It is said to be
responsible for "the bursting of the iron bands that once made
rigid the container of knowledge" (p 14). The fatal knowledge

that has burdened man for centuries, rendering him eternally guilty, has been released or lifted. The "weight of centuries of knowing" is carried "out of our reach." (p 14)

Like a divinity, the Gravity Star presides over the world of the novel. Though inexplicable, infinite and all-powerful, the phenomenon in fact has been scientifically recorded outside the world of the novel. The introductory note explains that a galaxy known to be distant appears to be close to the earth. Distant light focused "by the gravity of an intervening galaxy" causes the paradox.[5] The Gravity Star could be said to be a guiding star, for we are all guided through life towards death; the gravity of the earth draws us all into the grave. At the same time, the term acknowledges the forces of gravity that hold the seasons in balance, the earth in equilibrium and the universe in harmony. It is close to that concept of God which equates him with the creating, preserving, destroying power of nature within the entire universe. The Gravity Star can overturn life, transforming it into death, and it can overturn reality, transforming the known world into the world of the imagination. "Ordinary perceptions are denied, overturned" (p 12).

A first-person narrator speaks directly in an introductory note, in Chapters 2 and 3, and in the novel's concluding paragraph. John Henry Brecon creates a story in which his mother, Mattina Brecon, is the central character. The fact that he disavows her existence as his mother in the book's concluding paragraph serves to remind us of the writer's freedom to imagine and then to overturn characters and relationships. Until the final page, Mattina belongs within the Brecon family, wife of Jake and mother of John Henry. She is a wealthy middle-aged woman who travels from New York to a small imaginary New Zealand town to fulfil an "urgent need to know the lives of those distant from her" (p 19). She is, at the same time, searching for the wellsprings of her human heritage.

Mattina's quest parallels the action of the legend that forms the "threshold text". She travels to the gardens and orchards of

Maharawhenua, "an attractive horticultural centre" (p 19), growing "roses, carnations, kiwifruit, berryfruit, apples" (p 177). In an
effort to gain a particular kind of knowledge, she makes "a collection of people whose lives and 'truth' she discovered and *knew*."
(p 75) Mattina gathers the memory of the land; like the legendary woman of Puamahara, she later releases "the memory" by
recounting it to her husband and son on her return to New York.
Her 'disappearance' is her death. Her memories form the seed
from which John Henry's novel springs. The novel itself is the
memory's flowering.

In the course of Mattina's trip from New York to New
Zealand, time and distance are transcended and destroyed as they
are by any jet travel. Mattina is delivered "in a shredded state
of mind where hours equalled years and the time became . . .
striped with the past, present and future" (p 95). She enters a
different world, the world "Down Under" (pp 163 and 176). It is
quite unlike any other underworld, although there is one allusion
to Dante's Hell. Dante placed the forebears of many Italian citizens under the earth in a Hell with an opening to the Antipodes.
Mattina journeys to the antipodes of her own being. In contemplating the danger of "falling beyond the fabric", Mattina
"remembered that Dante had entered Hell through a doorway of
the Antipodes—or had that been the exit?"[6] (p 89) It is indeed
the exit, but in this context exit or entry is unimportant. The
world Mattina enters "down under" is her own "inner world of
searches" (p 11). She is contemplating the forebears who have
helped to shape her essential being. She is intrigued by the idea
of a gap in "the fabric" that will allow her to reach back to her
own heritage.

Mattina enters the neighbourhood of Kowhai Street,
Puamahara, like a person from a different sphere. She observes a
life-in-death existence, emphasised by the image of Kowhai
Street as on the one hand, an ordinary suburban street and, on
the other, as an accommodating and attractive graveyard. The
impression of a graveyard is a reminder of the community's

fragile tenure of the surface of the earth. But, more important, it emphasises the idea that the bones of generations of forebears are present within the earth: "the fertility of the soil is fed by the crushed bones of vanished rivers and the blood of former generations" (p 12). Kowhai Street resident Hercus Millow says that there is "a heck of a lot of dying in Puamahara" (p 40). For his neighbour Renée Shannon, Puamahara is a "dump" where she is "buried" (p 54).

> Where are they, the long dead, the recently dead, the poets, the painters, the toilers, the housekeepers, the murderers, the imposters . . .? If you walk in mid-afternoon through the streets of Puamahara you might suppose you walk through a neatly kept cemetery where the graves are more spacious than usual, with flowers and vegetable gardens, fences, concrete paths leading to the door of the family mausoleum. The silence, cavelike, may be entered. (p 15)

Again, a flexible perspective is needed to make the imaginative transition from the "graveyard" scene to the tree-lined street in a small town: "just as you become certain that you walk in a cemetery, the sounds of the living intrude" (p 15). The insatiable "hunger for the 'goods'" (p 47), just as prevalent in Puamahara as in the Blenheim of *Living in the Maniototo*, is incongruous in a place poised "at the end of the earth" (p 156).

It is in this setting that Mattina carries out her research, recording her findings in a notebook. By visiting neighbouring families, she learns about people whose attention is devoted to their computer, motor vehicle or renovations. A computer is described as the "remaining member of the Shannon family" (p 54). The James family home includes "Internal entry. The car as part of the household." (p 73) Family links beyond Kowhai Street are tenuous, and within the street the residents are strangers to one another. Instead of relating to friends or family members, including those who might be elderly or handicapped, the people of Kowhai Street direct their energies towards home improvement: "even the fence posts, the patio, the barbecue were spoken of as living things. 'See, there's the barbecue,' they said as if they named a new grandchild, their son's best friend, their daughter." (p 155) The ironical equation between people and things reduces people to objects.

Mattina, too, is a consumer. Her acquisitive tendencies take the form of a passion for buying real estate throughout the world, an ironically insubstantial or 'un-real' commodity when a person can occupy so little space at any one time. For all her wealth, she is "not a happy woman" (p 18). Her own two-dimensional existence is reflected in exaggerated form in the insubstantial lives of her neighbours. She differs only in that she is a searcher or researcher.

Images of an inner journey are reiterated. As in other novels by Frame, a room provides an image for the inner being of a person. When Mattina becomes aware of the bulk of something alive in her Kowhai Street bedroom, she is projecting a sense of something within herself into a more tangible form. "She moved downwards to a new distance that became incredible in its nearness" (p 79). She envisages the presence of "an invisible creature collected from the depths of the storehouse of time or of her own mind." (p 80) Later, the presence becomes more clearly defined, forming "a blank two-dimensional triangular space" (p 100). The stylised representation suggests a failure to know and understand an essential "human force" (p 95) from the past.

Mattina's restless travelling has been prompted by an awareness that something is missing from her life. She has already, in a series of "desperate searches" (p 19), lived among the people of Nova Scotia, the Bahamas, Hawaii, Portugal and Spain. On her many diverting journeys she has sought those aspects of human nature which all people hold in common. She chooses Puamahara because, in the vicinity of the Memory Flower, she hopes to find "the land memory growing in the air, so to speak, with everyone certain as could be of the knowledge of the programme of time, learning the language of the memory" (p 60).

She imagines, moreover, that New Zealand will be "small enough for everyone to be neighbours; a family place . . . With everyone, all races, sharing the Memory Flower." (p 60)

Mattina's day trip to a Maori settlement far inland where "the eye of the interior . . . smoulders even in the traveller's absence, day and night, century after century" (p 83) is both a search for an ancestral heritage and a journey into her own interior. The Maori meeting house, in which Mattina rests, holds "yesterday's silence" (pp 85–86). Here she finds her own individual place within a wide community reaching back deeply into the past. A community that reveres traditional knowledge and knowledge of lineage contributes richly to the understanding for which Mattina is searching. The concept of heritage in this novel is not limited to the forebears of just one race but is concerned with the heritage of the human family.

Cultural and genealogical knowledge contributes to the formation of a self. The concept of self is explained in relation to the James family's electronic tuner. Neighbour Joseph James, a piano tuner, describes the device: "it's a nothing with no self. And although it's known as a third or fourth generation tuner, it has no ancestors and no ancestral memory." (p 73) Joseph James is among those who help or guide Mattina as she seeks knowledge of herself, a knowledge which many people tend to avoid. The human race is described by Kowhai Street character Dinny Wheatstone as "an elsewhere race" in which one is inclined to inhabit "all worlds except the world of oneself." (p 51)

The novel dramatises an entirely postmodern wrangle between two characters, Mattina and Dinny, each of whom struggles to convey her point of view. Dinny is seen, initially, through Mattina's eyes. Then, for a time, Mattina becomes a character in Dinny's manuscript. But Dinny admits that she is an imposter who lacks a self: "Imposterism or imposture comes from the core of your being because there's nothing else there. Your central being never develops a self . . . almost as if you were dead." (p 44) Through her careful gathering of memory—of the land, its people and their heritage—Mattina gains a greater sense of her "self". Eventually, she regains control of the point of view, thus ensuring that it survives within the novel.

Mattina wonders whether people everywhere will be torn like cardboard unless they create "both the stolen dimension and the new imaginative dimension" (p 107). Knowledge of a genealogical history and a sense of family has been "stolen" by a modern mobile lifestyle. The "imaginative dimension" is an aesthetic awareness that would see human energies being directed differently, so that artists could work "side by side with the house-cladders, the plumbers, the builders of rumpus rooms" (p 115). Mattina compares Puamahara with New York, which owes a debt

> to its artists, once strangers from distant lands, who created a new dimension for the city, gave it depth, shape, and even were the city in reality a flat two-dimensional world . . ., the shape and density given it by the artists lay unbroken in the world of imagination, so that when outsiders looked at New York they saw ... real people of flesh and blood and depth in an adamantine city of height and strength, of all dimensions.
>
> (p 104)

To develop "real people of flesh and blood and depth", the work of artists in Puamahara would need to be "trebled or increased a hundredfold" (p 104). Mattina sees creativity within a community to be an alternative to disappearing into oblivion, for people are "close both to the flower of memory and the seed of oblivion." (p 75)

Kowhai Street's closeness to the "seed of oblivion" is demonstrated in a surrealistic episode. In a bizarre inversion of events surrounding the fall, the residents are all expelled from their Kowhai Street gardens. Instead of acquiring forbidden knowledge, they have *failed* to acquire knowledge, or rather "failed the Memory Flower", which exists only as a stone "or was it plaster?" (p 115) replica with lost petals and peeling paint. Having failed to know history, imagination, memory, the residents have such slight anchorage that "one morning the street and the town may wake to find all is adrift in the space of anywhere" (p 93).

And that is what happens: the residents are "changed beyond belief" (p 126), transported to "the other side of the barrier of knowing and being" (p 129). The Gravity Star has intervened, causing a plunge into the abyss of "unbeing" (p 129). The over-turning process, which occurs at midnight, is signalled by cries and screams from the neighbours, to the sounds of which two recently deceased residents contribute. The realm of "unbeing" is, therefore, synonymous with death. Garden has been changed into wilderness, world has been changed into underworld, life has been transformed into death in which "the faces, the bodies, the clothes" are "smeared with a mixture resembling clay, mud" (p 126).

> The people of Kowhai Street had experienced the disaster of unbeing, unknowing, that accompanies death and is thought by man to mark the beginning of a new kind of being and thought and language that, in life, is inconceivable, unknowable. (p 129)

Within this new dimension there is no language. The residents have suffered "a loss of all the words they had ever known, all the concepts that supported and charged the words, all processes of thinking and feeling" (p 129). The loss of language, which of course accompanies death, is made visible as letters from many languages rain down on Kowhai Street. The two-dimensional lives, embracing values couched in outworn patterns of language, have been eliminated.

Like ghosts returning to graves, the people of Kowhai Street disappear into their homes at the first hint of dawn. They are mysteriously removed later in the day with the usual efficiency that accompanies modern dispatch of bodies. The events—Mattina's survival, the disappearance of her neighbours and the midnight rain of letters—disregard credibility. As in much postmodern writing, the author's manipulation of a changing story is made visible. Facts are quite blatantly adjusted to fit a new situation. As Mattina's ghostly neighbours are removed by a team of stretcher-bearers going from door to door, Mattina hides behind a virgilia tree and is "thankful she had packed her bags the day before and had them checked in at the airport out of town"[7] (p 147). Such an after-thought is one of the signals that Mattina exists within an imaginary realm constructed and presided over by words.

She survives the disaster by "clinging like an insect at the point of destruction to the Memory Flower" (p 151). Her "real" being flies home to New York three days after the catastrophe: "Perhaps . . . she had removed herself, her real being, to New York City, that is, to Memory, and while races and worlds may die, if they are to change, to resurrect as new, they must remain within the Memory Flower." (p 151) At the same time, she is returning from the journey "down under" or down into her own human heritage bearing memories gleaned from that investigation.

The night that fills Kowhai Street with wailing spectres provides Mattina with an intimation of her own inevitable death, bringing her suddenly closer than at any other time to her husband and son. The love between Mattina and Jake emerges as a central concern. The novel provides an example of a family's contribution to memory within a concept of culture which sees human beings as members of one family. "And was not part of the nature of love to include the world . . .?" (p 138) By sharing with Jake and John Henry her understanding of people in many parts of the world from whom she has learnt stories, beliefs, traditional knowledge, Mattina is contributing to the Memory Flower.

Memory is "not . . . a comfortable parcel of episodes to carry in one's mind". Instead, it is "a naked link, a point, diamond-size, seed-size, coded in the code of the world, of the human race" (pp 171–172). This philosophy was apparent 25 years earlier in Frame's story "Snowman, Snowman", which proposes that "seed is shed at the moment of death."⁸ *The Carpathians* forms a song of praise to the human collectors of memory, and to the bearers of unique plant memories, the seeds that ensure the survival of a multitude of living species.

The Orchards of Puamahara survive through the care of "Housekeepers of Ancient Springtime"⁹ (p 157). The memory or blueprint for regeneration endures from season to season and from century to century. The phrase "housekeepers of ancient springtime" alludes to Rilke's series of poems entitled *Verger,* meaning 'orchard' which are his most positive affirmation that life and tradition endure through art. In its positive philosophy, *The Carpathians* shares the spirit of the *Verger* poems. Tree-memory reaches far back into time; the capacity of trees to bear blossom and fruit which have their own beauty and perfection of form is a metaphor for the capacity of the mind to produce works that will endure. In *The Carpathians,* such works are created when the divinity of the Gravity Star conjoins with "the legendary seed of memory, the Memory Flower" (p 151). The creative imagination draws on memory "like a honey-sucking insect" (p 166). With imagination, "the eastern mountains of Puamahara would be the Carpathians; and weight becomes lightness; and the trees, as in Rilke's poem, have their roots in the sky." (p 194)

The creative imagination of the writer is nurtured by and expressed through language. To Jake, "Words were his only valued property" (p 194). He is a preserver of language through his literary essays and through his sensitive reading aloud to John Henry, fostering in his son a love of language and literature. John Henry's novel reflects in enduring form the values and concerns, the questions and customs of different communities. It is among the many works that are "trying to continue the memory, replanting the orchard" (p 167). Jake embodies Love of Words, Mattina embodies Memory. Fiction (alias John Henry) is the child of their union. We are reminded of the fictional nature of the book when John Henry concludes by suggesting that "perhaps the town of Puamahara, which I in my turn visited, never existed?" (p 196)

Frame replaces the story of the fall with a story of creativity. The novel challenges old concepts, and proposes new, positive ways of relating to the earth, the heritage of the land and the human family's "yesterday within the tomorrow" (p 11). Traditional knowledge is revered. A Maori expert in flax weaving, another of those who guides or helps Mattina in her searching, explains the importance of "knowing" flax, for flax is "always alive" (p 86). This is a knowing that acknowledges human relatedness to the earth and its plants. From a "new language" born "from a new way of thought" (p 101), humanity could be rescued from a "swamp of absurdity, contradiction" (p 101). Since the story of the fall has been replaced in this novel by a new myth, the allegory prompts us to consider whether or not the old myth has contributed to the "absurdity, contradiction".

The Carpathians discloses Frame's most subtle allegorical patterning, using a prior text as a point of departure into a world in which concepts are overturned by "an idea" (p 193). That idea had been with Frame for many years, having found expression in *The Rainbirds* when Beatrice observed that "the change from death to life defying the laws of gravity set the dreamers wheeling and spinning in their wakefulness."[10] (emphases mine) In *The Carpathians*, such "wheeling and spinning" is instigated by the Gravity Star, allowing dreamers, users of imagination, to create within their own mind worlds which allow them to escape a death-in-life existence. Whereas the Maniototo is the realm of a particular writer, the world of the Gravity Star and the Memory Flower embodies a continuum of creativity, providing an undying earthly paradise to which successions of makers can contribute. In *Owls Do Cry*, the imaginations of children transform a rubbish dump into a paradise; *The Carpathians*, the most positive of Frame's novels, suggests that the memory and creative imagination of adults can recover a paradise. "In the gift of the orchards of the Memory Flower, it seemed that lost became found, death became life" (p 114).

The Carpathians was first published by Century Hutchinson in Auckland and Braziller in New York, 1988. Page numbers in this chapter refer to the Century Hutchinson edition.

1   For further discussion of the "threshold text" see Maureen Quilligan, *The Language of Allegory: Defining the Genre*, p 53. *The Carpathians* would be among those allegories which "unfold as narrative investigations of their own threshold texts." Quilligan derives the expression from Edwin Honig's discussion of the threshold symbol or emblem—see notes 2 and 4 below.

2   Edwin Honig, *Dark Conceit: The Making of Allegory*, p 74.

3   The town of Puamahara has much in common with Levin, 50 kilometres south of Palmerston North and lying between the Tararua ranges and the sea. Levin, which like Puamahara has blue plastic regulation rubbish bags, is where Janet Frame lived during the mid-1980s. 'Mahara' and 'whenua' are both familiar components in Maori names, as in Horowhenua and Maharahara. Levin is the main town in the Horowhenua district, which like the Maharawhenua is "an attractive horticultural centre" (p 19).

4   Honig explains his concepts of the threshold emblem and symbol in *Dark Conceit*, p 72. Threshold symbols introduced near the beginning of an allegory encapsulate ideas or concepts that will be significant throughout the work.

5   Marion McLeod's interview with Janet Frame, in *NZ Listener*, 24 September 1988, relates information provided by Frame: "The Maori legend of Puamahara, the memory flower, is entirely invented ("I believe nothing is barred for a writer") but the discovery of the Gravity Star is real, though the name is hers. She read about the paradox of near and far in the *Dominion* (a Wellington daily newspaper)—"a galaxy that appears to be both relatively close and seven billion light years away . . ." She has the clipping somewhere, could find it for me . . ."

6   Dante, *The Divine Comedy I: Hell*, C34 138.

7   This preparation is the more unlikely because the airport is "a fifty kilometre drive" (p 177) away.

8   "Snowman, Snowman", p 83.

9   In an interview with Elizabeth Alley, Radio New Zealand Concert Programme, 12 November 1988, Frame explained that "housekeepers" was her

word, but that Rilke had written of an "ancient springtime". The words are from a poem entitled "Verger". Its two concluding verses are as follows:

Verger: ô privilège d'une lyre
de pouvoir te nommer simplement;
nom sans pareil qui les abeilles attire,
nom qui respire et attend . . .

Nom clair qui cache le printemps antique,
tout aussi plein que transparent,
et qui dans ses syllabes symétriques
redouble tout et devient abondant.

Rainer Maria Rilke, *Werke, Band II·2*
Gedichte und Übertragungen, 1974, p 286.

10   *The Rainbirds,* p 63.

I 4

Conclusion

"Hers is a difficult inward-looking world both tortured and tortuous; it is not an easy terrain."[1] Michael Morrissey's statement is a fair summary of the most widely-held attitude to Janet Frame's fiction. In response to the problem, noted by Patrick Evans, of discovering where "the centre" of her work lies, Robert Ross in 1987 proposed that "the centre, the core, lies in language"[2]. Such an observation does not take us to the centre of Frame's work unless we see her concern for language in relation to her use of allegory. Maureen Quilligan has noted that allegory "announces itself by a number of obvious blatant signals—most notably personification and wordplay—to be about the magic signifying power of language"[3]. The centre of Frame's work has remained elusive because of the subtlety of the word-play that conceals the allegorical dimension to her novels.

Many traditional allegories offer their significance overtly. When moral concepts are personified, bearing names such as Sloth and Giant Despair, there is no doubt as to their role or meaning. But in Frame's work, allegorical identities are hidden within language puzzles. Since there is no satisfaction in asking a riddle that no one can solve, Frame's text offers many 'clues'. These are sometimes placed in italics. One example is the word "*deal*". "The Garretts had specified in their will a *deal* coffin." (*Living in the Maniototo*, p 220) 'Deal' is a homophone for 'de'il', an abbreviated form of 'devil'. It seems strange that the couple has specified only one coffin, until we realise that the Garrett family parodies the Holy Family, including the concept of the three-in-one. Having provided the clue, Frame quickly deflects attention towards the 'deal' tables of 19th-century literature. This example shows just how much one word can both conceal and reveal.

Words spoken by an allegorical character are determined, not by verisimilitude or idiomatic rightness, but by the role to which he or she has been assigned. A man would be unlikely to speak out in the manner of Theo from *Living in the Maniototo:*

> 'When I look in the mirror I see my sun-tanned skin, my glossy white curly hair, my fine athletic body, and you will notice my habit of making some move or gesture to draw attention to my body, to let it and not I announce that my years are far fewer than sixty-five.' (p 144)

As C K Stead has observed: "The more successfully [Frame] uses a character to represent some quality or trait she dislikes, the less humanly complete the character becomes."[4] Though he does not mention 'allegory', Stead is describing one of the characteristics of allegory where (to quote Maureen Quilligan) "the words any given character speaks are controlled at least in part by the word that character *is.*"[5] Some of Frame's characters embody negative roles and attributes, like Tom Livingstone as Satan and Talbot Edelman as Death. Others, like Milly Galbraith as Innocence and Aisley Maude as Christ, embody positive qualities.

It is fair to ask how one can be certain about a character's allegorical identity. In *Scented Gardens for the Blind,* for example, one might think that Edward is Satan. On that assumption, the image of Edward's fat cheeks stuffed with "Paper, people?" (p 212) is not meaningful. If Edward is Death, however, the image combines the fact that until 30 years ago it was common practice for the cheeks of a dead person to be padded with cotton wool or tissue paper, and the fact that Milton's Death dines on "people". When the correct allegorical identity is established, every piece of the puzzle fits into place and the text confirms the correctness repeatedly. Frame includes no meaningless passages or gratuitous images. Figurative language is never used carelessly or casually. Metaphors may, as if by accident like Freudian slips, reveal attitudes, obsessions or intentions. This is especially true for the satanic characters in Frame's work, all of whom are deceivers. A figure of speech often provides an accurate description of an allegorical character or setting. Those who look "as if" they are sleep-walking in hell can also be seen as wraiths in that same setting.

It is often startling and amusing to find that a familiar or idiomatic expression must be taken literally. Although Rob Guthrie is described as a "joking devil" (*Living in the Maniototo,* p 46), we do not at first believe that the text means what it says. His knees are "carboned with blue" and he wears in his hat a "Red-Tipped-Governor" (p 45). Those who are not New Zealanders might be unaware of the contingent of Kiwi males who insist on wearing shorts even in mid-winter. But shorts would be appropriate in the heat of hell, whose fires would be responsible for the 'carboning'. Fishing flies arranged in the hat-band cheerfully announce a man's affiliation with a whole brotherhood of trout fishermen. Humour springs from the sudden and unexpected connection between the familiar fishing fly, the horn of a devil and the hook as a means of devilish punishment.

Much of Frame's humour has gone unremarked because it resides in irony, and the irony is at the service of the allegory. So, if the allegorical dimension has not been recognised, it is not easy to know whether Frame is being ironical. In her review of *Living in the Maniototo,* Lydia Wevers notes that Mavis promises to entertain us. But Wevers suspects that she is stating the opposite: "Doesn't laughter and crying, in the context in which we are offered it, merely reflect moral guilt that the world, others, more particularly *oneself* should be like this?"[6] Wevers has discerned Frame's irony but is not prepared to be dogmatic about it. Once one has seen the allegory, Mavis's ironical response to many situ-

ations becomes clear. But at the same time Mavis speaks truthfully. She does entertain us. Her entertainment is like that of
Samuel Beckett's comic characters: we perceive the abyss in the
midst of our laughter.

If we don't understand the irony within a text, we will miss
much of the pathos as well as the humour. Only after we have
decoded *Intensive Care*'s allegorical aspects can we be fully aware
of the irony expressing Naomi's pain as she speaks of her father's
kindness and the happiness of her childhood: "Dear First Dad,
our life was one of happiness and calm, as you wanted it to be;
and always your wishes came first. What happy times!" (p 88)
We would miss the impact of Edward's malevolence in *Scented
Gardens for the Blind* if we assumed that he is speaking metaphorically rather than ironically when he says, "It is the Strangs
who are permanent, who will go on and on like roasted vege-
tables in the ashes." (p 127) Without the careful questioning that
deciphering allegory requires, a key question might remain un-
asked: why should a myopic genealogist employ this horrific
simile?

Once we have recognised the allegorical, the work must be
re-examined in order to consider its ethical implications. Lydia
Wevers has compared Frame's novels to "biblical parables, moral
fables, and didactic fantasies" but complains that, unlike the
traditional fable or parable where "there is almost always the cer-
tainty that you will understand the moral, this is scarcely ever the
case in Frame."[7] The author guides the reader in assigning qualities and roles to the characters, but the reader then becomes the
producer of meaning. This implies a constant questioning of
prejudices and assumptions. It is not a matter of finding a simple
"moral". Within the allegorical parameters, a range of moral or
ethical positions will become apparent. But Frame does not ever
state her own ethical position, let alone offer a moral.

Allegorical characters draw attention to the ways in which language may serve aggressiveness, vanity, greed and will to power.

Those who wield power in Frame's novels are, for the most part, men. Greta, and Vera in her allegorical role, do not exert power, but they are as malevolent as the worst of the male characters. At the same time, some of Frame's mildest, warmest and most benevolent characters are men—Turnlung, Jake Brecon, Aisley Maude, Sandy Monk. Frame's work reflects, not an antipathy towards men, but the fact that Western ethics, culture, tradition and religion, making language their vehicle and agent, have given the greater share of power to men. And, having assumed power, men have retained it, buttressing their position by the exercise of rhetoric. They have evolved their own language of politics and law-making. George Steiner, observing the abuse of the politics of language, believes that "the matter of the relations between language and political inhumanity is a crucial one". He agrees with De Maistre and George Orwell in perceiving "how the word may lose its humane meanings under the pressure of political bestiality and falsehood."[8]

Frame belongs within a tradition of Western European writers who mistrust the received language because of its capacity to falsify or mislead. "How much confidence may a man put in his language, or in words themselves?"[9] This question is central to all allegorical narrative. Six of Frame's novels show the disintegration or radical transformation of language. *Scented Gardens for the Blind* concludes with unintelligible animal-like sounds instead of speech. Erlene foresees a silence in which "ideas were falling in drifts of sounds, words, human cries . . . How could anyone speak unless the new language were discovered in time?" (p 237) Erlene's plea is for an entirely new set of concepts that will see people taking full responsibility for their actions—without imagining that matters will be set right by a deity. *The Rainbirds* and *Intensive Care* expose lies and platitudes through strategic misspelling. In *The Carpathians*, the letters from many languages fall from the sky as midnight rain. *A State of Siege* concludes with a poem from the human heart which seems unintelligible to the rational mind. The reason for Frame's grievance against language may be found in a verse from *Daughter Buffalo*. Turnlung speaks of

> ... that ruined coast littered with language,
> with see-through words, glass words, bleaching words
>   indestructible synthetic words
> helping to complete the big fish- and people-kill. (p 34)

"Bleaching words" imply a whitewash through euphemisms. "See-through words, glass words" are empty of meaning. Packages of clichés become "indestructible" together with the language of propaganda. Language has justified any number of misguided policies, condoning killing, exploitation and the despoiling of earth, air and water. Words have conveyed knowledge and education of a kind that has not enriched, but impoverished, human understanding and compassion, giving the Edelmans of this world licence and power to "complete the big fish- and people-kill".

Frame's fiction also questions an education system which has reinforced traditional thinking and encouraged conformity. The human family is seen to be comprised of "dull parched souls caked with the footprints of an extinct education in grammar and written expression." (*Scented Gardens for the Blind*, p 117) Education has failed to impart a critical attitude towards authority that might help young people to resist the 'hard sell' and the 'soft sell' of the media which has contributed to a culture devoted to the accumulation of 'goods'. By her own example, Frame advocates an intensely conscious use of language. She envisages the stripping of "heavily fleeced words" to expose "their true meaning, their gaunt uncluttered bones . . . upon the slopes of thought" (*The Edge of the Alphabet*, p 124).

At the same time, language is the only means we have for stating a truth. *The Carpathians* is concerned with the creative possibilities of language as a means of making ideas visible, preserving history and contributing to a culture. Frame's latest work extends and develops a positive theme that has been apparent in every one of her novels. Poems, notebooks, novels or diaries, supposedly written by characters in Frame's fictions, use language creatively and imaginatively to produce Turnlung's "golden trophy", Mavis's "golden blanket" or John Henry Brecon's "Memory Flower". A succession of narrators who are also writers have offered treasures which will transcend death: "words ... continue the memory through centuries." (*The Carpathians*, p 196) Since Frame's writing is so immediate and believable that she tends to be accused of telling her own story, her response has been to gain distance by inventing, in eight out of eleven novels, writers who are telling *their* stories. Their roles and their degree of involvement with other characters have varied greatly from novel to novel. However, the writer-narrators authenticate language by shaping original treasures or trophies, demonstrating in eight different ways the importance of the created work in bringing warmth and meaning to 'living'.

In her interview with Marion McLeod, Frame observed that "Both fiction and non-fiction demand skills of shaping, choosing, composing a series of patterns that are or give the illusion of being complete."[10] Winston Rhodes, speaking of *Daughter Buffalo*, remarked that an assessment of Frame's achievement "should emphasise not the distortion but the symmetry of her vision"[11]. Symmetry and completeness are in keeping with the demands of allegory: "narrative allegory always pursues the goal of coherence."[12] But such a goal is by no means in accordance with the randomness and contingency of much postmodern writing.

Living in the Maniototo demonstrates the viability of a marriage between the allegorical and the postmodern, in spite of the obvious contradiction between the characteristics of the postmodern, and the demands of allegory. The postmodernist Donald Barthelme warns against "reading things into things".[13] Postmodernists tend to recoil from profundities. It is indeed both amusing and ironical to hide allegorical depth and significance in a text that affects a postmodern superficiality and playfulness.

Allegory and the postmodern mode share one significant area of common ground. In both, language is wielded self-consciously; both ask the reader to pay attention to the work as a text, rather than as a story, or as a study of character. Furthermore, postmodernism's lack of inhibition has allowed Frame's sense of humour free rein.

The Carpathians is not consistently postmodern in style. The account of Mattina's experience in the antipodes includes some postmodern features, whereas her family's life in New York and the reflections on her past are presented realistically. A disregard for credibility, when it suits her purpose, and a foregrounding of the text itself have long been part of Frame's style. She has always been conscious of the magical power of language to make and unmake worlds and characters. *The Carpathians* differs from the first nine novels in two respects: it flaunts and exposes the writing process to a greater extent and, when it disregards the assumptions of realism, it does so in a more extreme and nonchalant manner.

Before *Living in the Maniototo,* Frame's work was modernist rather than postmodern. While noting the postmodern nature of her metafiction and her language-oriented writing, Michael Morrissey considers that Frame may be "our missing modernist",[14] since her work reflects a stage of literary evolution that other New Zealand writers have avoided. Frame's delight in a dialectical balance between opposing concepts, often a feature of modernism, is apparent in all her writing, *Living in the Maniototo* included. Her exploration of the inner being and her interest in the long-term effects of trauma are both modernist concerns. So is her mockery of the contrivance and replication of 'civilised' living, though the flippancy and detachment of the critique may be postmodern.

Frame has always worked independently, refusing to bow to fashion, literary tradition or the market. C K Stead considers that to describe *Living in the Maniototo* as a *novel* might "arouse the wrong expectations. Perhaps it needs some classification like 'post-modernist fiction'". But, he adds, "that would suggest an exercise in theories Frame is probably indifferent to. She works by instinct, and what she offers is a mixed genre."[15] This novel, and indeed most of Frame's novels, is of "mixed genre". Mark Williams, speaking of *Living in the Maniototo*, notes her refusal "to limit . . . fictional strategies to any single style or formal orientation".[16]

Like Stead, Gina Mercer questions whether Frame writes 'novels'. She refers to Frame's "subversion of the genre" and her "disruptions of the novel form"[17], and observes that Frame repeatedly traverses the border between poetry and prose. Indeed, there are lengthy passages of verse or italicised poetic prose in *Owls Do Cry, A State of Siege, Intensive Care, Daughter Buffalo* and *Living in the Maniototo*. However, like the irony, the poetry in Frame's work is frequently at the service of the allegory, introducing, emphasising or reiterating the most significant allegorical ideas. Some of the poetry in *Intensive Care*, for instance, conveys Naomi's initial response to the gentleness of language and her subsequent anguish at the discovery that she has been tricked and trapped by it: "First speech a hook" (p 80).

Although Frame may have avoided a consistent style or mode, there is a remarkable consistency in the concerns and questions her novels express. Toby in *Owls Do Cry* is said to pursue "the wrong magic and the wrong fairy tale." (p 32) The "wrong fairy tale" reappears in *Intensive Care*. Milly describes mechanical dwarfs displayed in a shop window who dig for treasure in a jewelled mountain. (They are, no doubt, from "Snow White and the Seven Dwarfs".) Eventually, they are thrown on to a rubbish dump and buried by a "pretty yellow sight" (p 207) of daffodils. The implied fruitlessness of the dwarfs' endeavours is matched only by that of the stunted humans who pursue a similar search, having discarded the real treasure of daffodil bulbs which will endure from season to season. This theme recurs throughout Frame's work to reach its most positive expression in a reverence for the orchards of Puamahara and the trees of the Maharawhenua "strong in their year-long force of being" (*The Carpathians*, p 195). "Snowman, Snowman", *Daughter Buffalo* and *The Carpathians* likewise express reverence for the life force and regenerative force in nature.

This study has concentrated on discovering an allegorical dimension to Frame's novels. That does not diminish the significance of other approaches. A psychologically-centred reading is always rewarding. Episodes in *Living in the Maniototo*, for instance, show remarkable understanding of human motivation and reaction. Several novels are journeys of self-discovery, each quite different in its emphasis and area of exploration. Many studies of Frame's writing have concentrated on her linguistic virtuosity. To identify an allegorical dimension is to find even more richness and diversity in her texts; it is to pay additional tribute to her linguistic virtuosity. What has most often been overlooked in the failure to recognise the allegorical aspects is the humour and subtle irony, together with Frame's most vivid exposure of human inhumanity and folly.

Mark Williams describes *Living in the Maniototo* as Frame's "most distinguished work of fiction to date."[18] Its particular allegorical structure allows maximum flexibility as Mavis explores the human condition in the 20th century. At the same time, the book is satisfying as a varied, witty and entertaining novel. *Intensive Care*, Frame's longest novel, has the richness and diversity of an epic. To discover the allegorical dimension is to reveal a devastating social criticism and also to understand how the work coheres as a novel. Although an abundance of insight into human nature can be appreciated without knowledge of its allegory, this is one of several books by Frame that has been undervalued. Another is *The Adaptable Man*, which Patrick Evans has described as "the most underestimated of her novels"[19]. If it is read as a parody of 'the bestseller', some of its humour becomes evident. But a different, dark humour is apparent when the allegorical identities of the characters are seen. At the same time, it is an intensely serious work which considers what this techno-logical age may have lost to past ages of greater simplicity and greater harmony between human and the earth.

The products and effects of a technological age are significant in several novels. Among them are pollution, medical research, electricity and the power plants generating it, computer techno-logy and the Bomb. All are different forms of that "bogie" per-ceived in Frame's earliest story. Potentially, all could contribute to the overwhelming and silencing of an entire civilisation. Space travel is rejected by Turnlung. "It's futile going to planets and the moon, though it's a diverting wonder, and when the poets get there it will be a verbal indulgence that will only give the tyrant language more power to deceive." (*Daughter Buffalo*, p 120) The verbal applause, he is suggesting, will simply reinforce the misconception that such projects have value.

To Janet Frame, language is magical. But it can also be sub-verted into "the wrong magic" (*Owls Do Cry*, p 32), celebrating a direction which fails to take account of the "human compass" (p 139). Turnlung warns against the tendency to be mesmerised by language into uncritical acceptance of technological progress. Frame shows that language, in transferring culture and custom from generation to generation, is an instrument of immense power; it may create and preserve, or it may instigate destruction. In their allegorical roles, the Edwards, Toms, Colins, Russells and Edelmans of our age wield language for their own gain. The allegorical dimension in Frame's fiction warns against a gather-ing darkness which could make of this world an underworld.

1   Michael Morrissey, Introduction to *The New Fiction*, p 66.
2   Robert Ross, "Linguistic Transformation and Reflection in Janet Frame's *Living in the Maniototo*", in *World Literature Written in English*, Volume 27 II (1987), p 321.
3   Maureen Quilligan, "Allegory, Allegoresis, and the Deallegorization of Language: The *Roman de la rose*, the *De planctu naturae* and the *Parlement of Foules*", in *Allegory, Myth and Symbol*, pp 163–164.
4   C K Stead, *In the Glass Case. Essays on New Zealand Literature*, p 132.

5   Quilligan, *op cit*, p 169.

6   Lydia Wevers, "Through the I-shaped window", review of *Living in the Maniototo*, *NZ Listener*, 24 May 1980, pp 68–69.

7   Wevers, *ibid.*

8   George Steiner, *Language and Silence: Essays on Language, Literature and the Inhuman*, 1977 edition, p 95.

9   Quilligan, *The Language of Allegory: Defining the Genre*, p 46.

10   Marion McLeod, *NZ Listener*, 24 September 1988, p 26.

11   Winston Rhodes, *Landfall* XXVII 2 (1973), p 162.

12   Quilligan, *op cit*, p 184.

13   Donald Barthelme, *Snow White*, p 107. Cited by Douwe W Fokkema, *Literary History, Modernism and Post-modernism*, p 47.

14   Morrissey, *op cit*, p 66.

15   Stead, *op cit*, p 130.

16   Mark Williams, *Leaving the Highway: Six Contemporary New Zealand Novelists*, p 24.

17   Gina Mercer, "Exploring 'The Secret Caves of Language': Janet Frame's Poetry", *Meanjin* XLIV 3 (1985), p 385.

18   Williams, *op cit*, p 44.

19   Patrick Evans, "Janet Frame and the Art of Life", *Meanjin* XLIV 3 (1985), p 379.

Bibliography

Primary Sources
Arranged chronologically, and indicating editions to which cited page numbers refer.

AUTOBIOGRAPHY
To the Is-land. An Autobiography: Volume One. New York: Braziller, 1982.

An Angel at My Table. An Autobiography: Volume Two. New York: Braziller; Auckland: Hutchinson; London: The Women's Press, 1984.

The Envoy from Mirror City. An Autobiography: Volume Three. New York: Braziller; Auckland: Hutchinson; London: The Women's Press, 1985.

FICTION
The Lagoon: Stories. Christchurch: Caxton, 1951.

Owls Do Cry. First published, Christchurch: Pegasus, 1957. Edition cited in Chapter 2, Melbourne: Sun Books, 1967.

Faces in the Water. First published, Christchurch: Pegasus; New York: Braziller, 1961. Edition cited in Chapter 3, London: The Women's Press, 1980.

The Edge of the Alphabet. Christchurch: Pegasus; London: W H Allen; New York: Braziller, 1962. Edition cited in Chapter 4, Christchurch: The Pegasus Press, 1962.

Snowman, Snowman: Fables and Fantasies. New York: Braziller, 1962, 1963. Edition cited in Chapter 5, *You are now entering the human heart*, Wellington: Victoria University Press, 1983.

The Reservoir: Stories and Sketches. New York: Braziller, 1963.

Scented Gardens for the Blind. Christchurch: Pegasus; London: W H Allen; New York: Braziller, 1963. Edition cited in Chapter 6, London: The Women's Press, 1982.

The Adaptable Man. Christchurch: Pegasus; London: W H Allen; New York: Braziller, 1965. Edition cited in Chapter 7, Christchurch: The Pegasus Press, 1965.

A State of Siege. New York: Braziller, 1966. Edition cited in Chapter 8, Melbourne: Angus & Robertson, 1982.

The Rainbirds. London: W H Allen, 1968. As *Yellow Flowers in the Antipodean Room.* New York: Braziller, 1969. Edition cited in Chapter 9, Christchurch: The Pegasus Press, 1969.

Mona Minim and the Smell of the Sun. New York: Braziller, 1969.

Intensive Care. New York: Braziller; Toronto: Doubleday Canada, 1970. Edition cited in Chapter 10, Auckland: Century Hutchinson, 1987.

Daughter Buffalo. New York: Braziller; Toronto: Doubleday Canada, 1973. Edition cited in Chapter 11, Auckland: Century Hutchinson, 1986.

Living in the Maniototo. New York: Braziller, 1979. Edition cited in Chapter 12, London: The Women's Press, 1981.

You are now entering the human heart. Wellington: Victoria University Press, 1983.

The Carpathians. Auckland: Century Hutchinson; New York: Braziller, 1988. Edition cited in Chapter 13, Auckland: Century Hutchinson, 1988.

OTHER PROSE

Review of Terence Journet's *Take My Tip. Landfall* VIII 3 (1954), p 309.

"Memory and a Pocketful of Words". *Times Literary Supplement,* 4 June 1964, p 487.

"This Desirable Property". *NZ Listener,* 3 July 1964, pp 12–13.

"Beginnings". *Landfall* XIX 1 (1965), pp 40–47.

"The Burns Fellowship". *Landfall* XXII 3 (1968), pp 241–242.

"Artists' Retreats". Interview with Claire Henderson. *NZ Listener,* 27 July 1970, p 13.

"Janet Frame on *Tales from Grimm*". *Education* XXIV 9 (1975), p 27.

"Departures and Returns: Some Recognitions of the Cross-Cultural Encounter in Literature". *Writers in East-West Encounter,* ed Guy Amirthanayagam. London, 1982, pp 85–94.

"A Last Letter to Frank Sargeson". *Islands,* New Series Vol 1 No 1 (1984), p 17.

POETRY

The Pocket Mirror: Poems. New York: Braziller; London: W H Allen, 1967.

Critical Response to Frame

Arranged alphabetically by author surname.

Alcock, Peter. "Frame's Binomial Fall, or Fire and Four in Waimaru". *Landfall* XXIX 3 (1975), pp 179–187.

Ash, Susan. "Janet Frame: The Female Artist as Hero". *Journal of New Zealand Literature* VI (1988), pp 170–189.

Backmann, Annemarie. "Security and Equality in *The Rainbirds*". *Bird, Hawk, Bogie*, ed Jeanne Delbaere. Aarhus, 1978.

Bertram, James. Review of *The Reservoir and Other Stories*. *Landfall* XX 3 (1966), pp 290–292.

Crawford, Thomas. Review of *The Edge of the Alphabet*. *Landfall* XVII 2 (1963), pp 192–195.

Curnow, Allen. *Look Back Harder. Critical Writings 1935–1984*, ed Peter Simpson. Auckland, 1987.

Dalziel, Margaret. *Janet Frame*. Wellington, 1980.

Delbaere (or Delbaere-Garant), Jeanne. "Beyond the Word: Janet Frame's *Scented Gardens for the Blind*". *The Commonwealth Writer Overseas: Themes of Exile and Expatriation*, ed Alistair Niven. Brussels, 1976.

Delbaere, Jeanne, ed. *Bird, Hawk, Bogie: Essays on Janet Frame*. Aarhus, 1978.

———— "Daphne's Metamorphosis in Janet Frame's Early Novels". *Ariel* VI 2 (1975), pp 23-37.

———— "Le Domaine Anglais". *Le réalism magique. Roman, Peinture, Cinéma*. Lausanne, 1987.

———— "Memory as Survival in the Global Village: Janet Frame's *The Carpathians*". As yet unpublished, but due to appear in a new edition of *Bird, Hawk, Bogie*.

Dowling, David. "Brave New Worlds: Janet Frame's *Intensive Care* and Hugh MacLennan's *Voices in Time*". *World Literature Written in English* XXV 1 (1985), pp 169–181.

Dudding, Robin, ed. *Beginnings. New Zealand Writers Tell How They Began Writing*. Wellington, 1980.

Dupont, Victor. "Janet Frame's Brave New World: *Intensive Care*". *Bird, Hawk, Bogie*. Aarhus, 1978.

During, Simon. "Postmodernism or Postcolonialism?" *Landfall* XXXIX 3 (1985), pp 366–380.

Edmond, Lauris. Review of *Daughter Buffalo. Islands* 3 (Spring 1974), p 338.

Evans, Patrick. "Alienation and the Imagery of Death: The Novels of Janet Frame". *Meanjin* XXXII 3 (1973), pp 294–303.

_____ *An Inward Sun: The Novels of Janet Frame*. Wellington, 1971.

_____ "Farthest from the Heart: The Autobiographical Parables of Janet Frame". *Modern Fiction Studies* XXVII 1 (1981), pp 31–40.

_____ *Janet Frame*. Boston, 1977.

_____ "Janet Frame and the Adaptable Novel". *Landfall* XXV 4 (1971), pp 448–455.

_____ "Janet Frame and the Art of Life". *Meanjin* XLIV 3 (1985), pp 375–383.

_____ "The Muse as Rough Beast: the Autobiography of Janet Frame". *Untold* VI (Spring 1986), pp 1–10.

_____ "New Zealand Myth-Maker". Review of *Intensive Care. Islands* II (Summer 1972), pp 180–183.

_____ Review of *Living in the Maniototo. SPAN* XVIII (April 1984), pp 76–88.

_____ Review of *The Rainbirds. Landfall* XXIII 2 (1969), pp 189–194.

Hankin, Cherry. "Language as Theme in *Owls Do Cry*". *Landfall* XXVIII 2 (1974), pp 91–110.

Hannah, Donald W. *"Faces in the Water:* Case History or Work of Fiction?", *Bird, Hawk, Bogie*. Aarhus, 1978.

Jones, Lawrence. *Barbed Wire and Mirrors: Essays on New Zealand Prose*. Dunedin, 1987.

_____ "No Cowslip's Bell in Waimaru: the Personal Vision of *Owls Do Cry*". *Landfall* XXIV 3 (1970), pp 280–296.

Joseph, M K. Review of *The Adaptable Man. Landfall* XX 1 (1966), pp 92–95.

Leeming, Owen. Review of *Scented Gardens for the Blind. Landfall* XVII 4 (1963), pp 386–389.

Leggott, Michele. "*The Carpathians* Explores Farthest Realms of Fiction". *Evening Post,* 10 September 1988.

Malterre, Monique. "Myths and Esoterics: A Tentative Interpretation of *A State of Siege*". *Bird, Hawk, Bogie.* Aarhus, 1978.

McCracken, Jill. "Janet Frame: It's Time for France". *NZ Listener,* 27 October 1973, p 20.

McEldowney, Dennis. "Breathe in the Gas Mask". Review of *Intensive Care. NZ Listener,* 10 January 1972, p 44.

———— Review of *Daughter Buffalo. NZ Listener,* 21 May 1973, p 50.

McLeod, Marion. "Janet Frame in Reality Mode" (interview with Frame following publication of *The Carpathians*), *NZ Listener,* 24 September 1988, p 25.

Mercer, Gina. "Exploring 'the Secret Caves of Language': Janet Frame's Poetry". *Meanjin* XLIV 3 (1985), pp 384–390.

Morrissey, Michael. "Introduction", *The New Fiction.* Auckland, 1985.

Reid, Ian. "The Dark, the Dull and the Dirty". Review of *Intensive Care. Australian Book Review* Autumn 1972, p 258.

Rhodes, H Winston. "Preludes and Parables. A Reading of Janet Frame's Novels". *Landfall* XXVI 2 (1972), pp 135–146.

———— Review of *Owls Do Cry. Landfall* XI 4 (1957), pp 327–331.

Robertson, Robert T. "Bird, Hawk, Bogie. Janet Frame, 1952–1962". *Bird, Hawk, Bogie.* Aarhus, 1978.

Ross, Robert. "Linguistic Transformation and Reflection in Janet Frame's *Living in the Maniototo*". *World Literature Written in English* XXVII 2 (1987), pp 320–326.

Rutherford, Anna. "Janet Frame's Divided and Distinguished Worlds". *World Literature Written in English* XIV (April 1975), pp 50–68. Reprinted in *Bird, Hawk, Bogie.* Aarhus, 1978.

Skolil, Genevieve. *Symbolism in J. Frame's Short-stories and Novels.* Toulouse, 1977.

Smith, Shona. "Fixed Salt Beings, Isms and *Living in the Maniototo*". *Untold* V (Autumn 1986), pp 24–32.

Stead, C K. *In the Glass Case: Essays on New Zealand Literature.* Auckland, 1981.

Stevens, Joan. *The New Zealand Novel 1860–1960.* Wellington, 1962.

Taylor, Margaret. Review of *A State of Siege. Landfall* XXII 3 (1968), pp 331–335.

Wevers, Lydia. Review of *Daughter Buffalo. New Zealand Bookworld* I (1973), p 21.

_____ "Through the I-shaped Window". Review of *Living in the Maniototo*. *NZ Listener*, 24 May 1980, pp 68–69.

Williams, Mark. *Leaving the Highway: Six Contemporary New Zealand Novelists*. Auckland, 1990.

General

Arranged alphabetically by author surname.

Anderson, Atholl. *When All the Moa Ovens Grew Cold: Nine Centuries of Changing Fortune for the Southern Maori*. Dunedin, 1983.

Anglo-Saxon Poetry, selected and translated by R K Gordon. London, 1926.

Auden, W H. *Selected Poems*, ed Edward Mendelson. London, 1979.

Barry, Peter. *Issues in Contemporary Critical Theory: A Casebook*. London, 1987.

Baxter, James K. *Collected Poems,* ed J E Weir. Wellington, 1980.

Bloomfield, Morton W, ed. *Allegory, Myth and Symbol.* Harvard English Studies 9. Cambridge, Massachusetts, 1981.

Booth, Wayne C. *The Rhetoric of Fiction.* Chicago, Illinois, 1961.

Buber, Martin. *I and Thou.* New York, 1958.

Bunyan, John. *The Pilgrim's Progress and The Holy War.* London.

Chaucer, Geoffrey. *The Works of Geoffrey Chaucer*, ed F N Robinson, second edition. London, 1957.

Cïalinescu, Matei. *Five Faces of Modernity.* Durham, North Carolina, 1987.

Clifford, Gay. *The Transformations of Allegory.* London, 1974.

Coleridge, S T. *Poems and Prose,* selected and introduced by Kathleen Raine. Harmondsworth, 1957.

Curnow, Allen, ed. *A Book of New Zealand Verse 1923-1950.* Christchurch, 1951.

Curtius, Ernst Robert. *European Culture and the Latin Middle Ages,* trans Willard R Trask. New York, 1953. First published 1948.

Dante. *The Divine Comedy, I: Hell,* trans Dorothy L Sayers. Harmondsworth, 1949.

_____ *The Divine Comedy, II: Purgatory,* trans Dorothy L Sayers. Harmondsworth, 1955.

_____ *The Divine Comedy, III: Paradise,* trans Dorothy L Sayers and Barbara Reynolds. Harmondsworth, 1963.

de Man, Paul. *Allegories of Reading: Figural Language in Rousseau, Nietzsche, Rilke and Proust.* New Haven, Connecticut, 1979.

———— *Interpretation: Theory and Practice.* Baltimore, Maryland, 1969.

Eagleton, Terry. *Literary Theory: An Introduction.* Oxford, 1983.

Elliot, T S. *The Waste Land and Other Poems.* London, 1940.

Fletcher, Angus. *Allegory: The Theory of a Symbolic Mode.* New York, 1964.

Fokkema, Douwe W. *Literary History, Modernism and Postmodernism.* Amsterdam, 1984.

Fraser, Sir James George. *The New Golden Bough,* revised, abridged and edited by Theodor H Gastor. New York, 1959.

Frye, Northrop. *Anatomy of Criticism.* Princeton, New Jersey, 1952.

Furst, Lilian. *The Contours of European Romanticism.* London, 1979.

Gilkison, Robert. *Early Days in Central Otago.* Christchurch, 1930.

Grimm, the Brothers. *The Penguin Complete Grimms' Tales,* trans Ralph Mannheim. Harmondsworth, 1984.

Hall-Jones, John. *Fiordland Explored.* Wellington, 1976.

Hassan, Ihab. *The Dismemberment of Orpheus: Toward a Postmodern Literature.* New York, 1971.

Hawkes, Terence. *Structuralism and Semiotics.* London, 1977.

Honig, Edwin. *Dark Conceit: The Making of Allegory.* New York, 1966.

Jung, C G. *The Collected Works of C G Jung. Volume 15: The Spirit in Man, Art, and Literature.* London, 1966.

Kafka, Franz. *The Castle,* trans Willa and Edwin Muir. Harmondsworth, 1930. First published 1926.

———— *The Trial,* trans Willa and Edwin Muir. Harmondsworth, 1953. First published 1925.

Kaplan, Ann E. *Rocking Around the Clock. Music, Television, Postmodernism and Consumer Culture.* New York, 1987.

Laing, R D. *The Divided Self.* Harmondsworth, 1965. First published 1960.

———— *The Politics of Experience and The Bird of Paradise.* Harmondsworth, 1967.

Levin, Richard. *Tragedy: Plays, Theory and Criticism.* New York, 1960.

Levin, Samuel. "Allegorical Language". *Allegory, Myth and Symbol,* ed Morton W Bloomfield, Harvard English Studies 9. Cambridge, Massachusetts, 1981.

Lewis, C S. *The Allegory of Love: A Study in Medieval Tradition.* New York, 1958. First published 1936.

Leyburn, Ellen Douglas. *Satiric Allegory: Mirror of Man.* New Haven, Connecticut, 1956.

Lodge, David, ed. *Modern Criticism and Theory: A Reader.* London, 1988.

May, Rollo. *Man's Search for Himself.* New York, 1953.

Milton, John. *Complete Poems and Major Prose,* ed Merritt Y Hughes. New York, 1957.

Ministerial Review Committee Report to Cabinet. Clyde Dam Project Decision-Making. Wellington, September 1990.

Muecke, D C. *The Compass of Irony.* London, 1980. First published 1969.

Newton, K M, ed. *Twentieth Century Literary Theory.* London, 1988.

The Oxford Book of Light Verse, chosen by W H Auden. London, 1938.

The Oxford Book of Twentieth-Century English Verse, chosen by Philip Larkin. Oxford, 1973.

Plato. *The Republic of Plato,* trans and introduced by Francis MacDonald Cornford. New York and London, 1945.

Politzer, Heinz. *Franz Kafka. Parable and Paradox.* Ithaca, New York, 1962.

Quilligan, Maureen. "Allegory, Allegoresis, and the Deallegorization of Language: *The Roman de la rose,* the *De planctu naturae,* and the *Parlement of Foules*". *Allegory, Myth and Symbol,* ed Morton W Bloomfield. Harvard English Studies 9. Cambridge, Massachusetts, 1981.

————— *The Language of Allegory: Defining the Genre.* Ithaca, New York, 1979.

Rilke, Rainer Maria. *The Selected Poetry of Rainer Maria Rilke,* ed and trans Stephen Mitchell. New York, 1982.

————— *Sonnets to Orpheus,* trans J B Leishman. London, 1957. First published 1936.

————— *Werke, Band II.2. Gedichte und Übertragungen.* Frankfurt am Main, 1974.

Russell, Charles. *Poets, Prophets and Revolutionaries. The Literary Avant-Garde from Rimbaud through Postmodernism.* New York, 1985.

Saphira, Miriam. *The Sexual Abuse of Children.* Auckland, 1981.

Scholes, Robert and Kellogg, Robert. *The Nature of Narrative.* New York, 1966.

Shakespeare, William. *King Lear,* Arden edition, ed Kenneth Muir. London, 1952.

_____ *The Tempest,* Arden edition, ed Frank Kermode. London, 1954.

Southey, Robert. *Poems of Robert Southey,* ed Maurice Fitzgerald. London, 1909.

Stanzel, F K. *A Theory of Narrative,* trans Charlotte Goedsche. Cambridge, Massachusetts, 1984.

Steiner, George. *Language and Silence. Essays on Language, Literature and the Inhuman.* New York, 1977.

Van Dyke, Carolynn. *The Fiction of Truth: Structures of Meaning in Narrative and Dramatic Allegory.* Ithaca, New York, 1985.

Wilde, Alan. *Horizons of Assent: Modernism, Postmodernism and the Ironic Imagination.* Baltimore, Maryland, 1981.

Wilson, Colin. *The Craft of the Novel.* London, 1975.

Yeats, W B. *The Collected Poems of W B Yeats.* London, 1967.

_____ *Selected Prose,* ed A Norman Jeffares. London, 1964.

Reference Texts

Arranged alphabetically by title.

'The Book of Beasts' being a Translation from a Latin Bestiary of the Twelfth Century, ed T H White. London, 1954.

Concise Maori Dictionary, compiled A W Reed, revised T S K retu. Christchurch, 1984. First published 1948.

Eerdmans Bible Dictionary, rev ed Allen C Myers. Grand Rapids, Michigan, 1987.

Encyclopaedia Judaica. Jerusalem, 1971.

An Encyclopaedia of New Zealand, ed A H McLintock. Wellington, 1966.

English-Serbocroatian, Serbocroatian-English Dictionary. New York, 1988.

A Glossary of Literary Terms, ed M H Abrams. Third edition: New York, 1971.

Hall's Dictionary of Subjects and Symbols in Art, introduced by Kenneth Clark. London, 1974.

The Oxford Dictionary of Saints, ed David Hugh Farmer. Oxford, 1987.
The Oxford English Dictionary. Oxford, 1961. First published 1933.
The Saints, ed John Coulson. London, 1958.
Stadtmuseum Münster Catalogue. Münster, 1982.
Wise's New Zealand Guide. Auckland, 1987. First published 1952.